METRO

Alasdair Duncan

burninghouse

First published 2008.

A Burning House book.

www.burninghousebooks.com

Burning House is an imprint of
Beautiful Books Limited
36-38 Glasshouse Street
London W1B 5DL

ISBN 9781905636181

9 8 7 6 5 4 3 2 1

Cover design by Kate Forrester.
Printed in Great Britain by MacKays of Chatham.

What you see is a tracking shot – it's shaky because it's been taken on a digital camera and the person shooting it obviously didn't really know what they were doing. The whole thing lasts for about five minutes or so. The shot begins with a blond boy in dirty denim, who looks pretty drunk or high or something, sitting on a kitchen bench. There is a party going on around him – some guys grab beers from the fridge then disappear, and a pair of girls walk by, waving at the camera as they go, giggling. The sound is distorted and all you can really hear is this spooky echo from the music and the conversations going on all around, but the boy is talking to the camera – he seems to be saying 'Get lost', you can sort of get that from lip-reading, but from the grin on his face, it seems like he doesn't really mean it. The boy mugs for a while, goofing around, and the shot moves in really close. A hand tugs on his shirt and he laughs, makes a drunken grab for the camera without managing to get hold of it. After a minute or so of this, you see the boy pointing at something behind the camera – the shot swivels and you get a panorama of the kitchen. You can tell it's pretty nice, stainless-steel appliances and whatever else, and you figure the people who live here must have money. The shot moves, jerking out of

1

the kitchen and into the living room, which is also crowded with kids – holding beers or bottles of vodka and raspberry, talking, laughing. It's like whoever is filming this has started looking for someone. For a second the shot lurches sideways and then down – you can see the polished floor, people's feet, and then it closes in on this dog, a border collie. The border collie seems excited or confused, and you see a hand scratching behind its ear, a close-up of its tongue, which is lolling out. After a while the dog seems to freak out about something, or maybe it gets a better offer, and runs away, and the shot moves on, working its way through the party. The music has changed and you can hear hip-hop beats blaring from somewhere. A really tall guy in a trucker cap pretend-slaps the camera a high five, laughing. The camera swerves to avoid him and then finds what seems to be its target.

The dark-haired girl is holding a champagne glass, deep in conversation with someone – you can't see who because the shot focuses only on her. She doesn't notice the camera at first, but when she does, she shakes her head and looks down, blushing. It's like she's embarrassed about being filmed, which seems weird, since how could anyone as beautiful as she is be that insecure? Now you can see the hint of a smile on her face – she tries to duck out of the way, but the camera follows her. The shot steadies and catches the girl in front of a big picture window. Because it's dark outside, you can see the reflection of the person who's filming – it's a boy, and although most of his face is covered by the camera, you can tell he's young, blond, not bad looking. All the kids at this party seem to have that ruddy, well-kept look about them. The boy filming talks to the girl, motioning with his free hand, and eventually she gives

2

in – pushing some hair away from off her face, grinning at him, responding to his questions.

After a while, the boy seems to say something that the girl can't understand – she leans in for a second, confused, and when she figures out what he's asked her, she opens her mouth wide like she's pretending to be completely shocked. She shakes her head, as if her answer to the question is no way, then she looks away and points insistently at something to the left. The camera swivels again, and through a group of people you see a tall, good-looking guy in a Von Dutch shirt. He's standing on the deck, beer in hand, and hasn't noticed the camera. The dark-haired girl moves into the shot and blows a big, dramatic kiss at the camera. The guy in the Von Dutch shirt, who has seen the camera now, is looking right at it, shaking his head and grinning. With his free hand, he gives the finger and mouths something that could be 'Don't be a fag' but could also be any number of other things. The girl bounds over to him and puts her arm around his waist. You can't tell what happens next because the video cuts out right after that.

One

We could get caught, but that, perhaps, is the point. It was after midnight when we got here and that was a long time ago. Because it's so late, there aren't many cars around, but whenever we see headlights approaching, she'll start to giggle and pull me in close to her. We'll hug as tightly as we can until the car passes. For a second, we'll be caught in the glare of the headlights, and through the giggles she'll whisper to me, telling me to keep down, not to let them spot us, and I'll tell her I won't, that we'll be safe, and then the car will pass.

This started off as a joke. I guess maybe it's not fair to call it a joke, but it was one of those stupid things that don't feel like much at the time but, looking back, set the tone for a lot of what comes after. The first time we did it was one night, a Friday, early last year. There was this club that had recently opened on Ann Street and some girlfriend of Sara's was having a party there – her parents had booked out the top floor for this girl's eighteenth birthday or something. So it's all these ex-Somerville girls getting tipsy and giggling, the boy-friends hanging out by the bar dressed in suits and acting like the Sopranos or some shit, and Sara and I, who'd gotten there late, dancing to hip-hop, drinking champagne, mingling. After about an hour or so of this, we wound up talking with this Jesse guy, who was telling us all about his big career plans – how he was acting in a short film about these surfers, but was only really doing it to break into modelling. Then a girl I didn't recognise came up and started hugging him, asking him how he was doing and about the movie and stuff. While the two of them were talking, Sara grabbed me and whispered, 'Let's get out of here.'

I was actually having a pretty good time and wanted to hear the end of this Jesse guy's story; when I asked Sara why she wanted to leave, if she was feeling tired or what, she told me: 'This all feels fake. I want to go. I want you to take me somewhere else.' Then she gave me one of those looks – those *if you do what I want there may be something in it for you later* kind of looks that it's really difficult to say no to – so I gave in and I was like, 'Okay then, where do you want to go?' all serious and stuff, playing along. Then she started laughing and said, 'I want to go...to...Scandinavia.' Sara's always saying stupid stuff like that, just to see how I'll react, so I said, 'Fine, I'll take you to the airport then,' calling her bluff, telling her, 'Better get packing', things like that, and hustling her out. We didn't even say goodbye, just left, both of us upping the ante until eventually we ended up in my car actually on the way to the airport. We were on the airport drive, deserted because it was so late, when Sara said, 'Oh shit, we'd better pull over,' so I pulled over onto the grass.

We lay there for the next hour or so, under the NO STOPPING UNDER ANY CIRCUMSTANCES sign, me holding her, watching planes take off. It felt good. I guess some of the time, when I'm alone with Sara, it doesn't feel right. Not 'right' exactly, but... Why the hell am I telling you this? I know you think it's dumb, but I'll bet you have dumb rituals like this too. I'll *bet*. Anyway, let's just say, this night when the two of us were at the airport, it felt good – it felt good in a way that it hadn't for quite a while. I mean, I love Sara – and I know what you're thinking, I do, but love can mean a lot of things – and when it comes down to it, I just want her to be happy. And this stupid thing with the planes taking off, it made her happy. So it became a tradition – every couple of months we'd be out somewhere, at a party, or maybe we'd just be hanging out at Sara's house, and things would go silent and she'd say to me: 'I want to go...to...Scandinavia', and I'd bring her here. Here's where we are tonight, her parents' M4 parked on the grass beside us.

It's going to be the last chance we get for a while.

'I'm leaving in four days,' she says.

'I know.'

'I want to know...' She stops. We're looking up at a plane which is just a bright light disappearing into the darkness. 'I guess I'd just like to think that you're going to miss me.'

'Of course I'm going to miss you.'

'You're not very cute when you lie.'

'We've had this conversation before,' I say. 'You tell me how I don't love you, then I tell you it's bullshit, then we have a big fight, then finally we get over it and I start to do this...' I reach for that place on the inside of her leg that makes her go completely nuts when I tickle it.

'Stop it!' she says, squirming. 'Stop...' I keep trying to tickle her and before long she's smiling, trying but not really trying to push me away, and I guess for now everything's going to be okay.

Finally we settle. She lies with her head on my chest and for a while neither of us says anything. There are no planes in the sky now, just stars, but it's difficult to see them because the lights coming from the airport terminal pretty much obliterate everything.

'Four days,' she says again. Sara brings her face close to mine and stares at me for a long time. I don't know if the silence is my cue to say something reassuring – to tell Sara that I'm going to miss her so bad, that I'll think of her every day, that she looks so hot right now – because really, except for the last one, none of these is strictly true, so I say nothing. I lean in closer, kiss her. For some reason Sara seems to prefer it when I act like the strong, silent type. I slide my hand around the back of her neck; she leans back on the grass and I lie on my side next to her, my body touching hers.

She takes my hand, lets it go. 'It's not too late for you to change your mind.'

'What does that mean?'

'You could still come with me. If you wanted to.'

'In four days?'

7

'Well no, not so soon. It's only early January but you were talking about deferring your classes...You said you weren't sure about this semester. That maybe you wanted to take some time off and, y'know...rethink things.'

Did I say that? It sounds like something I would probably say.

'I don't know, Sara. Life's just so...confusing at the moment. With you leaving and everything...'

'You still want to be with me, right?'

I set myself up for that. 'Yeah. Sara, baby,' I say, pulling her in again, 'of course I want to be with you.'

'Then you can... If you want to, you can fly over there and meet up with me. Not now, but in a couple of months? You know, when you...when you decide maybe that you have it together. You could come over and meet up with me. In Italy...' She lays her head in the crook of my shoulder. 'We could meet up when I'm in Rome, and then we could go around together...You could come backpacking with me, and we'd be...y'know. We'd be together.'

Six months. Taking a semester off to go backpacking together. The plans we made always seemed really far off and abstract, as though we were discussing something that was never really going to happen.

The trip was something we'd been planning for a while, though it's always been more Sara's thing than mine. She'd make big plans for it – she'd write stuff in her notebooks like most girls write bad poetry – and it was always part of the plan that I was going with her, being the supportive boyfriend or something like that. We'd meet up on our breaks, she'd have just come out of

8

a law lecture and be looking so cute in one of those pink polo shirts she always seems to be wearing, and we'd go to a study room in the library, or maybe go out and sit on the grass if it was sunny, and talk about it. I even bought her this dumb Lonely Planet guide, which she's been through so much that the spine has cracked.

When it came to booking the trip, that was when I told her. She wasn't really upset. I mean, it's hard to tell with Sara. What she's thinking. She said, 'Maybe you'll change your mind' and we left it at that.

Sometimes I do some pretty shitty things to Sara. I feel bad about it, but she always seems to forgive me. I guess there are some things Sara doesn't know about.

'You should be careful,' Jay says to me after swiping the card. 'I know a girl who went to London last year, left her boyfriend behind. It was only meant to be for six months, but... Hey, that was credit, right?' The customer, this blonde girl who is in the middle of a conversation on her mobile, nods distractedly. '...so, while she was over there... Just sign down the bottom please. Yeah, sorry, so while she was there she met a guy who was meant to be an artist or something, this...skater who got paid, like, hundreds of pounds for doing graffiti, I think it was. So she broke up with her boyfriend – via *email* no less – got an assistant job at some magazine, and she's still over there.'

'This isn't some girl, it's Sara. What are you getting at with this assistant stuff?' I ask.

9

'Just that anything might...happen. When your girl-friend's in Europe. Six months is a long time. Either of you could... Look, I'm just pointing out that these things, these long-distance things, they don't always... work out.'

Jay stuffs a pair of jeans – hipsters, faded denim – into one of the Metro bags, and hands it to the girl, who is still talking on her phone. As she's walking away, she turns to wave at Jay and gives him this funny half-smile, biting on her bottom lip. Jay grins back and the girl's smile broad-ens – I think she actually *blushes* – before she scurries back out to the third floor of the shopping mall, heading off in the direction of the food court, where she will probably tell her friends about the *gorgeous* guy she saw in Metro.

'She was hot,' I say to Jay, who shrugs.

'I guess.'

'You were flirting with her.'

'No I *wasn't*.'

'Don't pretend like you weren't. You're *always* flirting with girls in here. You love it. You'd jump the fence for half of these girls, I'll bet.'

'Hey, unlike someone I could mention – who seems to have forgotten his girlfriend already, by the way – I *happen* to be a nice guy.'

'Right, right. I forgot, you're a homosexual, aren't you? Sorry.'

'*You're* already checking out other girls. Sara's not even out of the country yet,' he says, shaking his head.

'So what if she's not? That girl was hot. And you're still a homosexual.'

Jay grins, throws a pretend punch at me. 'Hey *dude*, at least I'm not repressing it...'

A decent comeback escapes me so I make a fist and take a series of lunges at Jay, who edges back further and further, laughing. Eventually, we get bored of this game and slump, Jay on the counter and me on this display case filled, for some reason, with record sleeves from the 1980s. I ask him if he's coming to Sara's going-away party tonight and he tells me yeah, maybe. That he might be bringing some guy, this Danish exchange student called Nils that he met at some club last week. I don't press him for the details. Don't get me wrong about Jay – he's a pretty cool guy, homosexuality notwithstanding, and I guess you'd say he's one of my closest friends. We went to Grammar together, we're sharing a house with another friend of ours in New Farm – on the proviso that he keeps his sexual escapades and drug-hoovering to one side of the house and hangs a sock on his door when it looks like we're going to have 'company' at the breakfast table – and he's the one who got me the job here.

Metro, where I've worked since late last year, is a shop that sells up-market surf and skate clothes to fashionable upper-middle-class brats – a demographic that I guess includes me and pretty much all of my friends. My parents are kind of hung up on the idea of me having a job, to get an idea of the value of money or whatever before I finish uni, so I guess I'm here mainly to humour them, but the people here are cool, and I get a tonne of free shit, so why not?

11

It's pretty quiet, deserted actually, through most of the afternoon. These two girls who seem to know Jay come in – when they see him they go completely nuts, running over and hugging him, asking, '*Ohmygod howareyou?!*' and telling him about a band they're seeing tonight, about what they did last weekend. Girls always go completely nuts over Jay. I guess you'd probably say he's cute – he is pretty nice looking, and never seems to be alone at any given time – but it's more than that. He's just, I don't know, an okay guy. Jay talks to the girls for about half an hour. I arrange a bunch of these foam-and-mesh trucker caps in boxes that are set into the wall, then rearrange them in a more interesting order. I hang around the counter and change the music over a couple of times. I put on this German electro compilation that I think belongs to Jay – lots of bored-sounding girls speak-singing about sex and how hard it is to be a fashion model – then some Primal Scream, then the German electro compilation again.

When the two girls leave, Jay drifts back over to the counter and tells me that he used to go out with one of their brothers – he and the guy broke up but Jay stayed friends with the sister. He tells me they're going to Family next weekend to see this very famous DJ. The event sold out weeks ago but one of their friends who works there can get them in and they asked Jay along. The invitation's apparently open to me too – 'If you're not still, y'know, grieving over the loss of your girlfriend by next weekend,' adds Jay when he passes this information on. I grab a sweatband and start flicking him with it. He picks up this trucker cap with a big picture of a moose on the front and throws it at my head. We rough each other up a bit and then get tired of it and stop.

Boredom begins to creep back. Essentially, it's a completely normal friday afternoon. Jay goes over to a rack of jeans and starts looking at them really closely. I think about changing the music again. I'm still standing at the counter pondering this extremely big decision when the boy comes in. When I see him, I forget all about the music.

'That's right, that is *so* right, oh Jesus, I knew you'd agree with me, Liam, I *knew* it.' Felicia grabs my forearm, gives me an extremely intense look that tells me now would be a good time to be paying attention. 'You're such a sweet guy – most guys are bastards but you're *so* sweet, I can *so* see why Sara likes you so much... I wish I had a boyfriend like you.'

'Thanks,' I tell her. 'That means a lot. And it really is true...what you were saying before, about the...'

Actually, I have no idea what we've been talking about. It's after eleven at Sara's going-away party. I'm on my fifth or possibly sixth Corona, so I'm not exactly responding to the subtleties of the conversation, and besides, you always end up 'relating' drunkenly and insincerely at parties like this. I've had about three of these exchanges already tonight, so I figure I'll just shut the hell up and let Felicia fill the silence, which she does after about a second and a half.

'Yeah, it's hard. I mean, I feel like a bitch, like I really shouldn't be complaining about it, but like, girls my age *really* do it tough.'

Felicia is short, but what she lacks in height she makes up for in *cute*. She's one of Sara's oldest friends – they went to primary school together and she's studying marketing or something but really wants to be an actor. I saw her in this play last year, some dumb student-theatre thing at a concrete hole in the backstreets of the Valley. Sara made me go, dragged me there. I can't really remember much about it – it was meant to be set in Afghanistan or Iraq or some godforsaken place and it was meant to be a comment on, like, that whole situation there and it was essentially fairly shitty, but Felicia was playing an army officer and she got to walk around dressed like a boy and carrying a submachine gun which was, at the time, a real turn-on.

'I mean,' Felicia continues, letting go of my arm, 'being a pretty girl is really hard. People go on about, like, racism and whatever else, but seriously, when you're a cute girl with nice breasts, it's like everyone is out to get you. It's like models – I feel so sorry for them, and I'm *not* saying I look like a model or anything, but it's like they've got all this *pressure* on them, you know?' Felicia is on a rant now, and I wouldn't be able to stop her if I tried. All I need to do is nod, let her keep talking. 'I mean, on the one hand, they've got all this criticism heaped on them by quote-unquote *feminists* who accuse them of letting the side down, these women who blame them for being the cause of, like, bulimia and anorexia and all the other problems that young girls have, when really they're just jealous. And on the other hand, they've got these disgusting guys who drool all over them and basically want them to keep their mouths shut and have sex on command. And it's so, like, demoralising, because...' She seems to get confused for a second and stops.

'So...' I say, thinking that the 'disgusting guys' she just described sound like pretty much every guy I know. I'm about to ask what her point is when she continues.

'I mean, back at school I used to go to these parties with these Terrace guys and they were disgusting. It's like, they thought they could do whatever they wanted with you. And it was like that for all my girlfriends. The guys just wouldn't stop. It's like, this one night, this friend of mine, Ingrid, got so drunk she was almost passing out, and these two Terrace guys...um...the story is pretty gross...They...' Without warning, Felicia stops talking, focuses on something behind me. Her eyes widen and she squeals: '*Ohmygod*, Chops! How are you? I haven't seen you in *ohmygod* I can't even think how long...'

I turn to look. This punk guy with athletic socks and a flatcap has come out onto the deck and is heading towards us with this massive grin on his face. Felicia introduces me to the Chops guy, telling me that the two of them go to uni together and he's absolutely the coolest guy ever, except for me of course. We kind of size one another up; he says 'Hey' and offers me his hand, and we end up doing one of those stupid elaborate hand-shakes that involve a lot of thumb and forefinger action and... I don't know, the shit that guys do with guys... It's some kind of power thing, like whoever controls the handshake has the advantage – like, deep down, girls are all moaning with pleasure over the guy with the most forceful handshake? I think not.

Felicia starts talking to Chops, asking him these questions about how Japan was and how his band are doing. I'm kind of glad to get a break from her. Tonight has been pretty intense, with Sara leaving and everything. I've been here since late this afternoon, helping set up and stuff. When I showed up, she asked why I was looking so pleased with myself and I thought of the dude from this afternoon then quickly put him out of my mind.

The party has been pretty good, I guess. As far as parties go, some interesting shit has taken place. Sara's parents live in a big new house in Ascot, set back from the road – the second floor is open, and all night people have been spilling out from the living room onto the deck, leaning over the railing, smoking cigarettes, laughing. Sara's dog, this border collie named Hamish, has been banished outside for most of the night. Earlier on, some friends of her little brother, Toby, gave him beer and he was sick all over the floor. Terrace fags – I mean seriously, what do you expect? They cut a swathe through the Moët, threw one of their friends in the pool and one of them flirted fairly embarrassingly with Sara's mother. As of about half an hour ago they were sitting on and around this big leather sofa formulating some fiendish plan or other, who the hell knows, but the little brats were looking worse for wear and probably too drunk to do any serious damage.

Sara has spent all night doing the rounds of the party, dutifully saying goodbye to school and uni friends, smiling and crying at the appropriate times. I had no idea she knew so many people, but all night the house has seriously been packed. Everyone has been hugging her, crying, wishing her a safe trip and saying how much they'll miss her – she has developed this glazed kind of expression, like she'd rather be somewhere else, but she continues going around and talking, drinking glass after glass of champagne, listening politely while older relatives tell her about the six months they spent in Paris or the time they went backpacking through India and how it was the best time of their lives and how it changed them forever or some shit.

I finish my beer, listening but not really listening to Felicia and Chops and cursing the fact that I don't have any cigarettes, when I spot Brad. It's not as if it's that hard to spot Brad – he's like seven feet tall or something – but he disappeared earlier in the night, drunkenly following some girl around, and this is his first appearance since. Brad's a bit of a fag, but essentially he's a nice guy. I went to school with him, and now we go to uni together. He's probably my best friend, whatever the hell that means. He's inside talking to a girl I don't recognise, but I call his name and when he turns and sees me, he bounds out onto the deck, this big puppy-dog grin on his face.

'Brad! Dude, where have you *been* all night?' I ask.

'I don't know,' he tells me. 'Around. Doing my thing.' Brad is pretty drunk, more so than I am. 'Listen, dude,' he says. 'Seriously, I got something good for you.'

'Okay, so, is this something good going to involve you blowing me?' I ask. 'Because I know you're into that faggy shit.'

Brad looks confused for a second. 'Dude, that's officially twisted. You know I'm not, like...' He trails off.

'Forget it,' I tell him. 'I'm just messing with you. So... something good?'

'Oh yeah!' he says, grinning again. 'I forgot. You know that friend of mine? With the...?' He starts bouncing up and down on the balls of his feet, looking around like someone might be listening, some parent or other responsible adult who might be waiting to catch him out in this killer scheme. 'You know, the thing? That I was, like, telling you about...'

'The what?' I ask, like I'm not fully aware of what he's getting at. It's fun to mess with Brad – he can be like a little kid when he gets excited about something.

'You know, the...' He starts making this frantic gesture that involves scooping up imaginary powder with his finger and then putting the finger on his tongue. Subtle. He's actually bouncing faster now. '*Dude...*'

'I know, I know.' I motion inside the house. 'Shall we?'

Brad sighs with relief, his face breaking into this massive dumb grin. 'Yeah, let's go.'

Brad follows me back into the house; as we're leaving, I tell Felicia that we'll be right back, but she is talking very fast at the punk guy and has already forgotten me.

On the way through the living room, we meet Sara.

She is in the middle of a group of girls but doesn't seem to be listening to the conversation. I walk up behind her, put my arm around her waist. When she turns to look at me, she seems pretty wired, drunk but also kind of stunned, like some little animal caught in a car's headlights.

'Liam...' she says when I let her go. 'I really want to talk.' She touches my stomach then pulls her hand away.

'Okay...'

'But I don't want to talk here.'

'You want to go somewhere quiet?' I grin, pull her in so her hips are touching mine. 'Maybe in your room?'

'That's not what I mean,' she says. 'This party is getting to me. Everyone's crying and wishing me a safe trip, and it's making me feel weird. It's like I'm going to *die* or something. It's only going to be six months.'

While this is going on, Brad is bounding around, saying hi to the girls, telling them what a great night he's having and asking them how they are and whatever. The girls are all too drunk to feign detachment so they play along with him. Sara's friend Isabel starts dancing with him, grinding up against him while holding her drink above her head, and he lets her do it.

'Listen, we'll talk later, okay?'

'Don't you want to stay here with us for a while?'

'Baby...' I look over at Brad, who is trying to touch one of Isabel's breasts. 'Brad and I have to do...something. I'll be back, okay?'

'Fine,' she says, shaking her head. Looking away and then back at me. 'It's important, okay? I really want to talk to you.'

'I know. Don't worry.' I kiss her and then grab Brad, who seems reluctant to be torn away from the girls, but after a while he takes the hint and follows me. We walk through the house, dodging people. Brad says hi to this girl he knows from uni. We end up in the nearest empty bedroom, which happens to be Sara's. The walls in here are painted dark blue; there is a big four-poster bed that takes up most of the room and black-and-white photographs of Paris on the walls. They're from, like, the 1920s or something and Sara told me who took them but I don't really remember now. I guess Sara's really into Paris.

'Dude,' Brad asks me as I'm shutting the door, 'is your girlfriend going to have a problem with, like, us...?' He's acting all nervous now, bouncing up and down on his feet again.

'No,' I tell him. 'She's fine.'

'Shit, do you think we should have asked her if she wanted some?'

'No,' I tell him. 'She doesn't. Come on, let's do this already.'

'Oh yeah,' he says, as though he'd forgotten about the drugs, which he probably had. 'I got this from William,' he tells me, fishing around in his pocket. 'He says it's really good shit.'

It's a little plastic baggie with yellow crystals inside. They stick to the sides and form this kind of scum, which is gross, but I guess you have to ignore that.

'So Sara's friend Isabel,' says Brad, trying to get the baggie open, pulling at the top of it with his long fingers, 'do you think she…?'

'Isabel? Yeah, I think she likes you.'

He's grinning again, giving me that puppy-dog look. 'You think? Cos, y'know, before…' Without warning, the bag comes open, and Brad nearly drops it. 'Dammit. Here we go,' he says, putting his index finger in and getting as much of the powder on it as he can before bringing it back up to his tongue. 'She's really pretty cute, and, oh *dude*, you have to do some of this right now, it's really strong, seriously.'

Brad puts his finger in the bag again and then holds it out, offering it to me. I stare at it.

'Dude, I'm not putting your finger in my mouth.'

Brad looks confused. 'Come on, dude, it's me, it's not like I'm going to tell anyone.'

'No, it's gay. I'm not doing it.'

'Fine.' Brad shakes his head and offers me the baggie. 'Always with the gay shit, Liam. I seriously wonder about you, you know that?'

'Yeah, I'll bet. You wonder about sucking my dick, don't you? You want some of this…' I make a grab for my crotch with one hand and the drugs with the other.

The speed is bitter and does, in fact, turn out to be very strong. 'Jesus, you're right, this is good.'

'Told you, and by the way, suck this,' Brad says, grinning and making a lunge at me.

'Dude…' I tell him, laughing, 'get out of here, that's like…that is so gay.'

We do some more of the speed and Brad tells me he'd really like to have sex with Isabel tonight but he hopes

Sara won't get upset, Isabel being one of her closest friends and all. I point out that Sara's going to Europe in three days, and anyway, what the hell does she care? Brad seems happy with this and we head back out to the party. On the way past the kitchen, we bump into Sara's dad, who asks how we're enjoying ourselves, makes some joking remark about my driving and the M4. Sara's parents both own Beamers — which they upgrade every two weeks or something — and normally I'm never allowed to drive them, so basically, the other night with the M4 was a big deal.

I'm feeling kind of edgy now and Brad is bouncing up and down at about a hundred miles an hour and luckily the conversation with Sara's dad is cut short when Toby staggers out of the kitchen looking like he's about to be sick. I grab Sara around the waist and kiss her, and when this song we both like comes on we start to dance. Later in the night, Brad and Isabel disappear together. Sara drinks glass after glass of champagne and one of her brother's friends is sick on the floor.

It's after two now and I'm lying on Sara's bed. She's pretty drunk — before, she was dancing around the room all crazy, singing that song she likes about going on a rocket ride and refusing to let me touch her, but now she's out of breath, leaning on a chest of drawers, playing with this dumb stuffed wombat that she has, and every so often looking over at me.

'It's six months,' she says. 'I know it's a long time, but I'd like to think that if anything happened, that you'd still...'

'I'd understand... I mean, if anything happened. If you met someone. Like...a boy. I mean, I'd be upset, but I'd understand.' Before Brad disappeared, he and I smoked a spliff to come down from the speed, and the two drugs are still mingling in my system, giving me this nauseous and strangely weightless feeling.

'Jesus, your heart really sounds like it's in this.' Sara puts the wombat down, then rearranges it in a different position. 'And anyway, that's why I wanted you to come...so that wouldn't happen. So we could be together.'

I sit up with my elbow on one of her pillows. 'Come here,' I tell her, 'then we can be together.'

She laughs, throws the wombat at me and stumbles across the room towards the bed. 'I hate you,' she says, but she's smiling and when she jumps on the bed next to me I can tell she doesn't really mean it.

She grabs a pillow and hugs that instead of me, squeezing it and then loosening her grip like she can't really make up her mind about it. 'You'll wait for me, right?' she asks.

'Yeah, I'll wait for you.'

'I just want to hear you say it,' she tells me.

'Say what?' I ask.

'Don't play dumb. You know what I mean.' She rolls over so she's on top of me. She pins my arms down, puts her face really close to mine and tells me, all serious, 'I just want to hear you say it.'

'I don't know what you're –'

'*Say it.*'

'I love you,' I tell her. Some of her hair gets in my

23

face and she leans down to kiss me. Now I'm pushing my jeans down and Sara is sliding her dress off, over her head, letting me kiss her stomach.

'I love you too,' she says and starts moving against me.

We spend ten minutes or so touching one another, haphazardly, drunkenly. I finger Sara for a while and kiss her breasts, which always seems to drive her nuts. We're whispering stuff at each other and she goes down on me. Sara's never been that good at giving head, it's always been more a matter of enthusiasm than technique on her part, though, really, why complain? After she finishes that, I still haven't come and she starts getting all apologetic. I tell her 'It's okay, it's okay', breathing quite heavily, but she starts giving me a rather determined hand job, which I brush off, jerking off frantically for a minute or so while fingering her again with my free hand. This elicits a series of small gasps from her, and when things seem to be building to a climax, she starts opening and closing her thighs, groaning. I roll her on her side and manage to fuck her for a fairly hectic five minutes or so. This is usually the way it goes – she seems to be into it, and even if I'm not so much, I suppose it's not that big a deal.

When I've finally come, Sara tells me she loves me then almost immediately falls asleep with her head on my chest. I should be falling asleep too – I'm weak, feeling completely lousy and thinking over all kinds of bad stuff that's happened, but the speed is beginning to reassert itself and sleep is probably out of the question right now.

I lie there, staring up at these mostly faded glow-in-the-dark stars that I guess Sara put on the ceiling as a little kid, and continue to deal with the weight of her head. When you're younger and fantasising in your own inexperienced way about what things like this are like, you fall asleep on a pillow pretending that it's a real person, but you never really get an idea of how heavy and uncomfortable a sensation it is until someone does it to you. That being said, I think it's better to have someone to fall asleep on your chest than not. Sleeping alone with a pillow is worse, nine times out of nine.

Don't get me wrong, I really do love Sara, though right now, even as I'm lying with my arm around her, part of me is thinking about other things. She sighs, dreaming of who the hell knows what, and presses herself harder into me. I should be feeling happy right now but I'm feeling pretty bad, thinking that for the whole time I was doing Sara, when I wasn't thinking of the mechanics of it and what to put where and when, I was thinking about what happened with that dumb, helpless fag in the car park this afternoon.

When the boy came in he was by himself. He had shaggy blond hair and these sad-looking eyes, a nose that stuck out and moist lips, and he was wearing a shirt with these little pictures of skulls all over it. That messy-but-not-really-messy look that I guess a lot of guys go for now. But he was... I don't know if you'd say he was cute, but

25

when he came in, something inside me went hollow. Sometimes when you see a certain guy, and something about the way he looks or the way he carries himself makes you think... Everything about him screamed *faggot*, screamed *I'll let you do whatever you want*. Some people have this look of pretend innocence, the kind that's very easy to corrupt. Something about this boy gave me the feeling that I'd be able to talk him into doing just about anything.

The boy had moved to one of the racks by the window and was looking at a shirt with a big, doe-eyed bunny rabbit on it. I walked over to him to ask how he was going, said something about how cool that particular shirt was, how the designer was from Melbourne and only made, like, half a dozen of them or something. I mean, it was pretty much bullshit, but I just wanted to talk to him, get his attention or maybe size him up. The boy, who seemed to be about my age, was acting pretty cautious, but he looked right at me and said that it was interesting, about the shirt. There were a few seconds of silence between us – the boy ran his fingers down the shirt slowly before putting it back on the rack, and kept looking at me. I asked him what he did, if he was studying or something, and he said yeah, I'm studying this and this – I don't remember what he said – but we made this stunted conversation until I was distracted by Jay, who needed help moving this heavy box, the pussy, and by the time I got back the boy had disappeared.

Not long after that, I went outside for some reason. I told Jay I was getting a coffee, asked if he wanted anything, and he said yeah, get me a Red Bull. I told him that shit eats away your stomach lining but he said get him one anyway, so I left. I wasn't really surprised when I saw the shaggy-haired boy standing at City Beach, looking but not really looking at these Quiksilver shirts that were out the front. When he saw me he hesitated for a few seconds before looking away. I went across to him and said 'Hi' and he looked up at me and sort of smiled and said 'Hi' back, and from then there was pretty much no doubt where this was heading. He asked me some dumb question about the music that was playing before – a question so completely transparent it almost wasn't worth answering – but I told him the CD was mine, a compilation from this German record label. I told him that I was playing a burned version, but I had the original in my car (a complete lie, of course) and he could come have a look if he wanted to. Sometimes you've just gotta go with it and say to hell with subtlety, y'know?

I wasn't really that surprised when he followed me to the car park. We got to my car, the WRX my dad bought me when I finished school, and he got in on the passenger seat beside me. Then he started acting all nervous and saying things like, 'This is kind of weird', and 'It's not like I'd normally do shit like this' and whatever else, and I really wasn't in the mood so I told him to shut up, leaned back in my seat and let him go to work. It was all over pretty quickly. He gave me this practised blow job that kind of made me doubt his *It's not like I'd normally do shit like this* statement somewhat, but it was pretty good nonetheless. When we were done, I locked the car again and went back inside, telling him not to follow me.

Okay. So I have been with guys before, but, in the end, it's about the sex – you know, they're into it, they seem completely grateful for the chance to suck my dick, and really, what's the big deal? I get to come, they get a story about going down on a hot straight guy to tell their faggot friends, and essentially it's all forgotten about as quickly as it happened. It's not like I'm into guys. I mean, I'm not. It sounds harsh I guess, but I'm not a faggot, and when you're in a certain position there are some things you can get away with even if you're not necessarily *meant* to. Lots of guys do things like this. *Believe me.*

Two

It's dawn when I wake up. There is a beeping noise that insinuates itself into a dream I've been having about a plane crash, but as the dream starts to wear off the noise continues, insistent and high-pitched. The noise, I rationalise after some initial anger and confusion, is the kind that comes from a mobile phone, and ignoring it is clearly not an option. I'm feeling what you might diplomatically describe as *worse for wear*, wondering firstly if my head will hurt less if I don't move, and secondly what could possibly have made me set my alarm for this ridiculous hour.

My legs have somehow become twisted in the sheets and as I struggle out of them, I try to remember where I might have left the phone, as the noise seems to be coming from somewhere on the other side of the room. Why the alarm? Was an apocalyptic event of some sort pencilled in for today and I've forgotten about it? Is the phone even *mine* – and if not, who else might have spent the night in my room? These and other questions assail me as I stumble across to my desk and blindly search inside a pile of shirts, under an open copy of *The Face*, but to no avail.

Finally, after thoughts of giving up, suicide, moving house, I manage to locate the phone – inside a shoe that is wedged for some reason between my computer monitor and the wall. After dislodging the shoe, I realise that there is also a piece of paper inside with a note scrawled across it in black marker. The note reads:

Your girlfriend leaves for Europe today.
Get out of bed you lazy motherfucker.

The note, it's fair to say, clears quite a few things up. It's all coming back... Sara's flight leaves at ten – London via Dubai, as I now remember her explaining – and by implication I'm supposed to be at the airport before then to see her off. We discussed it in a vague way yesterday before I left her house. She said she wanted to spend her last night with her family or something and I said yeah, okay, and the whole situation reminded me of that Mexican movie where the two guys sneak around their girlfriends' parents the night before a big European trip, and I was going to bring that up with Sara but didn't. I remember making plans with Brad instead. He's picking me up at my house...when? I think at around eight, but I could easily be wrong.

There is a floor-length mirror near the desk, and I move in front of it to get a look at myself. I'm wearing only boxer shorts and socks – which I guess I forgot to take off – and I take a look at my chest and stomach, happy with how toned they still look, even though I haven't done rowing for, like, more than six months. My hair's messed up from being in bed, but it's messed up in an attractive way. Basically, I feel like shit but look fantastic, and that's really all that counts. I notice a stamp on the inside of my wrist – the kind they give you in clubs, with the words KILL THE DJ in smudged purple ink – and other things from last night begin to come back. I need to shower – if Sara sees the stamp on my wrist she'll almost certainly get upset, ask me what I was doing, and I really don't need that kind of aggravation this morning.

In the shower, I let the cold water hit me right in the face as I try to piece together a decent account of what happened. My recall is sketchy at best, but I remember getting home from Sara's in the afternoon, a weird conversation with Chloë, who lives here too, and then...what? Getting mashed on some rather excellent weed that Chloë had scored from her new German boyfriend, then going into the Valley to see Jay, who was DJing at some offensively hip new place on Brunswick Street and had ordered us to come along and check him out. Jay's set was good, if somewhat heavily reliant upon trendy tech-house, and the place was full of yuppies and metrosexuals, whom we pilloried mercilessly until Jay came down on a break and scored us all complimentary vodkas from the bar. A few of those turned into many and after a while the night becomes a series of fractured images: standing on the street making fun of some clothes in a window; girls from either Somerville House or All Hallows; snorting speed on a fire escape that overlooked a vacant lot; loud trance music in a poorly ventilated space; and finally, collapsing alone into my bed.

I emerge, finally, from the shower and prepare to face the horrors that lurk beyond my bedroom door. Our house is at the Teneriffe end of New Farm, staggering distance from the Valley, which means that on any given morning there can be up to ten people crashed out – or in one instance last month, actually *having sex* – on the floor. My housemates bring them home – friends, acquaintances, people they've just met, all of them trailing along like lost, drunken puppy dogs.

In the living room a cluster of strays, emo-ish kids I've never seen before, is passed out on one another. A boy with black hair covering one eye and a pair of Converse sneakers is unconscious on the sofa, while a blond boy with a hooded sweatshirt and tattoos down one leg is slumped across him. The blond boy is holding the hand of a Kelly Osbourne-ish girl who is half propped up on the sofa. There is one more, lying face down, but the gender of this last one is kind of difficult to determine and it's too early in the morning for this shit anyway. These people might be friends of Chloë's, or Jay's, or we may have taken them in as part of some Adopt-A-Subculturally-Challenged-Kid program, but whatever, I find it difficult to even express how much I don't care.

When I get to the kitchen, Chloë is sitting at the table with an empty coffee cup in front of her, looking a little blurry around the edges but otherwise impeccable.

'Big night?' I ask her.

She grins, looks me up and down. 'Not as big as yours,

cowboy. Here,' she says, pointing at her cheek, making
these kissing noises. 'Kiss me and you'll feel better.'

I do as I'm told and she closes her eyes and scrunches
up her face in pretend delight. 'Now sit,' she says. I do.
Chloë only moved in two days ago but already the
dynamic in the house has shifted and she has taken
control. Chloë gets away with things like this simply
because she's Chloë. The two of us have kind of a routine going – we've been friends since about halfway
through high school and she's always doing stuff like this.
Not just to me, to all kinds of boys. Boys are *all*, to some
extent or another, in Chloë's thrall – if she asked you to
bark like a dog or chase a stick or something, believe me,
you'd probably do it.

Chloë does some modelling, though she also studies
fashion design and is basically allergic to anything that
amounts to work. She was a door bitch at some club in
the Valley for a while but gave it up because it was boring and she'd rather be inside partying anyway; at the
moment she shows up, like, two days a week at this fashion shop called Fashion Shop, but it's boring too, so she
tells us, and she's probably going to quit soon. Chloë was
in a series of Mambo ads last year. She was the blonde
girl sitting on a bathroom sink staring off into the middle distance behind a reasonably good-looking fag in
distressed denim and a 'Frankie Say Relax' shirt. The ads
were on billboards and in magazines. One of the billboards was near my old school, but it was defaced and
they had to take it down.

Disinclined as Chloë is to actually, you know, do

anything productive, the cash flow thing never seems to be that much of an issue. There's always Daddy's money to fall back on, but regardless of that, she always seems to be getting involved with guys who try to take care of her – people like bankers and club owners and property developers, otherwise sane and rational guys who fall for her wacky charms, who cheat on their girlfriends to be with her, who take her out to cocktails, buy her ridiculous, expensive shit and tell her they love her. I'm not even kidding when I say that – believe me, being a guy, I know how averse we are to displays of emotion in any form, genuine or not, but Chloë just brings it out of them, has them tripping right over their tongues. At one point last year there was a guy who used to fly her down to Sydney all the time and might or might not have proposed marriage; we never quite got to the bottom of that one.

There's always been a weird sexual tension between the two of us – I've always gotten the feeling that she wants me and a couple of times, well okay, this one time, we got completely fucked up together at some party or other and we *did* fool around a bit, but I stopped it before it went too far. She got angry after that and asked why I wasn't into it and I told her it was for Sara's sake, that I wanted to be faithful to her, which I guess was the truth. Chloë told me she understood and it didn't screw up our friendship or anything like that, but ever since then there's always been this... I guess you'd call it an undercurrent.

It was just a weird twist of fate that our old room-mate

moved out as Chloë was looking for a place, so we're renting one of the bedrooms to her. None of her furniture has arrived yet so she's been sleeping on a sofa in the living room – she said something about sleeping in my bed, and though I'm pretty sure she was kidding, she gave me this look when she said it, and...well. Truth is, I'd kind of like to have hooked up with her that night and I'm not really sure what went wrong, but I guess it's in the past now.

She sighs dramatically, puts her legs up on a chair, then changes her mind and crosses them underneath her.

'Who are those people?' I ask her. 'In the living room?'

She glances disapprovingly in their general direction. 'Friends of Jay's, maybe. I'm pretty sure they smoked the rest of our shit. I couldn't find it this morning and I looked for it, like, *really* hard. I *wasn't* very happy about it.'

'Little fuckers. I'll beat it out of them later. Where's...' I try to think of her boyfriend's name and end up drawing a blank, '...the German?'

'Lukas?'

'Yeah.'

'Lukas,' she says, pausing for an intake of breath, 'is the reason I *never* date guys my own age. And he was a *backpacker*. I mean fuck, I would *never* have gone out with someone like Lukas, but I let my standards slip because he was fucking *gorgeous,* even you have to admit...'

'Do I?'

'His accent was cute too. They always sound so *earnest,*

German guys. I love it, it's like, even if they're asking you for fucking directions or something they sound so *serious* about it. It's adorable. But it doesn't matter now. Lukas is finished.'

'Meaning?'

'Meaning he's no more. We went back to the Sun Bar last night, after we split up with you, and he ran into this guy he knew – another German, I think – and they started drinking these awful German beers together. The beer was called...I can't remember, Stein...herts...von... somethingorother, and it was fucking *ungodly*.'

'So you left?'

'I stuck it out. I thought, he's *gorgeous*, the least I can do is get a root out of him. I love going to bed with a guy who has an accent; y'know the way they say, like...' Adopting a breathy tone of voice, writhing, she demonstrates: '*Ja! Ja!* or whatever the fuck the word is for yes wherever they come from...'

'Um...'

'So we end up sitting on one of those big vinyl things and Lukas and this guy start getting all pally, and he starts snuggling up to me on one side and the friend on the other, and then the shithead asks me if I want to have a three-way with the two of them, asks me if it's *cool* – and I was *so* insulted, I was like, *no*. I mean, it's not something I'd rule out, but you don't just spring something like that on a girl, y'know? It's like... How fucking sleazy can you get? So Lukas and the friend went home.'

'Okay.'

'Together.'

'No shit.'

'And I'm like...*Jesus*.'

'That's no good.'

'They're all gay,' she says.

'German people?'

'Boys. All the boys I know are gay. Those awful fucking kids in there are gay. Homosexuals! All of them! I'll bet *you're* gay too.'

'No I'm *not*.'

'I'm kidding. Why do you take things so *seriously*, Liam?' she asks. 'Oh, forget it. Kiss and make up?'

I kiss her again.

'Why are you up so early anyway?' she asks.

'Sara,' I tell her. 'Leaves today.' It feels different now I've actually said it. The words hang in the air. 'Yep,' I add. 'Today. For Europe.'

'You and Sara...' She trails off.

'What?'

Chloë looks me up and down again, re-crosses her legs in a different way, says nothing.

Brad arrives at around eight. I hear him pull up to the house and then blow the horn. Having been awake for a while, the idea that Sara is leaving has had time to sink in, and the whole situation fills me with a vague sense of unease. Brad blows the horn again and I call out that I'm coming, not that it's going to make a great deal of difference. The little Valley brats are still passed out in the living room, and as I'm leaving, one of them – the one with the hair across his face – wakes up and asks me if I know where Matthew went, but he falls asleep again before I have the chance to tell him I have no idea what the hell he's talking about. The morning sun is almost sarcastically bright, and it seems way too much to handle in my fragile state, so without giving it much of a second thought I steal a pair of aviator sunglasses from one of the sleeping kids as I make for the door. Serves the little faggot right, I guess.

Brad is pulled up across the driveway in his mother's Lexus. When I get in, he reaches across to offer me one of those elaborate handshakes, which I return before slumping back in the seat. Brad immediately pulls away from the kerb, turns without bothering to look, and starts heading back down Harcourt Street. He starts telling me about what he did last night, a story that involves some friends of his brother's and some nitrous oxide. The word 'dude!' seems to be coming up quite frequently, but I'm finding it difficult to pay a great deal of attention. How Brad can possibly be so awake, so goddamned *bouncy* at this hour of the morning is beyond me, but I guess Brad's always like this. By the time we reach Kingsford Smith Drive, things have moved on and Brad has turned his attention to the stereo. He changes the station a couple of times and then starts fumbling around in a big black CD wallet. You really have to admire the guy's carelessness – he's paying no attention whatsoever to the road, one hand on the wheel, telling me, 'We need a soundtrack, dude – keep it fresh, keep it real.'

'Keep it *real*? I'm sorry, but who died and made you

P Diddy? Dude, watch where we're... Dude! *Brad*!'

A red Mitsubishi with two girls inside is slowly pulling away from some traffic lights ahead of us. Brad only swerves to avoid it at the last available second.

'No way!' he laughs once it looks like we've managed to cheat death. 'I would *not* have had a fun time explaining that one to Mum and Dad. Dude – you remember when I wrote off that Volvo? Whoa...'

'Jesus,' I say, making a grab for the CD wallet. 'I remember. Give it to me. What do you want to listen to?'

'Put on...shit, I don't know. Put on...' He looks down at the wallet, which is now on my lap.

'Look at the road, dude!'

'Put on Good Charlotte. No, don't... Um... This is confusing.'

'Here.' I find an old Beastie Boys album and slip it into the CD changer. Brad seems satisfied with this and turns his attention back to the road. The traffic is pretty light and he draws level with the girls in the Mitsubishi, then pushes the button to make his window go down. At first they seem kind of hostile to his advances, what with his nearly turning them into roadkill and everything, but Brad waves at them, goofing around, and after a while they seem to loosen up somewhat. Before long they're actually grinning at us, flirting with Brad as we drive along. One of them blows him a kiss. Pretty impressive shit, actually.

When we pull up to another set of lights, we're still next to the girls. Brad leans out the window and asks them how they're going, still messing around, and they giggle, tell us their names and that they're on their way to their friend's apartment in Noosa. Brad tells them to forget that and meet up with us at the airport, but the light goes green and pretty soon we've lost them.

We merge onto the freeway and after a few close calls we're on the airport drive. We pull into the temporary parking, which is weirdly deserted considering the time of day, and after sitting in silence for a couple of seconds, Brad asks me: 'Do you wanna get fucked up?'

'Absolutely.' Didn't even have to think about it.

Brad pulls a bag of weed from under the seat and starts to skin up as I check out the airport terminal, wondering if Sara and her family are already inside. I imagine them at the luggage check-in, her mum getting impatient with the person at the ticket counter, the blank, impassive look on her dad's face.

'We need to have the windows down, okay?' Brad says. 'Dad's going to crack the shits if he finds out I've been smoking weed in Mum's car again.' Seems logical. 'Do you remember when I wrote off that...'

'Yeah, I remember.'

He lights the joint and then passes it to me. The morning is just starting to seem salvageable when, in spite of how obviously deserted the car park is, an old couple in a black Audi pull in right next to where Brad is parked. It might be some kind of atavistic response – primitive urge not to stray too far from the herd or something – but it's *typical* of the shit that seems to happen to me. Needless to say, when they get out to lock their doors, the woman, who is wearing pearls and looks more middle-aged than old now, sees us and starts to smile, but then she smells the smoke from the passenger window and the look changes to one of deep disapproval. She whispers something at her husband and it seems the two of them can*not* scurry away fast enough.

'Fan-fucking-tastic.'

'Maybe we should've asked if they wanted some,' says Brad, still grinning. 'I wish those girls were here, from before. The blonde one was cute. We'll need to get you a girl...' he continues. 'One of them for each of us.'

'Dude, a little respect for Sara, please?'

'Right, sorry. You're a gentleman. I forgot. Seriously, how could you *not* have slept over at her house last night?'

'I don't know...family time?'

'That's obscene, dude. That's retrograde. This is the last chance you'll get for six months. If it was my girlfriend, I'd still be there. I mean, *man*, I'd be in bed for like four days or something. I wouldn't want to leave...'

'I had, like, her parents to think of and stuff. She wanted to spend the last night with her family and you can't really argue with that, it's pretty understandable...'

'Yeah, but even so, I'd be over there saying, like, you've seen enough of your daughter, I'm taking her upstairs now, seeya. *Dude.* Six months? Will you even last that long?'

'You're asking me if I'm planning to sleep with other girls while Sara's away?'

'I mean, not to disrespect you and Sara or anything, but I haven't gone that long since I was...since I was *fourteen*, dude, you know what I'm saying?'

At this point I punch his closed fist with mine, a gesture of solidarity that's meant to say *yeah, nail those bitches* or something along those lines. It has to be done. It's like being on autopilot. It's so much easier when you can switch shit off and just go with it.

'I think you're crazy. Sara's gorgeous – no offence – and she's gonna be, like, alone. In Europe. For six months. Think of all those hot European guys. You've seen the movies, like, late at night on SBS and shit...you know what I mean?'

'Are you saying you want to do one of those European guys? Because if you want to, y'know, come to terms with your inner homosexual, I'm completely cool with that.'

'Dude, enough with the gay shit. I'm being serious. I'm talking...like, Italian guys, they have sex all day long. In, like, olive groves and at the Arc de Triomphe and shit.'

'I'm pretty sure that's Paris.'

'*Whatever*, dude. I'm talking about buff guys named Giancarlo and Antonio. Sex, that's all they do. And Sara, going into the middle of all that, alone...'

'Dude, if you don't stop talking about my girlfriend this way I'm going to impose some serious sanctions on your behaviour, some UN-style shit...'

'Sorry, dude, all I'm saying is –'

'You think I should be going with her?'

'That's what I'd do.'

'I trust her.'

Brad's face breaks into one of his trademark grins. I can feel some serious bonding coming on. 'Dude,' he says. 'Dude, that is so awesome. I mean that. You and Sara...' He leans across and hugs me with one arm. 'I don't mean to doubt you, and you know I'm really sorry... Because, you guys... What you have is special. You're the best couple. And I mean that, dude.'

'Jesus, are you on ecstasy or what?'

'Dude, that's funny.' He stares out the window for a second. 'Hey, do you wanna try and get some pills for this weekend? Might cheer you up,' he says with a weird, annoying music in his voice, 'what with Sara leaving and stuff.'

That particular leap of logic was stellar, even for Brad. 'Funny shit,' I say.

'What?'

'Never mind... Yeah, this weekend. I think we should.'

As we approach the terminal, it becomes clear that the weed has had no effect whatsoever on Brad – if anything, it has made him *more* hyperactive than usual. He points out planes as they fly overhead, starts telling me how he flew down to Melbourne with a friend of his to party, and how we totally have to do the same one weekend. When he spots an old man struggling with one of those luggage trolleys, he bounds over to help out. I'm feeling somewhat more reticent but I'm glad to have Brad around, as I guess the two of us cancel each other out. As we are getting out of the lift into the main part of the terminal, a group of tall, Nordic-looking blondes is getting on, and he almost loses it completely.

'Did you see those girls? Did you *see* them? We have to follow them. We have to, like, welcome them to our country and shit!'

'On the way back,' I tell him.

We walk through the terminal, past the check-in desks, and try to spot Sara. There aren't a huge number of people around this morning – it seems mainly to be worn-out business travellers and kids my age with backpacks. This bored-looking guy at one of the check-in desks looks me over and I look him over and then keep hunting for Sara.

I see her before she sees me – she's standing near a large potted plant, holding a pillow and surrounded by a group of her friends and relatives, all of them fussing over her to varying degrees. She looks smaller, more fragile in this huge setting, and her skin seems very pale. She has that same glazed expression from the other night, and a look of relief comes over her when she spots me and Brad.

'Sara!' yells Brad, running towards her in a pantomime of slow motion. 'Don't gooo with-ooooout meee...'

'Hey, Brad,' she says, like she's trying to laugh but not really succeeding. Then she turns to me.

'Liam.' Her tone of voice gives nothing away. 'You're here.'

I grab her shoulders, brush some hair away from her forehead and give her a kiss there. She hugs me, tightly, then reaches up to take my aviators off.

44

'I want to see you,' she says, then, looking at the sun-glasses, 'these are nice. When did you get them?'

'I've always had them.'

'Really? I guess I never noticed before.' She reaches up to touch my face. 'Where have you been?'

'Couldn't find a park. Sorry.'

Sara hugs me again. 'You were almost too late. I have to leave in, like...' She looks up at one of the departure boards 'Like, really soon. I'm so nervous.'

'I'm sorry. We're here now. You'll be fine.'

'Liam.' She says my name and that's it.

The various friends and family have all fallen silent. I've had my turn with Sara and the hour of her departure is fast approaching, so she goes back to her parents for some final words of advice or whatever. She playfully hits her little brother but then hugs him tightly, and he pretends to look embarrassed, trying without really trying to squirm out of her arms and then hugging her back. Amongst the group of girls here is Isabel – I have no idea what happened between her and Brad the night of the party, but she seems happy to see him and the two of them have gravitated towards one another.

We have about ten minutes before Sara leaves. She does the rounds of her friends again, all of them hugging and crying, making promises to email, telling Sara to have 'the most awesome time'. It's way too bright in the terminal and I'm kind of suffering without my sunglasses, but I leave them off for Sara's sake, hoping her parents won't notice my eyes, which I'm sure must be extremely bloodshot by now. Her father drifts over to me, but, fortunately, Mr Chase exists in a perpetual daze and is almost incapable of talking about anything but the M4 and his architect firm. We talk about the car and the practice for a while – and by 'talk' I mean he talks at me while I squint and try not to give in to my creeping paranoia – that *he knows his daughter's boyfriend has been smoking weed in the car park.* Luckily, he doesn't.

Over near the escalators, Brad is teasing Isabel, moving in like he's going to tickle her and then pulling away, and she seems to be eating it up, laughing and pretending to push him out of the way. I guess those Nordic girls are off the agenda for later then. By this stage, Sara has covered everything with her friends and has drifted back towards me. The word 'drifted' really isn't an exaggeration when it comes to Sara – it's like she's so light she moves around on currents of air, as though one day she might just decide it's time to fly away and that will be that. The obvious is not lost on me at this moment.

Sara takes my hand, looks up at the departure board. 'I guess this is it,' she says. I put my arms around her waist and we kiss for what feels like a long time. When she whispers 'Love you' in my ear, her breath feels hot. I tell her I love her back. Then she turns and seconds later has disappeared down the escalator.

It's sometime later in the afternoon. The thought of going home, dealing with my room-mates and the various other hangers-on, leaves me cold, so Brad and I make an executive decision to go back to his house and get fucked up instead. The Caldwells live in one of those places along the river in St Lucia; all the houses around here are big, set back from the road and surrounded by bush. I guess the suburb is kind of what you'd refer to as *leafy* – that's probably what the real estate agent told Brad's parents when he was giving them the grand tour; how quiet the area was, close to the university, a great place to raise a family and shit. You have to feel sorry for the Caldwells – I mean, if I remember correctly, the main reason they bought this house was that they were thinking of the boys' future, about their education and keeping them out of trouble and everything else. Knowing Brad, that must have been the disappointment of the fucking century. The Germans have a word for that, so I remember reading once, *schaden*...fucking...whatever, doesn't really matter.

Anyway, Brad's parents are away this weekend – 'Mum has this thing down the coast' is all he offers by way of explanation – and his brother doesn't seem to be around, so the two of us basically have the place to ourselves. Brad's socked feet are on the coffee table next to a large bong and what was once a fairly hefty bag of weed. We're both sitting on the couch, watching an old episode of *Degrassi Junior High* on cable with the sound turned down and old Beastie Boys blasting at a ridiculous volume from the stereo. We were planning to call some of the guys, hang out at Indooroopilly or go for a drive or something like that, but we sort of lost the will to do so some time back. Classes go back next month so

I guess you have to take these opportunities to just hang out whenever you can get them.

Brad slumps down in his seat, picks up the remote like he's planning to change the channel and then, after staring at the multicoloured buttons in something like bemusement, puts it down again. 'So Dad's getting wound up again,' he tells me after a while.

I motion towards the weed, kick it across the table a bit and give him a questioning look.

'It's not that. Not directly anyway. It's like...He was going to buy me a car this year – we've been talking about it for ages – but now he's saying that he's not going to do it until I improve my GPA or something. It's bullshit. But part of the deal is that I'm banned from bringing weed into the house... Since, y'know...'

The *y'know* Brad's referring to is an incident that occurred several months ago, when his parents, suspicious about his marked academic decline, conducted a raid on his room and found an eighth of weed in his sock drawer. This was the explanation they were looking for – *this* was all the evidence they needed. The eighth was, of course, bullshit, and his parents probably knew as much. I mean, I've seen Brad so strung out that he did nothing but sit in front of his brother's Playstation staggering bong hits and nitrous oxide for something like six hours, and this was in high school. The drugs were nothing new. His parents' reaction to this rather pitiful amount of the stuff was reassuring at least – proof that people see what they want to see. 'When did you start doing this?' they asked. He told them university was to blame, some other kids on campus, bad influences, kids who were involved in leftish political groups...*AND THEY BELIEVED HIM*. Never underestimate the power of denial.

Parental drug busts can be a real fucking drag. It happened to me once, this time in grade eleven when our Yugoslavian housekeeper found my bong in my cupboard and freaked out. She ran out to the landing holding it above her head, shouting, 'What is? What is?' in her wide-eyed, broken English, playing innocent, like she wasn't fully aware what the fucking thing was. It was just bad luck that my parents happened to be home at the time and caught this hysterical display. Later, when they'd managed to sedate the bitch and send her on her way, punishments were being meted out and I asked them what exactly Irina was *doing* going through my cupboard in the first place. I hinted darkly at invasion of privacy, going on to point out that the bong itself was the product of an illegal search and therefore inadmissible as evidence. You'll find this shit works on *Law and Order* but it doesn't go down so well in other contexts. I can't remember how I weaseled my way out of that one, but I guess I must have, because after a while the subject just stopped coming up.

'Uni's hard work,' I tell Brad, reassuring him, though I don't know that second-year business is really that much of a challenge. *I'm* doing it, for fuck's sake, so really, how hard can it be?

'Hell, yeah, it's hard work. I told Dad I was doing the best I could – I'm passing stuff, and it's like, what *more* do you require? But he wants me to try for honours or something.'

On the screen, a punkish girl in pink and black is sulkily carving something on a desk while sitting in detention: every so often it cuts to a shot of a blond boy sitting in a bathroom stall, crying. It's not clear if the two events are connected, and I might never find out. I turn my attention back to Brad. 'Honours? Fuck that. You can get your degree and then get, like, a thoroughly decent job, and you'll be on... I mean, you'll be earning, like...'

'It's bullshit. I have this friend down the coast who's a property developer, and he's, like, *our age*. He did it straight out of school, and this guy, he's pulling in, like... an obscene amount of cash. And for what?'

'Family business?' I ask.

'Could be, I'm not sure, but it's like... What am I even going to uni for? It's stupid. Hey, you know Isabel?'

The subject tends to change fairly rapidly around Brad, and it takes me a second or so to catch up. 'Yeah,' I say, 'what about her?'

When I turn to look at Brad, his trademark grin has come back. 'The two of us...the other night...' He's nodding now, grinning even wider, and reaches across to tap my closed fist with his. 'She was hot. She was the *shit*.'

'No *way*, man. Why didn't you tell me this sooner?'

'Forgot, I guess. I got her number though, and she was texting me, like, all the next day, calling me up and shit.'

'Did you hit it yet?'

'I'm working on it. I think she might be one of those girls who don't want to fuck you until like the time's right or whatever.'

'To hell with that shit, man. That's cruel.'

On the screen, the blond boy is no longer crying; he's in someone's darkened bedroom, staring into a mirror. He's saying something to himself, but I can't hear what it is, which annoys me for some vague reason.

At a certain point Brad decides he feels like a drink – or maybe I decide, it's all very unclear – so we head back through the lounge, past a leather suite that I haven't seen before, past bookshelves stuffed with airport novels and books about Nazis, and head into the kitchen. This part of the Caldwells' house is large and well-lit; there is an island in the centre and I lean on that while Brad goes through the fridge, searching for beer, muttering about how his brother's friends better not have drunk it all.

'We could go out and get some more,' I tell him. 'We could go for a drive, go to Toowong or something.'

'Yeah, but I know there's some here,' he says. 'There was stacks of it.' Brad takes out a container of grape juice; he looks at it for a while, like he's confused about what might be in there, then he shakes it and puts it back.

'Hey.'

We both look up – Brad's little brother, Kristian, has somehow materialised in the kitchen. He is holding a pink and white trucker cap and he messes around with it for a while, passing it nervously from hand to hand before finally putting it down on the bench. He stares at the two of us. 'Hey, Liam,' he says after a while.

Kristian is almost as tall as Brad, even though he's two years younger or something, but he's a lot skinnier and kind of awkward-looking, like he hasn't figured out what to do with all the extra height yet. He has this nervous sort of look that's hard to place exactly; his hair is brown and kind of shaggy, and he has the same dumb smile that Brad does but he hides it most of the time. He's... I don't know, nice-looking. I guess if you were a fag you'd say he was cute.

'Where have you been?' asks Brad.

'I don't know. Around.' Kristian is silent for a second; he looks in my general direction then back at Brad. 'I was on the net before. I think the computer has a virus.'

'What the hell?'

'I don't know. This, like, weird stuff kept happening. But I think I fixed it.' He doesn't say anything more, just stares at the two of us. Weird.

'Good. Hey,' Brad asks him, 'what happened to all the beer?'

'Um, I think my friends got through most of it. There's like some more, in the cupboard, but it's not cold.'

'You'd think that would be fairly self-evident.'

'Um...yeah.'

There is silence again. Kristian picks up the trucker cap, messes with it some more before putting it down again.

'Hey, Brad,' he asks, 'can you drive me to the city later?'

'Why?'

'I don't know. Meeting my friends.'

'So you can hang out on the mall and suck each other's dicks?'

'*No.* I don't know. We're just planning to, like, hang out or something.'

'Don't be a faggot, Kristian.'

'I'm not.' He looks at me then back at Brad. 'Can you drive me in?'

Kristian is basically this little skate brat – he and his friends hang out in the city with boards they don't really know how to ride, attempting to look streetwise or menacing or something, even though all of them live in Toowong and Ascot and their parents send them to Grammar. Kind of like Brad and I were at his age, though we'd both be loath to admit that now.

'I'm not driving you in. It's dumb; forget it.'

'I'll tell Mum you brought weed into the house again.'

'No you won't. Anyway, I'll tell her you're a faggot.'

'Come on, part of the deal with you having the car was...'

So the negotiations continue. Eventually Brad gives in, telling Kristian to get his shit together, that we'll be leaving in five minutes and that he owes us one. Kristian looks at me and then away again. Brad takes the grape juice out of the fridge and swigs from it; he offers the container to me but I shake my head. Kristian picks up the trucker hat and leaves.

I don't know, I guess I think about Kristian sometimes. It's weird, not least of all because he's my best friend's brother and everything, but I think about what it might be like to fuck him, to have him suck my dick, in his room maybe, or in the pool. This one time last year I was meant to be meeting Brad, but when I got over here, he hadn't come back from uni yet and it was just Kristian and me. The two of us watched movies on cable for a while; I caught him looking at me a few times and he pretended that he wasn't, and things were just starting to get interesting when Brad got home, and I guess I'd forgotten all about it until now.

I think of Kristian hanging out in the city with his friends, standing on the corner near Hungry Jacks, trying to look tough. I wonder if I could talk him into letting me fuck him, if it ever came down to that. Not that it ever would.

'Dude,' Brad asks, snapping me back into the moment. 'We ready?'

'Yeah,' I tell him. 'Let's go.'

Three

So it's the three of us sitting on the back deck of the house in the shade of that big pine tree – it's way too early in the morning for this shit, but we're in the middle of what basically amounts to a major crisis. We've figured out that those stray Valley brats the other morning did, in fact, smoke the last of our weed – we have no idea how they got through it all, we had no idea such a feat was even *possible*. Resilient little bastards, I guess. But the fact remains that it's all gone. We've been calling friends, trying to work out what options might be open to us, but so far, nothing.

At least part of the mystery is solved – we've figured out that the kids were here with Jay. He'd picked one of them up earlier in the night – some little first-year design brat named Matthew, as he explained it, and the friends came as a package deal. Jay and Matthew met at some place on Ann Street and – after what I can only imagine was a lot of drinking, 'accidental' touching and 'relating' on various faggy subjects – when Jay asked Matthew to accompany him home, Matthew was like, *great, but can* FIVE OF MY ANNOYING BASTARD FRIENDS *crash at your house as well?* I guess Jay must have weighed it up and decided that the potential irritation from this was far outweighed by the potential irritation of *NOT GETTING LAID FOR ONCE IN HIS LIFE*, so he said yeah, sure, that's fine. So they staggered back to Harcourt Street – I can only imagine what that walk must have been like; I somehow have a mental picture of the two of them stopping to kiss drunkenly and feel one another up every two minutes, with everyone busy trying not to look on – and that was pretty much that.

Anyway, after I left that morning, Chloë saw the first-year design brat leaving Jay's room and put two and two together. The story, apparently, came gradually over the course of the day...We may never know the whole truth; the only real information Chloë was able to glean was that 'Matthew was pretty bad in bed' (Jay's words) and all of our weed was gone. We figured that, as this was the case, the responsibility for replacing our shit should fall on Jay. He didn't quite see it that way. We argued the point quite extensively – he reminded us that he hadn't smoked any of it as he was clearly busy at the time, so if anyone was to blame it was the design brat's friends, an interesting if not entirely convincing defence, and we countered with the fact that he was the one who brought these people into the house, these strangers who might have murdered us in our beds. But in the end we decided to hell with it, in times of crisis everyone has to pull together. It's like Winston Churchill or some shit. For the good of the empire.

Chloë, in a Mötley Crüe shirt and a pair of aviators, is

leaning back on one of the deckchairs, holding a bowl of cherries that she so far hasn't touched. I'm sitting nearby; every now and then I'll unlock my mobile phone and scroll through the list of names, trying to figure out if there's anyone I haven't called yet, anyone I might have forgotten about. Each time I come up with nothing and end up locking the phone in disgust. We're not getting much out of Jay, as we gather he's had kind of a big night. He was out with Matthew – who obviously can't have been *that* terrible in bed – and the two of them got in pretty late. He mentioned something about attending a friend's art show, tequila shots, a condom lost under the bed, but the account we got was scattered at best. At present he's leaning against the railing wearing only a pair of jeans, his eyes hidden behind sunglasses, and we can only tell he's not asleep by the periodic grunting noises in response to the various questions we ask him.

Chloë has made a couple of calls – to old boyfriends, a girl she used to work the door with at Family, to this wakeboarder she knows from the Gold Coast who is 'dumb but, like, the *best* fuck I've *ever* had ever', but as she warns us, 'nobody ever answers their phone'. This turns out to be pretty accurate. I've called a few people too, but so far no luck. My regular guy is Seth, and at the best of times you'd refer to him as *a bit unreliable*. Seth and I went to Grammar together and he went on to do a semester of software engineering at UQ but then lost his shit completely – something to do with some bad acid, we think, or a girl – and dropped out. Now he spends most of his time writing computer viruses, making this weird electronic music and selling weed. Seth's not answering, and nobody else seems to have any shit, even Brad is running low, so basically we're at a bit of an impasse.

'I've tried everyone,' says Chloë. 'Everyone. If *Jay* could be bothered to *wake up...*'

'I'm *awake*,' says Jay through gritted teeth, still not moving. 'I've *tried*. Nobody's coming to the *rescue*. Don't think this doesn't affect me too.'

'Well, I've been through, like, my *whole* address book,' says Chloë, '*twice,* and I'm not getting anywhere. This is ridiculous. It's inhuman. We're white middle-class kids in a first-world country in the twenty-first century. If we want drugs, drugs should be made available to us.'

'Maybe we can just deal with it for a few days. You know, go without it,' I venture.

'*Not* an option,' says Chloë with a noticeable edge in her voice. Jay is actually motivated enough to lower his sunglasses and glare at me.

'Well, I'm *not* getting any help from either of you.'

'Look, a little consideration, okay? This is, like, a really stressful time for me,' says Chloë. 'It's awful. Classes go back, like, next week – and there's, like, my job to worry about, *and* there's this whole thing with Annabelle, and I'm just really not feeling up to it.'

This whole thing with Annabelle is actually a major source of anxiety for Chloë. An old school friend of hers, also a model, is currently part of a reality TV show being filmed in Melbourne. The basic idea is that twelve attractive youngsters are put up in a hotel and put through their paces in the modelling world; each week one of them is kicked out of the hotel until the last one standing scores a contract, as well as all kinds of other offers, you'd imagine. Chloë has worked herself up into a near-psychotic state 'hoping that Annabelle makes it through this whole thing okay'. There have been a number of tense mobile phone calls – Annabelle, weeping uncontrollably when a boy she liked was evicted – and a number of offers to fly down to Melbourne so Chloë can be by her side. Chloë, naturally, is seething with not entirely repressed resentment, and secretly hopes that the bitch gets kicked out as it clearly should have been *her* in the competition all along. I guess that would be a source of anxiety for anyone, but Chloë really knows how to take this shit to the next level.

'We'll deal with this situation, okay,' I tell her. 'We'll get through it.'

'We'd better. I'm not going without weed. Jesus, I'm a bundle of nerves – I'm, like, freaking out as we speak. And I need to be strong...for Annabelle...'

'Why don't you call *her*?'

'She doesn't smoke weed, you dick. She's, like, asthmatic or something. And anyway, they're only allowed to do drugs when the cameras are off, which makes it really hard.'

'I was *kidding.*'

'Just think, is there *anyone* else who can help? Jay, what's going on over there? Anybody home?' Jay groans at us, and his sunglasses move a little as though he is screwing up his eyes beneath them.

'Hey,' he says slowly, 'what about that friend of Sara's?' Then, after a few seconds, 'That Zoe girl?'

'Who?' asks Chloë, suddenly all perked up again.

'You know,' says Jay. 'Zoe. That friend of Sara's from UQ. She introduced us that time...'

'That's right,' I say, my mind slowly beginning to tick over. The more I think about it, the more I start to realise we might actually be on to something. 'Zoe is this arty type. She's studying post-feminist thought or something like that, but she's nice. I went to her house once. With Sara, I mean. It was never like that...'

'Yeah, I'll bet,' says Chloë. 'So what's the story with the drugs?'

'Well, it's not her, not directly, but she was telling us that she had this room-mate...this German guy...' I remember now. This was a party a year or so ago – I'd gone along with Sara, not knowing anybody, to this weird house right near the river. The place was crowded with arty types and fags but there were some cute girls there, including Zoe, who spent a lot of the night talking to me. She told me about her room-mate, Reuben, a German exchange student who almost always had more shit than he could use, and she said that if I ever needed anything, I should come to her. He hadn't been at that particular party though – he'd disappeared a week before and nobody was quite sure where he was, but they weren't worried, because apparently that kind of thing happened all the time.

When I explain this to Chloë, she says: 'Great, let's do it. You got her number? You'd *better* have her number,

Liam, or I'm making you call Sara, I swear to God.'

I begin scrolling down to the 'z's, remembering the rest of the conversation, remembering the warning that came attached, and some darker things that Zoe had hinted at. 'Reuben is what you'd call, um, troubled,' she told me. Apparently Reuben's English isn't that great and he's an alcoholic who gets a bit temperamental. She went on to tell me that he sometimes locks himself in his room for a really long time, that he was studying but he stopped going to class and they're not sure if he's even enrolled any more, he won't tell them. Immigration may or may not be after him. The whole situation is basically very fraught.

Surprisingly, Zoe's number is indeed right there under 'z'. I guess the last time I looked through my phone I gave up before getting that far. When I call her up, she answers on the second ring. We talk for a while; she remembers who I am. She sounds a little vague on the phone, and when I ask if she's feeling okay she tells me she's recovering from a party they had last night that got a little out of control. It's pretty difficult getting straight answers out of her as she still seems a bit scattered, but I ask her about the crazy German and she tells me that he still lives with them, and that scoring some weed from him shouldn't be any problem at all. I hear noises on the other end of the line; Zoe tells me to hang on a second and I hear her shout something that sounds like 'I don't know where Paris Hilton is' but could probably be anything. She tells me she has to go and I hang up.

It's with great relief that I relay the information about the weed to Chloë and Jay. They nominate me as the one to go pick up our shit. Jay is going back to bed and Chloë insists she has to work soon; I'm like, yeah, in about three hours, but she gets grumpy and reminds me of how fragile she's feeling right now, so I guess it's up to me to save the day. We pool our resources – Chloë and Jay have two hundred bucks between them, and I throw in another hundred and fifty. I might have forgotten to mention earlier, but in terms of cash flow, one of the sweetest parts of the set-up here is that I don't really have to pay rent. My parents own the place, they bought it a few years back as an investment or something, and they basically let me live here for a token amount every week. My brother and some of his friends used to live here until they went on to bigger and better things...Now the place is mine. I mean, I have my job and everything – it doesn't really seem appropriate to hit my parents up for cash *too* often – and I probably sound like a spoiled brat to you, but if you had an arrangement like this, wouldn't you make the most of it?

Chloë eats one of the cherries, flicking the seed over the verandah railing. Jay doesn't move. 'It's probably still under there,' he says, though I really don't want to know what that's about. I get my shit together and leave them to it. Onward and upward.

I still have the aviators that I stole the other morning, and I need them when I head outside. The distance isn't even that great, but it's really early in the morning, like ten-thirty, and the sunlight is still way more than I'm able to deal with. Looking one way up Harcourt Street you can see the office buildings in the city – shiny and clean on this smog-free morning – and looking back the other, the last traces of warehouses and industrial shit which will probably all be apartments soon. Things feel kind of fresh this morning; all the trees along the street are in bloom, and it starts feeling like it might actually turn into a good day.

Zoe's house, around the corner, is almost right on the river, this weird little place that's sandwiched between a pair of warehouses and looks like it probably should have been knocked down years ago. I stare up at it. The house is two storeys, but they only occupy the top bit, and you need to walk through a narrow, overgrown gap between the fence and the house to actually get inside. I've never seen anywhere like this before, but it makes sense that this is the kind of place someone like Zoe would live. I head through the tiny space, my jeans catching on prickly weeds and God knows what else, and after what seems an epic struggle finally manage to fight my way through.

When I make it out into the backyard, Zoe is standing on the wet grass looking mildly confused, and she does not seem to register my presence. Evidence of the party remains all over the yard. Right next to the stairs, there is an inflatable pool, the kind that's usually meant for little children. It's covered in cartoon pictures of smiling dolphins and seahorses. The pool is filled with mostly melted ice and has various bottles in it; some Beck's and Coopers and, strangely, a bottle of absinthe. Nearby, on an old wooden table, some guy with a white-boy afro is passed out with empty beer and vodka bottles all around him. I begin to wonder if the guy is alive, then decide it's probably best to leave that one alone.

I walk up to Zoe, tap her on the shoulder. She turns, and when she sees me, her face breaks into a big grin. 'Liam!' she says, giving me a dramatic hug and kissing my cheek. 'It's good to see you again. Wow, this is so freaky.'

'Yeah, it's good to see you too,' I tell her. 'Who's that?' I point to the guy on the table.

She looks around, laughs nervously. 'We don't know,' she says. 'We think he's from the party last night.'

'Is he alive?'

'Hard to say... Come on, Liam, I need your help.'

'What's wrong?'

'I'm looking for Paris Hilton. I've lost her.'

'Why... Why would Paris Hilton be here?'

'You've met her, haven't you? She was here the last time you came. Oh come on, don't be dense, Liam. Help me find her. We'd better find her before she gets out. She might get hit by a car or something.'

Zoe grabs me by the hand, leads me around the back-yard, calling out 'Paris! Paris Hilton!' over and over. The guy on the table stirs at the noise but does not wake up. Someone who didn't know Zoe would probably think this whole situation was weird, but for her it's actually a pretty normal day.

'Maybe she's upstairs,' says Zoe. 'Come on, let's look

there.' As she leads me towards the staircase, which looks as though it might collapse at any second, I ask her about Reuben and the drugs. 'Oh yeah,' she says. 'Reuben's home. I told him you were coming. He has heaps of the stuff. It's scary.'

We head up the stairs, over a rickety landing and into the kitchen. The kitchen is a strange, dark little area that seems to have been tacked onto the side of the house – there is a plastic water dish in the doorway, like you'd have for a cat or something, although I don't see a cat around here anywhere. The cupboards are the kind that haven't been popular since about the 1950s, and lino of an unidentifiable colour is peeling off the floor in several places. All around the window the wall is covered with postcards – a pair of lips, full, red and garish on a white background, a sad-eyed panda bear, an eight-armed Hindu goddess, a boy with lipstick smeared all over one cheek, a bottle of Absolut Raspberri. There are dozens of others. The whole place seems to be plastered with them. There are no dishes on the sink, just empty vodka and gin bottles.

'Who the hell drinks gin?' I say to Zoe.

'I don't know, who?'

'I'm asking you.'

'Oh. Sorry, I thought it was a joke.'

'No.'

'They're probably Reuben's. Reuben drinks anything. At our last party we ran out of beer and all we could find was Campari so he started drinking that. Straight out of the bottle. It was gross.'

At this point a guy who I assume must be Reuben comes into the kitchen. He's wearing only a pair of boxer shorts. He's blond, kind of toned and smooth all over, and if he is a massive alcoholic, it hasn't started to show yet. If you were a fag, you'd probably think that Reuben was pretty hot but I'm not so I wouldn't. He's looking vaguely wasted or perhaps hungover, but still smiles when he sees me. Zoe introduces us and he says, 'Hi there, Liam' in heavily accented English.

A cute girl, who looks kind of like that French actress or something, emerges behind Reuben. She's wearing an oversized men's dress shirt, carrying a bottle of vodka. 'A new person!' she squeals when she sees me. She does a pirouette across the room and kisses me delicately on the cheek. 'I'm Audrey,' she says. 'Lovely to meet you.'

'Audrey lives here too,' Zoe tells me helpfully.

While all of this is going on, a fluffy grey cat pads into the room and cautiously looks everyone over.

'There she is!' says Zoe when she sees the cat. 'That's Paris Hilton! We have to be quiet... We don't want to scare her. I couldn't find her *all* night. I think the party freaked her out.'

Audrey totters towards us, still clutching the bottle of Absolut. 'She's giving me the *saddest* little look. I think she wants a drink, don't you, puss?' Audrey begins to laugh. 'Paris Hilton's an alcoholic,' she whispers to me.

'Audrey, *don't*,' pleads Zoe, but it's already too late. Audrey unscrews the cap, takes a fairly large swig. She wipes her mouth with the back of her hand and then, unsteadily, starts pouring vodka into the water dish.

'You're wasting good vodka,' I tell her, hoping to be of some help.

'There's always more.'

Reuben has been watching this display from across the room. 'I don't know if you're meant to give vodka to cats, baby,' he says slowly, shaking his head as though he's offering up some incredible pearl of wisdom.

Audrey begins to giggle uncontrollably as the cat takes some tentative steps towards the water dish, sniffing it uncertainly.

'Come here, puss,' says Zoe, rushing to pick the cat up. 'Come here, Paris Hilton. I won't let them do this to you.' She holds the cat to her chest and squeezes it very tightly like a child being too affectionate with her favourite stuffed toy. Paris Hilton has this look on her face like she's clearly not interested in any of this shit. Her two front paws are sticking straight out, her back legs kicking uselessly at the air. Zoe puts her face close to Paris's, swinging her from side to side, telling her what a good girl she is, what a good kitty cat. The kitty cat begins to make unhappy noises, *growls*; she starts to squirm, finally managing to struggle free of Zoe's grip and leaving a trail of scratches that actually look pretty deep down her arm.

'Fine,' Zoe says as the cat disappears out the window, knocking over an empty Jägermeister bottle. 'Fucking cunt. To hell with her.'

'Forget Paris Hilton,' laughs Audrey. 'She's over.'

'I'd better find her. I don't want her to get hit by a car. That would be bad. If she got hit by a car.' With that, Zoe turns and is out the door, leaving me alone with Reuben and Audrey.

'Beer?' he asks.

'It's ten-thirty in the morning,' I say, but not before I've actually spent a moment considering it.

He shrugs.

'I'll take one,' says Audrey.

Reuben walks to the fridge and cracks open two Beck's. He asks me if I'm sure I don't care for one, and I really have to make myself say no. He hands a beer to Audrey and she kisses him on the cheek before waving me goodbye and skipping away, disappearing back into the other part of the house.

Reuben and I stare at one another for a few seconds, and neither of us says anything.

'So...' I begin tentatively. 'Reuben, um, Zoe mentioned to me that you might be able to, um, hook me up with some of your...like...'

His smile fades and he gives me a blank look, but after a while he breaks into a smile and says: 'Ah yes, I forget. I...um...I forget these things sometimes. My English. Come.'

Whether it's his bad English or his drug intake that makes him forgetful, I'm not sure. He beckons for me to follow into the main part of the house – he leads me down a hallway, past a grand piano and a room with sheets draped from the ceiling, turning a corner into what must be his bedroom.

I don't know what I was expecting but this definitely isn't it. There is a large set of windows, open, on the far wall, and in spite of all the junk in here – records, decks and computers in various stages of disrepair, lying all over the floor, stacked on top of one another in almost unimaginable quantities – the room still feels pretty big and open. There is a large unmade bed that takes up almost half the available space; there are lots of posters, including a big one with the words INTERNATIONAL DEEJAY GIGOLO RECORDS and another, just beside, with the word HELL written in white on black.

'I keep it here,' Reuben says, fishing around under the bed, 'so it's safe.' He pulls out an old shoe box – the word KUSTOM written over and over on the outside – and opens it up to reveal seven or eight ziplock bags, all of them stuffed with weed. Zoe wasn't kidding. 'How much?' he asks.

Reuben gives me the requisite amount and then puts the rest back. I hand over the cash and he starts explaining to me about how he wants to be a DJ but his broken English keeps interfering and I'm still kind of overwhelmed by the sheer amount of weed in the shoe box. I wonder what other fun things might be stashed around the room, but now probably isn't the best time to ask. He leads me back out to the kitchen, says, 'I'll see you soon? Yes?' and I tell him most definitely. He smiles, shakes my hand then leads me to the kitchen door. He says if I need anything to call him, and I'm on the verge of saying I don't have his phone number but it probably doesn't matter. He waves me off, takes another swig of his beer. I don't care what Zoe says, Reuben seems like a pretty decent guy to me.

Zoe is out in the yard when I leave, holding Paris Hilton, who still doesn't look happy about it. I tell her we'll probably be heading out into the Valley at the weekend – last gasp before uni goes back and all that – and Zoe says great, she'll be in touch.

'Yeah, see you there, Liam...' she says in a strange tone of voice as I'm turning to leave, and it's almost like she's flirting with me, but it's too much to deal with at the moment so I get while the getting's good, head back to my house. I mean, I can't be flirting with other girls; I have Sara to think of.

Sara called me from London last night. We've been exchanging a whole lot of text messages and she has sent a number of emails I haven't replied to yet, but we've only spoken once or twice since she left. The call was kind of unexpected but I guess it was good to hear her voice again, and we ended up spending about an hour on the phone. She's been in London for a while – she says it's fantastic. It took her some time to adjust – strange place, strange people – and there was a mix-up with the youth hostel she was meant to be staying in, but she's staying with a friend in Hampstead Heath now and is starting to get used to things. She said something about how the boys in London were really cute – mentioned some South African guy named Martin or Marcus or possibly Abraham who was living in the house with them – as though she was trying to...what? Get some sort of response from me? I really don't know. I told her,

'Yeah, cool', and the conversation moved on to something else. She sounded kind of nervous but you can tell she's going to fit into the whole European thing pretty well.

She asked me what I'd been doing and I told her nothing much, which was pretty close to the truth. I mentioned that my older brother Euan – recently back from London – had moved down to Melbourne with an Australian girl he met while he was over there and was urging me to go and visit them. She told me that sounded like a good idea, that a weekend in Melbourne might be good for me, and I told her I'd think about it, even though I hate my brother and probably won't end up going at all. Sara told me she loved me and I told her I loved her too and I'm pretty sure I meant it, and after that she asked me if everything was okay, and I was like 'Of course it is' and didn't bother to say anything else.

It was a weird, vaguely awkward conversation and afterwards I thought about how much I was going to miss Sara. Then I started to think about Brad's brother again but that was dumb so I put it out of my mind. Jay and I got messy together and played video games for three hours and then I went to bed.

Four

Today a bunch of us are going to uni to check things out. It's orientation week, which means a variety of extremely boring events that none of us will participate in are going to take place, but it also means there's every likelihood of a party at one of the colleges tonight. This is a far more exciting prospect; it being a Friday and there being a bunch of eager first-years around, it seems almost certain. This is basically a very encouraging thought.

So we're in my friend Lachlan's WRX, driving too fast through the city, and it's a case of unbridled hilarity and adolescent hormones gone wild, and it's basically all been done before but it's a ritual, one of those times you just have to go with the flow. I'm in front in the passenger seat, Brad and Callum are somehow crammed in the back, in front of a large set of speakers that are pumping Death Cab out at about six billion decibels, but we're all managing to carry on some semblance of a conversation; the potential for partying tonight seems pretty much to be the dominant theme.

'There better be some bitches there, some fucken first-year girls,' says Callum.

'For real,' says Lachlan, turning his head to look at the guys in the back, and every so often glancing up at the traffic. 'It's gonna be like, oh yeah, I'm a second year, oh yeah, business, you seem like a really nice girl, oh yeah, I'll show you around, oh yeah, oh yeah, who's your fucken *daddy*, bitch?' The guys all laugh and Lachlan attempts to slap us all high fives while still somehow paying attention to the road.

'We need to hook you up with some of that, Liam,' says Callum, laughing.

'Hey,' says Brad. 'Liam's a saint. Liam's faithful to Sara.'

'But man, it's *first-year* girls. Sara never has to know. What happens on campus...'

'*STAYS ON CAMPUS*,' the other two echo. You have to forgive my friends; if they end up sounding too much like the guys in one of those *Spring Break Girls Gone Wild* videos, it's only because they are.

'Guys,' I tell them. 'I can look, okay, I just can't touch.'

'Oh yeah... Touch this, Liam,' Callum, I think, says.

The music is still blasting out of the back of the car as we head down Ann Street. Lachlan tailgates a silver four-wheel-drive for a while then veers out into the right lane and overtakes at about eighty. The guy in the four-wheel-drive doesn't exactly seem pleased but we've already left him behind for bigger and better things. Callum and the guys keep talking about bitches and pussy for a while but I kind of lose the momentum of the conversation, space out for a while and stare out at the river, which is going by very rapidly thanks to Lachlan's driving.

'...so he's letting me DJ at this party he's having,' Callum is saying when I return to reality, somewhere near the Regatta. 'It's gonna be sweet. It's gonna be *awesome*.'

'You know he's a fag?' I hear Brad asking.

'Who's a fag?' I ask, actually interested.

'You are if you don't get yourself one of those first-year girls tonight. Dudes! Am I right?' Callum reaches forward like he's trying to shake hands or something, so I grab his fist and we make our gesture of solidarity.

As we get closer to the university campus it becomes abundantly clear that we're not going to be finding a park any time soon. Lachlan swears under his breath as we circle to check all the obvious spots; we head up steep hills, down various side streets, but all the spaces, even the illegal ones, seem to be taken up.

'This is so typical,' he says, making a fist and punching the steering wheel. 'O-week. Jesus Christ, I should have known.'

'Dude!' Callum calls out from the back. 'First-year girls, okay? Just focus on that. *Think of the girls.*'

Lachlan shakes his head, swears again under his breath. 'This is fucked. We're never going to find one.'

Callum continues, affecting a high-pitched voice which I can only assume is meant to be that of a first-year girl. '*Lachlan,*' he says, '*don't leave me here all alone... I need some of your hot man-juice tonight.*'

'Dude, will you, like, *please* cut it out with the hot man-juice? That's disturbing on so many levels...'

'*But Lachlan...*'

'I'm not fucken kidding, okay?'

As we are circling around near the sports fields, a parking space suddenly becomes available – two girls in an old Volvo are pulling away from the kerb. We all seem to spot this at the same time, and Lachlan puts his foot down. As we are approaching the park, a standoff develops between the four of us and an old couple in a Mercedes who have been approaching from the opposite direction. Their right indicator is on and they have already started manoeuvring when Lachlan pulls into the park. The old couple linger for a few seconds and blow their horn at us before driving away.

'Fuck that shit, man,' says Lachlan. 'This is ours. This is our *territory*, right, guys?'

We all pile out and start heading towards the main part of the campus. There are quite a lot of people hanging around; kids circling alone and in packs. It's all about trucker caps and distressed denim again this year. Guys walking around in Billabong and Quiksilver, girls in Roxy, most people looking like they haven't really come back from the beach yet. There are groups of girls sitting around on the grass, some of them laughing and others, probably first-years, looking thoroughly freaked out. There is a lot of flesh on display, but it's still summer, and anyway, flesh on display is rarely a bad thing. As usual there are loads of tables set up around the perimeter of the great court, people offering you free shit if you join the Hip-Hop Society, Queer Kids For Jesus, the Drama Club. There's also the odd table with political types behind it, pale and earnest-looking kids all but weeping about shit like, I don't know, refugees or post-structuralism or whatever. And still more first-years. The idea that we're coming back here for another semester begins to sink in.

'My dad's really getting stuck into me this year,' Lachlan says, unprompted, as we make our way out onto the grass. 'He wants me to get first-class honours. I've told him it's a long way off but he's always bringing it up.'

'I wouldn't worry,' I tell him. 'Of all of us, you're the only one who actually does anything resembling study. You're, like, built for this shit.'

'I guess,' he says, 'but it's a lot of pressure. I don't think I'll be coming out with you guys much this semester.'

'What do you mean?'

'Well, my GPA is on, like, a six-point-four, but Dad keeps telling me it can be higher. He keeps, like, threatening to take my car away if I don't spend more time studying.'

'You practically *live* in your books,' I tell him, 'it's obscene.'

'Well yeah, but I'd really like to get him off my back, and if that means staying at home, y'know, studying, then...'

'But it's law... It's tough. I know people who've failed subjects, like, two and three times.'

'Dad wouldn't cope well with that. Anyway, to hell with it. I'm just saying. What are you guys doing this year?'

'I don't know,' I tell him. 'There's this micro-business subject. It looks like bullshit.'

Brad begins to explain about the class, which he's

enrolled in as well – although for Brad, being enrolled in something isn't necessarily a guarantee of much. I'm half listening to him and half staring off at the people around us. This is when I see the boy for the first time.

He walks by in a group with another boy and a girl. Something about him kind of...I don't know. Something about him is interesting. He's shorter than I am, with glasses and this deliberately messy hair, but he has that look, that slightly nervous, fragile look, which makes me think of the way the shy ones always go mental when you get them into bed. As he walks by, he notices me looking at him and he looks back. I wait for a second or two before averting my eyes, and after he and his friends have walked past, I turn my head slightly and see from the corner of my eye that he's looking back at me. If I were a fag, this would probably be an interesting development, but I'm not, so it isn't.

'...dude?' Brad's asking me.

'What?'

'You sign up for the tutorial yet?'

'No. Yeah. I don't know. I think so. Yeah.'

'That's very...um...precise of you.'

'Yeah, I try.'

As we continue on to the other side of the great court our attention is drawn to these girls who are standing behind the table at the Law Students Association. 'Here we go,' says Lachlan, and we head over to talk to them. This one girl in particular, blonde, white cotton top, seriously cute, seems to recognise him, and as we stand around in front of the table, the two of them try to figure out where they know each other from. Lachlan introduces himself, the girl flirts back. Nice. We talk to the rest of the girls for a while – Brad asks them how they like law; they ask him if he's studying it too and he tells them no, he's doing business, and they start getting all faux-sympathetic, which Brad absolutely eats up. Eventually, the blonde girl, whose name is Anna, asks Lachlan if he's here to actually sign up for anything or if we just plan to keep wasting their time. Lachie asks for the form to sign up and the blonde girl hands it to him, followed by the pen, lingering over both.

I look back out into the crowd of people in the great court, unsure of what I'm looking for, but whatever it is, I'm not having any luck. At this point, Anna asks us if we're going to the party tonight, over at Saint Martin's College. Lachie's like, no, we haven't heard of it, and Anna tells us, 'Ohmygod, you have to come.' We tell her we'd be happy to, that we'll see them all there. She says, 'Hope so,' looking across at Lachie when she says it.

As we walk back out onto the grass, the first objective of our mission achieved, we see these two guys who are almost certainly from one of the colleges running across the great court. They are dressed only in togas and are painted blue. This must be some kind of faggy initiation ritual or something; later on tonight, the bigger boys will probably tie them up and sodomise them or something.

'Jesus,' laughs Callum. 'College guys.'

'Those girls were hot,' Brad says.

'Dudes, that was our first step. What time should we rock on over to the party?'

I keep scanning the crowd, but whoever I'm looking for doesn't seem to be here.

Our plans more or less established, we leave campus to pick up supplies and devise a plan for the conquest of the first-year pussy. Consensus among the group seems to be that, absent girlfriend or no, I'm a filthy homosexual if I don't bag myself a first-year tonight.

'Think about it,' says Callum as we loiter in front of the fridges at the back of some bottle shop in St Lucia Village. 'These girls are just out of high school, they're horny as hell, they're *tight* as hell and the bitches are all begging for it. They want a real man. They want a *uni student.*'

'He has a point,' says Brad, who is drawing on a patch of condensation with his finger, making what looks like a dollar sign. 'It's part of the university experience. They're *expecting* to get drunk and have sex with some random dude at the party tonight... It's a sign that they're, I don't know, grown up or some shit.'

'It's some kind of, fucking...what's it called?'

'It's a rite of passage.'

'That's the one!' Brad and Callum slap one another a high five and trade a handshake so elaborate it seems to take half an hour or so.

This whole situation sort of reminds me of this one night last year, when I took Sara to one of those college parties. It was our first year then, and I remember her having too much to drink, dancing with her friends to some song we all liked at the time. This college guy came over and started hitting on her in a very obvious way, and knowing that I was there, she let him do it, flirting back with him, laughing at some dumb joke of his, touching his arms, his chest. When I intervened to tell her I was taking her home, the guy started making threats at me. I told him in no uncertain terms what I'd do to him if he touched my girlfriend and I guess it worked because he disappeared after that. Sara was pretending to pout at me, teasing me about being the protective boyfriend, but when I got her home she grabbed a hold of my T-shirt and pulled me into her room in the dark. She wanted me to fuck her and she kept asking me to over and over, twisting the sheets around her legs, touching herself, but for some reason I couldn't do it. Fuck her, I mean.

I told Sara I didn't know what the problem was, that I needed a beer, a joint, something. She looked at me, just looked at me in the dark, and the silence seemed to go on for a very long time until eventually, almost at the point of laughing, she made this exaggerated sigh, whispered loudly, 'Well, what a disappointment.' I started to apologise, but she ignored me. She sat up instead, pulling a sheet around her, and asked, 'If I were Toby, would you want to fuck me then?'

The question kind of hung in the air for a second. I told her the whole idea was crazy, told her Toby was her *brother*, told her she was drunk and didn't know what she was saying, but you could tell by the edge in her voice that it possibly wasn't the first time she'd considered this. I was kind of shaken after that; perhaps it showed a little more than I realised, because Sara started apologising to me, grabbed me around the waist and pulled me into this very tight hug, telling me that I seemed so distant sometimes, asking how she could ever know where she stood with me. I told her not to worry, told her again that I loved her and then she pulled me into bed. Although I didn't actually manage to fuck her, we spent the night together.

'Tonight's going to be grand,' I tell the guys.

'For real,' says Brad, who is still drawing on the glass, just making these weird shapes. 'Do you think there's some code? I mean, do you think the college guys will be pissed off that we're invading their territory?'

'They won't care. It's every man for himself at these things. They know that.'

'Did you *see* some of those girls around campus today?' asks Callum. 'Things are looking good. Things are looking very good.'

'Do you really wonder if that's their great ambition?' I ask. 'Do you really think all first-year girls just want to get drunk and fuck guys like us?'

'Not all of them,' says Brad.

'Yeah,' adds Callum. 'Some of them are dykes. Yee-aaahhh!' He and Brad slap another high five.

'Should we get a carton or what?' asks Lachie, emerging from the cold room.

This may be the hardest decision we have to make all day.

We've been at the party for about an hour and even though it's only early in the night, the place is crowded and things are already starting to get pretty noisy. We're in the common area – with this carpeting that could only be described as retro and a series of plaques and photographs of old boys up on the walls – and there are people all around us talking, laughing. Hip-hop beats are blasting from somewhere, and everyone is young and everyone is dressed more or less the same and everyone wants to get fucked up and, basically, there is a sense that we are among our own.

The crowd is essentially made up of drunken jocks in testosterone overdrive, tanned guys in surf gear and polo shirts, shaking one another's hands and stroking their respective egos while dewy-eyed girls stand around admiring them, with lips that say *I wanna suck your dick* and bare midriffs and other pieces of flesh strategically revealed. There are various breakaway groups: the girls who are either not forward enough or not yet drunk enough to make a play for one of the alpha males stand around nervously in groups of two and three, while several of the more awkward-looking boys hang around the edges, joking with one another and getting progressively more hammered while secretly wishing they had the balls to get a piece of the action themselves.

Our group has already been reduced to three. About half an hour ago we spotted Anna from the law society, standing over by a window with her friends. One of them looked across at our group, and then all of them did. She saw Lachlan and smiled, waved at him before returning to the conversation. We basically told Lachlan that this was his chance and he wasn't a man unless he could *stick it to the bitch*, something along those lines, but he needed little by way of encouragement. He walked over to talk to her, and whatever he said to her must have worked as they disappeared into the crowd some time back.

Meanwhile, Brad and Callum, much to my consternation, have gotten us involved in some kind of drinking game with two of the burlier jocks. The jocks drifted our way a few minutes ago – humorously, gregariously drunk – and started talking to us. There is a brunette guy with huge arms, and a blond – blue polo shirt, upturned collar – who if you were a fag you'd probably say was the better looking of the two, but if you were a fag you'd probably be entertaining fantasies of the two of them taking you to someone's room and gang-banging you or something like that, so the distinction would be sort of immaterial. After a great deal of shaking of hands and slapping of backs, Callum let slip that we weren't actually from Saint Martin's, we were interlopers, crashing their party on the presumption that some first-year pussy might happen to cross our path. The college guys grinned and made a big, joking pretence of being upset.

'You pack of bastards,' said the blond one, whose name might have been Damien but I wasn't really paying that much attention. 'We should kick you out.'

'Yeah,' his friend added, 'or kick your arses.'

'What's the matter?' asked Callum, smiling. 'You think

we're too much for you? You think all those first-years are gonna fall for our immense charms instead?'

'Yeah, I think they're nervous,' said Brad, laughing. 'I think they can sense the competition. Isn't that right, Liam?'

'...Yeah,' I said after a while. 'Can't handle the pressure.'

After some calling of names and some throwing of pretend punches, the college guys decided that we were a bunch of amateurs and the only rational way to settle the argument was with a drinking contest. They provided us each with an unopened can of beer – I pointed out that the contest was gay but agreed to it anyway as the thought of letting a drink go to waste was too sad. The idea, from what I can work out, is that everyone opens their beer at once, and whoever can chug theirs the fastest is the better man, and thus entitled to the aforementioned first-year pussy.

We're all standing around in a loose circle and the blond guy, grinning, looks each of us in the eye. 'Ready?' he asks. 'Three, two, one...'

Everyone cracks open their beer, begins to chug. I make a half-hearted attempt to keep up with the guys and at first it seems easy, but before long very little of the beer seems to actually be going in my mouth, and I'm beaten after about halfway. Not wanting to look like a pussy, I keep the can more or less level with my mouth, keep my head tossed back and wait until I hear victory declared. It's ridiculous, like the handshake thing; like secretly, girls are wetting themselves with delight over the guy who can drink his beer the fastest?

'Yeaaah!' I hear someone yell. It's the dark-haired college guy who has managed to finish first, and though he has this slightly cross-eyed expression, his arms are thrown up in victory and he is grinning broadly.

'Good work!' his buddy yells, drunkenly throwing an arm around him and almost knocking him over.

Nonchalant, I take another sip of my beer. Callum, who is slightly unsteady on his feet and wiping his mouth with the back of his hand, says that the competition was unfair and demands a rematch. The college fags seem to have no problem with this and the four of them head off, arms thrown drunkenly around one another, in search of fresh beers. I leave the bastards to it and begin circling the party on my own, bored, maybe looking for people I know.

I strike up a conversation with these two blonde girls, both of them holding plastic cups filled with beer. They tell me that they're first-years, studying business, and the taller of the two is flirting with me fairly heavily. I flirt back for a while, bored. The conversation turns to my rowing – which I haven't even done in ages, but for some reason it never fails to impress. The girl who has been flirting with me feigns surprise, tells me that most rowers she's seen have been pretty toned, and I tell her she can see for herself, lifting up my shirt so that she can look. The girl is impressed and actually reaches down to touch my stomach. While she does this, her friend rolls her eyes, and I am starting to wonder where this whole thing might be heading, when I spot him again. The boy from earlier this afternoon, the nervous, fragile-looking first-year.

He knows I've seen him looking at me, and he looks away a little too quickly, embarrassed or something. He's standing by himself near where the DJ is set up, and he has this extremely earnest, wary sort of expression on his face, which makes it that much more interesting. That look is like an invitation to get them in bed. That's what I like about guys – you can talk them into doing basically *anything*. Most of the time they don't even take that much convincing. That just isn't the case with girls. He looks back and when he sees that I'm still looking at him, he turns away again.

The taller of the blonde girls has finished inspecting my sixpack and is now making small talk about...I'm not sure what, actually, as I'm trying to think of ways to extract myself from the conversation, something I can say to make this whole thing go quickly.

'So I had, like, twenty minutes before the exam started and no way of getting there, and I so wasn't coping with the situation...' the girl is saying, 'but that's when I remembered...'

When I look across, the boy is staring at me again. He starts looking thoroughly freaked out, like he's preparing to make a move, so the time to act would pretty much be now.

'Hey,' the girl's friend interrupts, this slightly pissed-off edge in her voice, like we've been freezing her out, 'I'm going to get another *drink*. Are you okay?'

'Um...' the other friend starts.

'Actually,' I tell them, 'I think I see this dude I know over there. If you guys want to...' I motion in the general direction of where the beer is, '...I can...' motioning with the other hand, '...and then maybe we can, y'know...'

'Sure,' says the taller of the blondes, slightly uncertain, but she's still smiling at me.

'Great. Well...' I start heading off in the other direction.

'See you...soon?' says the girl hopefully.

'For sure.'

I catch the boy as he is moving towards an esky filled with beer and those berry-flavoured Vodka Cruisers. He is reaching down to grab something from inside it when I say: 'Hey.' He turns around, surprised, gives me this look like he doesn't know what I'm about to do to him. 'Do I know you?' I ask.

'Um...I don't think so. Sorry.' The kid is holding an unopened beer, his hand still wet from the ice.

'Ah, don't worry. You look like someone else. I think I've seen you around before.'

'Um, yeah. Could be.' He gives me this nervous smile. 'Did...you want one of these?' he asks, motioning towards the beer.

'Sure.'

He hands me the Carlton Draught that he's been holding, then grabs another for himself, cracking it open, taking this long, nervous gulp from the bottle. From the way he's acting, I'm pretty sure this beer isn't his first.

'It's probably my mistake,' I tell him. 'I thought

you looked familiar, and when I saw you looking at me before...I figured maybe you recognised me from somewhere.'

'Yeah,' he says. Slightly embarrassed, clearly pretty drunk. 'I was just...yeah, looking. Was that your girlfriend or something?' he asks. Well, the little faggot obviously has some sense of initiative.

'No,' I say to him pointedly.

'Well, she seemed to like you anyway. She was...she was hot.'

'You think?' I ask him.

'I don't know.' He looks down at his beer, then back up at me. Objectively speaking, the little brat is pretty cute; he has fine features or something, and if he wasn't looking so fucking wary, he'd probably even have a nice smile.

'Do you have a girlfriend?' I ask him.

'No,' he says, trying very hard not to give away any hint of anything.

I open my beer and start to swig from it, wiping my mouth with the back of my hand. 'You're a first-year, aren't you?' I ask.

'...Yeah.'

'I can tell. Well, there's still time for you at least.'

'What's that mean?'

'Come on,' I say to him, giving him this thoroughly patronising look. 'I saw you standing over here by yourself. I used to do the same thing at parties. I can tell you're out of your depth here, right?'

'Well...' he starts, 'I've been to parties like this before, but this is my first since I came here... I guess it's weird, not knowing anyone...'

'You know me,' I say, really laying it on thick.

'I guess so,' he says, his expression completely unreadable.

'So I can help you out. The thing to remember is confidence. That's all you need. Just let them know you're not afraid to take what you want and you're set. They like that.'

'Who does?'

'*Girls*,' I tell him. 'Like that girl before... The one you thought was *hot*?'

'She wasn't that hot,' the kid says.

'Just let me ask...' I begin, grinning. 'If you could have any girl in this room, which one would you have?'

'I... What?' That nervous look has started to come over him again.

'Come on,' I say. 'Which one do you like the look of? If you could make a play for any of the girls here, if you could *fuck* any one of them you wanted to, which one would you go for?'

The kid seems to be struggling to come up with a decent answer. 'I don't know...'

'Come on, there must be one.' I look right at him. 'You were looking at that girl before, weren't you? Either that or you were looking at me.'

He says nothing, just stares at me like a deer in the headlights or something.

'Look,' I continue, 'don't take this the wrong way, but have you ever done it before?'

'Have I ever done what?' he asks.

I don't know where the hell any of this is coming from, it's like being on autopilot, but it's hilarious how easy this is turning out to be. I almost break out laughing. 'Have you ever fucked a girl before?' I ask.

'I...yeah, sure, I mean...' He's really lost for words now, really struggling.

'You *are* into girls, right?' At this point I look *right* at him, and the implication becomes somewhat clearer.

'I...' Once again, he's lost for words.

I smile, move in closer.

Twenty minutes later and the little fag is leading me down a carpeted hallway towards his room. As we were leaving the common area downstairs I was on the lookout, making sure none of the other guys were watching, but Lachlan had long since disappeared with the blonde girl, while Brad and Callum were in the thick of yet another drinking contest and seemed pretty much oblivious to everything else.

When we get to his door the kid is swaying a bit – drunk, excited, probably both – and as he starts looking for his key he keeps telling me how 'weird' this whole thing is, that he had been looking at me but he'd 'never thought...' He told me his name before but that piece of information is lost to me right now. I keep listening to him go on about what to do 'if anything happens, I mean, between us...' and 'if anybody finds out' and the whole thing is sort of annoying but I endure, mostly because of the fairly large boner I'm nursing and the pretty high likelihood that it's about to be taken care of.

Finally, we make it inside. I don't know what I was expecting the place to look like, but as far as first-year rooms go, I guess this one's fairly typical. There are posters for Bright Eyes, The Faint and various other emo-ish bands up on all the walls, clothes strewn haphazardly all over the floor, a new-looking laptop on the desk along with a half-empty bottle of Absolut, books lying open and closed all over the place. I walk across to the bed, push some clothes out of the way and sit down. The kid looks at me, like he's about to make a move, but he ends up staying over by the desk. He sits down on it then stands up again, looking away and then back at me. He picks up the bottle of vodka and takes a swig from it, gagging a little as he does so, licking his lips. Seeing this turns me on, though I'm not sure why exactly that is.

'Um...do you want a drink or something?' the boy asks.

'No,' I tell him. 'Come on.'

'Maybe I should, like, put some music on. Or not. Whatever.'

'Put on whatever you want,' I say. 'It doesn't matter.' I lean back on the bed, undo my belt, as if any more hints need to be dropped at this point.

He replaces the bottle of vodka on the desk, keeps staring across at me, looking wide-eyed and sort of frightened. 'Sorry,' he says, 'it's just that I never...here, I mean, and...we have to be quiet, so nobody will, like...'

'Nobody's going to hear,' I tell him. 'Everyone's down-stairs. We'll be fine.'

'Yeah...' he says, flicking off the light. 'It's just that, I've never, and...if anyone...'

Jesus. The whole situation is starting to get beyond what could be considered funny. I don't plan to hold the little faggot's hand through this. 'Dude...' I tell him, 'just...stop talking now. I want you to shut the fuck up and come over here. Is that okay with you?'

'Okay,' he says. 'Sorry.'

My dick is so hard it's actually kind of starting to hurt, and I really hope that he'll just get on with it. He walks over to the bed, sits down next to me. He leans in close, touches my forehead, and I let him kiss me for a while, my hand in the small of his back. His lips and tongue are all over the place and his mouth tastes very strongly of the vodka, and, to be honest, the kiss really isn't doing a lot for me. I start to push him away, ignoring the resistance, and when we finally part, the boy's eyes are still closed and he is breathing fairly heavily.

'You can...' he says to me after a few seconds. 'I mean, we can... I don't care, just... Just don't fuck me, okay?'

To be honest, I hadn't actually considered that as a real possibility, and I'm surprised, if not to say sort of turned on, by the fact that he had. 'Yeah,' I say, sighing. 'That's fine. Whatever you want,' acting like it's such a big sacrifice on my part but I won't try to fuck him because that's just the kind of nice guy that I am.

He tries to kiss me again but I direct him downwards,

gently at first and then more forcefully, until eventually he gets the hint and he slides down to his knees on the floor, his face basically in line with my crotch.

It's weird, but in the dark, looking at the kid with his shaggy brown hair, you could almost imagine that it was Kristian down there. Now that I think about it, the little fag *does* kind of resemble Kristian – the hair, the pout, that nervous and slightly stupid expression. I start to wonder whether Kristian has done this kind of thing before, with guys, and more to the point, if it *was* Kristian down there, would I be more interested in this than I currently am? As soon as this thought has occurred to me, I start to get angry with myself. Determined to put Brad's brother out of my mind, I start helping the kid along, telling him to 'Suck it, you fag, come on.'

Slowly, nervously, he starts to undo my zipper, and I help him as he pulls my jeans and then my boxers down over my hips. He whispers something to me but I don't hear what it is and really couldn't care less at this point. With no further need for encouragement, the boy starts giving me this drunken and fairly sloppy blow job. He's not that good but there's really no point complaining; he sucks on my dick determinedly, stopping every so often for breath, and after a while it actually starts to feel pretty good. I grab the kid's hair, encouraging him to start sucking it harder, which he does, and I start groaning, moving my hips up and down and essentially just enjoying the warm, wet feel of his mouth.

Some minutes later, when I start to come, I'm still

thinking about Kristian. I begin to groan louder, push the kid's head right down, and I get the sense that he might be uncomfortable, out of breath, but at this point I really don't care. When I close my eyes, I see Kristian again, standing in Brad's kitchen with that stupid expression on his face.

I come, and for a second my whole body goes limp. The boy leans back on the floor, panting to get his breath back, looking up at me as though he doesn't quite understand what's just happened, as though he's expecting... What? Sympathy of some kind? Fuck that for a joke.

I clench and unclench my fists and for a moment it occurs to me that it might be fun to beat this kid up, hurt him a little bit, but that seems like a lot of effort and at this point I'm basically keen to get the hell out of here.

'Thanks,' I tell the boy, already completely bored by the whole thing, sliding my jeans back up. 'That was... great.'

'I'm...yeah. I'm...glad. That's good.' The kid sits down on the carpet, leaning against the bed. He wipes his mouth with the back of his hand, then does it again – an awkward gesture that seems to bear out how drunk he probably is. 'Was it really?'

'It really was.'

He looks at the ground a couple of times, then looks at me, keeps looking, like he's expecting me to say something. 'Do you...'

'Do I what?'

'Nothing.'

'Okay,' I say, going over and opening the door. 'Great.

Listen, I'm going back to the party. It might be better if you don't follow me, okay? You wouldn't want people to find out what we did up here.'

'Um... I don't really feel like going back anyway,' he says. The little fag is attempting to look nonchalant and it's not working and suddenly his shoulders start heaving and the whole thing has become way too much to deal with.

'Listen,' I tell him, 'I have to go.' The expression on his face when he looks up at me again, sitting in the triangle of light from the open door, is sort of hard to describe. 'Look,' I'm compelled to add, 'I don't know what you were expecting, but... I have a girlfriend. Sorry. This has been fun. I hope this uni thing, y'know...works out for you...'

He mumbles something I can't make out, and I leave, closing the door behind me. Whatever. We'll always have Paris. Faggot. When I get back to the party, one of the drunken college guys has his arm around Callum's shoulder and they are half talking, half shouting things at one another, toasting with plastic cups of beer. A lot of the beer seems to be spilling on the floor, but this doesn't seem to be a problem. Callum grins when he sees me.

'Liam,' he says, slurring. 'Motherfucker. Where the hell did you get to?'

'What do you mean? I've been here the whole time.'

'Yeah,' he grins. 'I saw you talking to those two girls...'

'I don't know what you're talking about,' I say, but

I smile when I say it, letting Callum think what he wants.

'Ye-eeah!' he yells. He offers me his closed fist and we tap our knuckles together. A song we both recognise comes on and a lot more people start to dance, girls pressed up against boys, girls dancing in twos and threes at the centre of the common room. We all turn to look at them. One of the blonde girls from before, the taller one, is on the outer edge of the group. When she sees me she smiles, waves to me, and I wave back.

Five

All of the parking spaces in the street are full, but by sheer coincidence, some guy in a white Beamer is pulling out just as Lachie and I are pulling in, and his spot becomes mine. It's a Saturday night, and Anna – the girl who Lachlan has been very conspicuously *not* fucking for the last several weeks in some attempt to act like the perfect gentleman – is having a party at her parents' house in Toowong. It took an effort to even get Lachlan out tonight – we talked it over on the phone this afternoon and the shithead kept giving me excuses, telling me that he should be studying, how hard his father was going to come down on him, but I pointed out firstly that it was Saturday night, and secondly, that he was a pussy if he didn't make more of an effort to try to fuck Anna, who was playing hard to get but was plainly begging for it. Eventually he agreed, telling me to give it an hour or two and then pick him up.

My car is parked in a back street near the bottle shop at the Paddo, because we'll be heading in there later to pick up some beers, but first we're heading into Subway for some much-needed nutrition – you know, warriors preparing to go into battle and all that shit. When we get inside, the music — some Gwen Stefani song that I'm pretty sure Sara likes — is turned up very loudly, and there is only one very stoned-looking dude behind the counter, dealing slowly with the not insignificant number of people waiting for sandwiches. Lachlan curses under his breath and we take our place in the line.

'This shit with Anna is getting ridiculous,' I say to him. 'It's time to seal the deal. Even if you don't fuck her tonight...' The girl in front of me turns around briefly to glare at me. '...even if you don't, you need to give some indication that you might be *planning* to fuck her. At least that way she'll know you're not a fag.'

'It's always this gay shit with you, Liam. Why do you even care?'

'I care about you, my friend. If there's anything you'd like to tell me, I'd be okay with it. I'm very open-minded... Does she know?'

'Know what?'

'...*That you like it the wrong way*,' I whisper.

'I'm *not* gay, Liam.'

'Whatever you say.'

Lachie shakes his head. 'I'm taking my time with Anna. She's...nice.'

'Right. Nice. Has she even given you a BJ yet?'

'What the fuck do you care?'

The girl in front turns around again, but I stare her down this time and she turns away.

'Has she?'

Lachie half-smiles at me.

'Was it good?'

His smile breaks into a grin and, shaking his head, he reaches out to slap my hand with his and do the secret dude handshake.

Gwen Stefani changes to the voice of an annoying radio announcer and then some hip-hop song I don't recognise. When it's finally our turn at the counter, I ask for a chicken fillet on white bread but the dude tells me that the plain white bread has run out so I reluctantly order the parmesan kind instead. The dude – I guess you'd say he's not bad-looking, even though he's spacey and vague and his eyes are incredibly bloodshot – forgets my order several times, and ends up putting the wrong kind of cheese on it. In the end, Lachie and I don't really care, we just pay and sit down at one of the tables inside.

Lachie, who has been weird and distant most of the night, sips a Coke with a faraway look on his face, leaving me to look around at the other people in the restaurant. Soon after we've sat down, a group of kids – little emo and skate fags, who are all wearing identical pairs of Cons and look like carbon copies of every kid you see hanging around the city – trail into the restaurant, one behind the other. They are muttering darkly at one another, their conversation peppered with a lot of 'fucks' and 'faggots' as they move towards the counter, but watching them walk by, you can pretty much tell that the whole thing is an act, that they're all a bunch of plainly ineffectual private-school kids play-acting at being tough.

'I wonder if Katrina's serving...' one of them says.

'She can serve *me* any time.' Laughter.

As they gather by the counter, I notice that one of them has turned away from the others and is staring at me like he knows me or something. I keep trying to ignore him, to focus on what Lachlan is saying, but when I look back, the kid is still there, still looking, and it takes me a second to recognise him – he and his friends are, after all, basically interchangeable – but I realise that it's Kristian, Brad's brother.

Lachlan is saying, 'The thing with Anna is that she just broke up with her boyfriend, and you know how these things are that drag on from high school...' But I'm no longer paying attention.

Kristian turns, says something to one of his friends, and the two of them break away from the group and start walking towards our table. The other kid looks to me like John-Paul, Isabel's little brother, the kid who, I'm pretty sure, ended up being tossed in the pool at Sara's going-away party.

'Hey,' Kristian says to me, nonchalant.

I nod at him. 'What's happening?'

The two boys look across at each other, as though they're trying to decide which one of them's going to do the talking. Kristian shrugs. The one who I think is John-Paul shakes his head, grinning, and then looks back at me.

'Hey man,' he says, looking at his feet for a second before looking back up at me, one of those bullshit male things that you do to establish which one of you is the alpha dog or whatever. 'It's John-Paul. Remember me?

Your girlfriend's party, man. I was so *blind*...' He draws out the word 'blind' like he's expecting me to laugh along with him or something, but I don't, which makes him falter a little.

'So yeah,' he says when it becomes clear I'm not going to take the bait. 'We were wondering if you could...you know. We need you to help us out with something.'

'What do you need?'

'Well...We're going to this thing later...this party with these All Hallows girls, except, like, we don't have any ID on us, and the dude at the Paddo won't let us buy anything. I'm like, *What the fuck, our money's no good here*? But he said no. I mean, the dude has acne, looks like he's younger than *us*, you know, but the fucker still won't help us out. And it's like, these All Hallows girls, man...' I think I can work out what the little prick is getting at, but I let him continue. John-Paul is bouncing up and down on the balls of his feet, a nervous gesture that definitely sits oddly with the tough-guy posturing. 'So we're wondering,' he offers, 'would it be possible for you to, like, buy us some vodka or something? I mean, we need it, because there's this Jacqueline girl who's going to be at the party, and you know how it is, brother...'

Brother? I'm still reeling from the fact that John-Paul has called me *brother* when the little faggot grins at me and extends his closed fist – hoping, perhaps, that I'll knock it with mine, telling him to 'nail that bitch' or offer some other tidbit of brotherly advice. It's pathetic, but in an odd, hopeful way, and I can't help but recognise a bit of myself in their behaviour.

101

Who am I to deny him this relatively benign request? I would have expected nothing less when I was this little fucker's age.

'Okay,' I tell him. 'I'll get it for you...'

'Brother, I owe you one...'

'...I'll get it for you,' I continue, 'but listen. For inexperienced drinkers – which I'm assuming you all are – it's better to buy beer.'

Something passes between John-Paul and Kristian. *Did you know this? No – did you? Is he fucking with us?* They trade significant looks before John-Paul turns back to me.

'I've never heard of that,' he says, challenging me.

'Listen,' I tell him. 'Against my better judgment, I'm giving you guys some advice, so you can choose to ignore it or...'

'Fine,' says Kristian, 'we're listening.'

'Good,' I say, looking him up and down. 'Now, the most important thing to remember is that you can pace yourself with beer. You can drink only so much of it at a time. You show up with a bottle of vodka, you end up mixing your drinks half and half, and before long, *bang*: you're babbling at strangers, you're taking a piss off the deck, you're passing out in the swimming pool at nine-thirty.'

'I hear you, brother,' says John-Paul.

Jesus. I glare at him. 'But worse than that, say you actually manage to hook up with these All Hallows girls – whom I don't see around here, by the way, but I'll have to trust you on that one – you run the risk of

not being able to...well...*perform* at the critical moment.'
I look at Kristian when I say this and for a second he seems almost embarrassed.

'What?' John-Paul asks.

'He's saying you...um...can't get it up,' Kristian tells him.

'Hey, fuck that, man, I can go all night.'

'I'll bet,' I tell him.

'Oh yeah, you want some of this, don't you?' he asks, pretend dry-humping the back of a chair.

'Um, maybe later. So listen, do you fags want me to buy you some beer or not?'

John-Paul stops humping the chair, shrugs. A vaguely doubtful expression on his face, he turns to the rest of his friends, who are still standing near the counter, snickering. One of them, this little fucker in a pink trucker cap, attempts to stare me down, without much success.

'Fine,' John-Paul sighs after a few seconds. 'Do it. Whatever.'

'A carton's fifty bucks,' I tell him.

'No it's not!' Kristian says, animated all of a sudden.

'It is for you guys. There's a ten-dollar surcharge for being faggots. And because JP called me brother.'

'That is so not fair,' says Kristian. 'I'll tell Brad.'

'Tell him what? That you overpaid for beer? That you're a fag?'

'I'm *not*,' he says. 'That's so fucked up.'

John-Paul and Kristian close ranks again, muttering darkly at one another. After a while they seem to have come to a decision. John-Paul pulls out his wallet – white Quiksilver, attached to his suitably-faded jeans by a chain – and removes a fifty-dollar note. This is the best he can do tonight. Grudgingly, he hands the money over.

'Pleasure doing business,' I tell him.

Lachlan and I screw up our sandwich wrappers and leave them on the table – John-Paul and Kristian slink back to their friends, a victory of sorts having been achieved. 'Meet you outside the Paddo,' I tell them as we leave.

Lachie and I head across the street. Some tipsy girl at the Paddo is trying to buy a four-pack of those watermelon-flavoured vodka drinks, but she keeps entering her PIN wrongly and laughing about it to the dude behind the counter, who looks like he'd rather be anywhere else in the world but here.

I pick up a carton of Hahn Premium for us and one for Kristian and his friends – we debate about whether to get them light beer instead, just to fuck with their heads, but decide that this would be too cruel a thing to do, even for us.

'Those fucking kids...' Lachie says to me as we are waiting to be served. 'Were we that annoying when we were their age?'

'I don't think so. Must be something they're putting in the water.'

'It's weird though, isn't it?'

'What's weird?'

'To think that we'll never be that age again... All that shit that they're going through, you know, hormones and girls and having to scam their way into buying beer...All that's over for us. You never realise how fast it goes...'

'What the fuck are you talking about?' I ask.

'Nothing, sorry,' he says.

I don't know, Lachie's a really great bloke, but he has days where he tries to bring you down with weird shit like this. I mean, why can't he lighten up? The fucker's always acting like his girlfriend or his dog just died, and I'm not comparing the two or anything, but you know what I'm getting at, right?

There must be a lot of people at Anna's party already, because when we draw close to the house there are so many dinky European hatchbacks parked around it that I end up having to park in the next street over. Anna's parents live in a quiet part of Toowong – every second driveway around here seems to have a Mercedes or a Beamer parked in it, and almost all of the houses are Queenslanders, tastefully and expensively renovated to the point where they look pretty much identical. I like this part of town a lot, and I can actually see Sara and me living somewhere like this one day.

Lachie is finishing his first beer as we get out of the car. He sets the empty bottle down on the footpath, and when he goes to open a second, I remind him that it would probably be bad form to show up to his own girlfriend's party with a half-empty Hahnie in hand. Grudgingly, he agrees.

The same song that was playing at the Subway earlier

is playing at the party, and we can hear it getting louder as we walk up the hill towards Anna's house. 'Eyes on the prize, okay?' I say to him as we approach, and he grunts in response.

We climb the stairs and follow the sound of the music down a long hallway full of family photos, and into a tastefully lit living room filled – overflowing – with Anna's friends, most of whom, it seems, are exactly like Anna. I can see the odd boy here and there – beefy-looking guys in Tsubi shirts and Havaiana thongs, nodding politely at conversations or occasionally talking amongst themselves – but the overwhelming majority of people here are girls, and hot ones at that. The whole house, in fact, seems to be vibrating with them – ex-private school girls with fair hair and good teeth, girls whose fathers probably bought them Alfa Romeos when they finished high school, laughing and swaying to the hip-hop that is playing from somewhere, drinking vodka or red wine out of Slurpee cups.

The girls – and some of the guys – seem to size us up when we come in, stopping for a second to look at us before returning to their conversations. One of the girls, a tall blonde with skinny legs and the most gravity-defying chest I've seen outside of one of those beer commercials from the 80s, breaks away from the pack and approaches.

'Hi there,' she begins, all sultry, while we are both still vaguely lost for words. 'I'm Caitlin. I'm the *welcoming* committee,' she says, and then laughs, though it wasn't immediately apparent that she'd been making a joke. We laugh along with her. 'You must be Lachlan! Anna's *told* me all *about* you...' She leans in to kiss Lachie on the cheek. 'Come in! It's nice to meet you. And you're Lachlan's *friend*...'

It takes me a second to get my bearings, as all of this has taken place fairly quickly, but I realise that Catherine, Kristin, whatever her name is, must be talking to me, so I smile back. 'Liam,' I say. 'Great to meet you.'

'Great to meet you too, *Liam*,' she says, emphasising the 'Liam', drawing it out. 'Anna's outside.' She takes Lachie by the arm. 'I know she's *dying* to see you. Why don't we go find her?'

She sets off with Lachie in tow, and I follow close behind. We negotiate our way around the throng of girls, through a narrow kitchen and a dining room with a table pushed to one side and a temporary bar being manned by a pair of guys who have that drunken, dorky younger brother look about them. Though she's holding on to Lachie, Katharine/Christina spends most of the time talking to me, possibly because she has identified me as the single one.

She asks me questions about what I do and the things I like, the kinds of questions that you might ask a little kid if you were being friendly, but she seems fairly consistently amazed by my responses, *oooohhh*-ing when I tell her that I go to UQ, that my dad is a partner at Smith McTiernan & Kelly, where Lachie hopes to do his internship.

We find Anna on the narrow back verandah of the house, surrounded by even more cute, tipsy-looking blonde girls and their boyfriends, all of whom size Lachie and me up mistrustfully as we walk towards them. There are several eskies near the door, and as soon as I open one and put our first six-pack – which is now a five-pack – on ice, Lachie grabs another Hahnie and cracks it open. Anna approaches and takes Lachie by the arm. They kiss and she seems genuinely pleased to see him. Introductions are made, but the names wash over me and I forget them straightaway, not bothering to correct Caroline/Katie when she introduces me as 'Lachie's gorgeous and more importantly *single* friend Liam'. Soon after this, Lachie is being gushed over by a not-bad-looking older woman, probably Anna's mother. Anna pretends to be mortified by the spectacle while Lachie himself seems to actually be responding to the attention, less morose than I've seen him all night.

I'm about to grab a beer and join the party when, in my pocket, my phone begins to buzz. I hesitate for a moment when I see the number that comes up on the display – Sara's. She has been calling and texting me a lot over the last few days – I guess she's been missing me and it's only natural. I've been faithfully responding to all of the messages, telling her how much I love her and miss her, telling her about the boring, routine stuff that has been making up my days lately, but it never seems to be enough. When I see the number on the display my first thought is that I might be able to ignore the call – make up some excuse like I didn't have my phone with me or I didn't hear it ring – but doing that would probably be a bad idea, and it's not like Anna's party is shaping up to be that great anyway.

'Hey babe,' I say when I answer.

'Liam!' Sara says, sounding mildly relieved, perhaps at the fact that I've answered the call. 'How are you? Sorry to call so late at night – is it even that late there? I don't know – but I woke up this morning and I really missed you.'

'Babe,' I say to her, 'it's never too late for you to call. I've been missing you too.' I excuse myself from the verandah – though Lachie, who seems to have his hands full, probably doesn't even notice – and walk back through the house to find somewhere we can talk.

'It's noisy where you are,' Sara says. 'Sounds like you're out enjoying yourself.'

'In a manner of speaking,' I say.

'Where's the party?'

'It's not really a party. It's more a get-together.'

'Where's the get-together?'

'It's at some Anna girl's house.'

'Sounds mysterious...'

'Not really. She's just this girl that Lachie's seeing. It's her birthday in a few days so she's having this thing at her place in Toowong.'

'You silly boy,' Sara laughs. 'I'm glad that you're out having fun. You're not just sitting at home pining over your girlfriend thousands of miles away.'

'I've been a mess for weeks,' I say, not sure if we're playing this sarcastic or sincere right now. 'Seriously. Ask anyone.'

'Well, I'm glad you're having fun,' she says again. 'I just wanted to call you because I've really been

109

missing you.'

'I miss you too,' I tell her.

'Really?'

'Are you kidding? It's weird not having you around. I'm still getting used to it. I think about you all the time.'

I walk through the party, in search of a quiet place, and end up ducking into a bedroom off the main hallway. I guess the room must belong to Anna – there is a big bed in the centre, a desk with an iMac and various framed photographs on it, and clothes scattered everywhere. As I take a look around, Sara starts telling me that she is staying in a hostel in Prague right now, that she has just woken up and is about to head out to breakfast with a friend.

I listen, vaguely interested, but the flow of her speech is so dense that it's all I can really do to interject with the occasional 'Yeah babe, I'll bet' whenever she says something along the lines of 'Oh, I wish you'd been there, it was so much fun'.

I'm picking up random items on the desk, examining law textbooks, a photo of Anna and some other girl I don't recognise, when the words '...and I met the *nicest* boy, so sweet' jolt me back into the conversation.

'What?' I ask. 'Who's this?'

'When I got to the hostel,' Sara says, sounding mildly irritated. 'Here in *Prague*. Don't you remember? I was telling you how they got the booking wrong and I was going to have to wait, like, twelve hours to get into a room and I was almost crying...'

'Yeah,' I say. 'That. The booking. Of course I

remember.'

'There was a boy there called Miles, who was waiting for a room too...'

'Miles? Who's that?'

'I'm *telling* you who he is now, Liam. Miles is from Scotland, he's a backpacker too. He saw how upset I was about the room, so he told me not to worry. He had a word to the girl at the desk – she was really rude but he just wouldn't take no for an answer, and he made her keep looking on the computer until she found places for both of us. It was *so* nice of him to do –'

'Sounds like a wonderful guy,' I say, deadpan.

'I *know* what you're thinking, Liam, but it wasn't like that. We went out for coffee afterwards and he showed me around the city...'

'You went out for coffee?'

'It *wasn't* anything like you're thinking, Liam. Miles behaved like a perfect gentleman.'

'Is he a fag or what?' I ask.

Sara is silent for a few seconds. 'Not that it's any of your concern, but yes, Miles does happen to identify as homosexual.'

'Thought so,' I say. 'That's all right then.'

'You're so jealous,' she says. 'You were never like this when I was at home.'

'I'm just protective,' I say.

'Not protective enough to come to Europe with me...'

'What's that supposed to mean?'

'Nothing,' she says. 'Nothing at all. Look, Liam, I've

just woken up.'

I can sense her backing down, trying to avoid whatever confrontation we were heading towards. I could call her on that last one; perhaps here and now the two of us could have the significant discussion that we've been saving up for months, but the prospect of an hour or more of this weighs down on me, and instead I say: 'You know I love you, Sara.'

Pause. 'I love you too, Liam.'

'You know I would never do anything to hurt you. I'd never see anyone behind your back.' I try my best to sound genuine when I'm saying this, ignoring the strangely nauseous feeling in my stomach.

'Neither would I.'

'I'm glad you've met this Miles guy,' I say after a while. 'It's good you've got someone to show you around.'

'Yeah,' she says. 'He's lovely. You'd really like him.' She sounds a little doubtful on the last count.

'I'll bet I would,' I say, conscious of how forced the conversation has suddenly become.

We talk for a while longer before Sara says goodbye. 'I'll call you in the next few days, okay?' she says.

'I love you,' I say.

'Love you too.'

I replace my phone in my pocket and prepare to head back out to the party, but moments after Sara and I have hung up, I hear the sound of a text message coming through. It has to be Sara again, I'm thinking, apologising for what she said before. She's feeling bad about it already, which is typical of Sara, but also kind of sweet.

When I flip back the screen, though, the number on it is one I don't recognise.

The message, when I open it, reads:

> hey liam, kristian here (brad's
> bro) just txting to say thanks
> for the beer & i hope yr party
> thing is going all right, owe you
> one – kristian

Owe me one what? I wonder. I read the unexpected message over several times, not sure if I should even bother responding, and if I do, how to go about it. I don't even know how the little fag managed to get my number – from Brad's phone, I'm guessing – but that's probably not the most pressing issue here. I consider my response for a while before writing:

> that's fine, always glad to
> contribute to the declining
> moral standards of underage
> drinkers. have fun with those
> all hallows girls

It's not like me to wait around for a reply when I send off a text message, but this time, as I watch the icon on the screen – an old-fashioned envelope with a set of wings attached – fly away, I realise that I'm somehow too intrigued not to wait around for what comes back. Sure enough, seconds later:

yeah the girls are all right not
really that interesting – tell
me if i can ever do anything in
return

I wonder, not unamused, how many of those beers the little fag must have gotten through already. I reply:

i'll hold you to that ;)

...not even sure if the little wink thing looks amiably retarded or menacing, but fuck it. I slip the phone back in my pocket and head out to the party. When I leave Anna's room, the music has changed – someone has put on The Strokes, or another indie band who sound identical to The Strokes, it's hard to tell – and the girls in the living room have begun to dance a lot more purposefully, some of them roping their boyfriends in too. When I get to the kitchen there seems to be some sort of commotion going on in the room with the bar – people have started to crowd around the doorway – and I can hear someone yelling: 'Clear a path! Come on, clear a path, guys!'

The next thing I see is Lachie being led into the kitchen by a guy I don't recognise. He is looking somewhat worse for wear, his right hand wrapped in a towel, and immediately after noticing the worried expression on the guy's face, I look down and see the blood on the towel.

'Fuck, man,' the guy is saying. 'What were you thinking? We need to get some ice on that now.'

'I'm fine,' Lachie is saying. 'It's...' he winces in pain. 'It's nothing.'

Anna rushes into the kitchen, ahead of both of them. 'Liam!' she says when she sees me, pulling me along with her to the sink, trying and failing to open a bag of party ice. 'Help me with this.'

'What happened?' I ask her.

'He was...' she says, 'he was, oh, shit! I can't open the bag!'

'Here,' I say, tearing at the plastic, 'let me. What the hell happened?' When, finally, I manage to make a hole in the bag, party ice begins clattering out into the sink.

I watch as the dude leads Lachie over to where we are standing, shuddering at the sight of his hand, slick with blood so dark that the source is not immediately apparent.

'He was playing around with a beer bottle,' the dude says.

'I was showing Anna my trick,' Lachie cuts in.

'I told him not to but he *insisted*,' Anna is saying, 'he flicked it up in the air and tried to open it on the edge of the table, but it came down on the table too hard, and there was broken glass everywhere, and...'

I'm familiar with this 'trick' of Lachie's – he managed to ruin at least half a six-pack of Coronas practising it at my house last summer – but I've never seen him try it in public before.

'It would've worked,' Lachie is saying, 'if the table wasn't –'

'Don't worry about that. Here, give me your hand.' The cold water rinses off the worst of the blood, revealing a series of gashes, some of which actually look reasonably deep, across his palm and fingers.

After we pack the wounds in ice – a difficult process, as an angry, drunk Lachie keeps pulling away, saying that it's nothing – Anna's dad steps in and insists on driving him to the hospital. Anna wants to come, but Lachie tells her to stay, not wanting her to miss her party, and when he starts to cry, I tell them that *I'll* follow Anna's dad to the hospital in my car, and stay there with Lachie while they stitch him up.

I promise Anna that I'll call and let her know how Lachie's doing, and she thanks me, looking very shaken up nonetheless. As we are leaving, Lachie, who is muttering about making a fool of himself in front of his girlfriend, about what his dad is going to say, asks me for another beer, but I pat him on the back, tell him it's probably not a good idea the shape he's in.

Later, as I'm getting into my car, Kristian responds to my message:

bet you will ;)

It's a week later and that night is nearly forgotten when a phone call wakes me up. It's overcast and I feel like shit, but the ringing noise is not something I'm going to be able to ignore. My head is hurting, and as I step into a pile of dirty jeans and T-shirts, I try to piece together a decent account of last night.

From what I can recall, we started out at some art gallery on Brunswick Street, where some Fine Arts student – a dude who looked like Chloë Sevigny, a dude that Jay might or might not have been fucking – was having an exhibition of his work. Beforehand, over drinks at the Fringe Bar, I'd asked the guy what he did and he told me 'multimedia', and I basically took that as a cue not to ask him anything else. The show itself was pretty grim. It was meant to be a comment on something, but I couldn't really figure out what. It featured a videotape of a boy dressed in an army uniform and walking down a dark tunnel that played, on a seemingly endless loop, American flags with fake bloodstains on them, recruiting posters, canvases with words like IMPERIALISM and CHOMSKY and HEGEMONY on them and the whole thing was basically too boring for words, but there were girls walking around with glasses of champagne and I drank an awful lot of that, which almost made the whole thing bearable.

Just as I was preparing to chew my own paw off, Callum showed up, and after a few more drinks we fled to Family. The line to get in was un-fucking-believable – a queue of ravers and fags and girls in low-cut things stretching almost to the end of the block – but Callum was friends with the girl on the door and she let us in straightaway, which was a massive relief. We headed to the upstairs bar, drinking beer, knocking it back, and talking about how much we hated the Valley until these two girls approached us and started flirting fairly openly. We talked to the girls about how we came to Family all the time, impressed them by telling them that we were friends with the DJ downstairs (a statement that was complete bullshit, but the girls were too drunk to even question it). A few drinks turned into a lot of drinks, and now, returning to consciousness, I realise that I'm actually quite hungover.

The ringing of my phone is actually hurting my head and I realise there is probably no choice other than to answer it. The display shows Kristian's mobile number, which I saved on the night of the vaguely inappropriate text messages. I try to figure out why the little fucker might be calling me at one on a Saturday afternoon, wonder if it might be an emergency of some kind, but a reasonable rationalisation is beyond me. I answer it after a few rings. 'Hello?' I say.

'Hi, um, this is Kristian,' he says, then, after a pause, 'Brad's little brother.'

'I know,' I say, playing it cool. 'Yeah. Hey. What's happening?'

'Yeah, um, not much, I just wanted to... I mean... How are you?'

'Good,' I say, then, after a few seconds, 'how are you?'

'I'm pretty good. Y'know, school's back and stuff...it's pretty boring, but it's okay.'

'Yeah,' I say.

'Listen, um, I was wondering... I'm sorry to bother you, but do you have any... I mean, the reason I thought I'd call you was that...'

'What is it?'

'I wanted some, like... I was hoping to get some weed.

I kind of wanted some and none of my friends have any and I thought I might call you...since...I thought you might, um...You might have some.'

'Why didn't you talk to Brad?'

'I didn't want to ask him. I thought it would be, I don't know, it would have felt weird or something.'

'What makes you think that *I'd* have weed?'

While we're talking, I'm looking myself over in the mirror. My skin is a little pale and there are some dark circles under my eyes, but my chest and stomach still look pretty good and basically, when it comes down to it, I'm in fairly fine form.

Kristian is silent for a second, like he's not quite sure what to say. 'I thought you'd be... I mean... I didn't know who else to call. You seem like you'd...'

I decide not to torture him any longer. 'How much do you need?'

'I don't know. Not much. If you had a quarter then maybe like half of that?'

'That shouldn't be any problem.' I have a fairly large quantity of weed at the bottom of my sock drawer, along with several pills and a point left over from a bender Callum and I went on several weekends ago.

'Really?' he says. 'If you do, that would be awesome. I mean, I wouldn't have called you, except...'

'It's fine,' I tell him. 'I've already plied you with alcohol, I might as well make your descent into after-school special territory complete. When do you need it by?'

'Well, like, I'm home by myself right now. Nobody else is here. So if you're free this afternoon...'

'Yeah,' I tell him, 'that should be okay.'

'It's just me,' he says. 'Nobody else is home. Brad's gone over to Isabel's house. I'm here by myself.'

I wonder why exactly it is that Kristian has chosen to emphasise this – his bet you will ;) returns momentarily to my thoughts – but whatever, it doesn't really matter at this point in time. 'Great,' I tell him. 'I'll be there in an hour.'

We say our goodbyes and hang up; I look myself over again in the mirror, running my hand across my stomach. I take a shower and realise I still have a boner from when I woke up; I consider jerking off but decide not to. There are assignments I should be working on this weekend, but the chances of my actually doing them are fairly remote and the idea of heading off to Kristian's seems somehow more interesting.

The Caldwells' house is near the top of a steep hill. I park what I assume to be a safe distance behind a black Mercedes, then almost roll into the back of it when I'm putting the handbrake on. Jesus, *that* would've been a nice one to have to explain, these crazy bastards and their cars.

The eighth that's intended for Kristian is in the glove box; I pull the bag out, weigh it in one hand, sniff it. My car still smells pretty new and that mixed with the scent of the weed is a weird...juxtaposition. That's the word that Sara would probably use. I wonder why, when Jay asked me where I was going, I didn't tell him.

I wonder what Brad would say if he knew I was going to see his little brother in the middle of the day, if he'd care. I look at the bag of weed for a while; I put it on the seat next to me and consider driving off. Instead I get out of the car, lock the doors and start walking back up the hill. I've been here hundreds of times before but it looks somehow different today, knowing that Brad isn't here, that it's Kristian, normally just a presence in the background, who is waiting for me inside. The whole thing feels weirdly out of context, but kind of intriguing at the same time.

This is my best friend's little brother. I start to think about all the reasons Kristian might have had for calling me – aside from the drugs, obviously. There are those text messages to think of, for a start. He is always kind of quiet and nervous, he seems to hang out on the edges of things, but you get the feeling that under the right circumstances he'd go wild. Under the right circumstances, it probably wouldn't be hard to talk him into... No, to hell with it. I'm being a faggot. The only reason Kristian called me was because he wanted some weed. It's completely innocent, and nothing that I wouldn't do for anyone else. Except that this is my best friend's little brother.

At the front of the house there is a high wall with an intercom. The Caldwells have one of those modern houses, built with protection in mind, with the intention of keeping the world out. *Too late*, I think as I push the button.

At first there is no response. I wait for a while, finger the bag of weed in my pocket, then push the button again. After a few seconds Kristian's voice comes on the intercom. 'Um... Hello?' Even through the static he sounds nervous, kind of weirded-out.

'It's me.' I tell him. 'Liam.'

'Oh yeah. Hey... Um, come in.'

I hear a clicking noise as the gate comes open. I walk in, pushing it closed behind me. There is a courtyard at the front of the house with this fussy, Japanese-style garden – it's all stepping stones and tiny white pebbles, little bushes everywhere and one of those weird bamboo water-fountain things. The silence here is a little oppressive and as I wait, staring at my reflection in the big glass doors, I pick up one of the pebbles, run my fingers over the surface of it; after a while, I get bored of it and toss it over the wall.

Finally, I hear footsteps coming from inside. When Kristian slides the door back, a frenzied streak of fur comes bounding out after him, panting, wagging its tail furiously.

'Henry,' he calls out after the dog, 'c'mere.' Kristian looks up at me for a few seconds, nervous, like he was about to say something but he's forgotten what it was. 'Sorry,' he says in a shaky voice, looking back down at the dog. 'Henry's not meant to be out here...'

Henry is the Caldwells' golden retriever – he's so energetic, so relentlessly fucking *bouncy*, he could actually be two dogs. He rushes over, really affectionate, and starts jumping all over me, going nuts in that dumb, helpless way that dogs get when they're excited.

'Great guard dog,' I say, crouching down to pat him,

scratching behind his ear. 'I could be coming in here to beat you up or something.'

'He's not supposed to go outside,' says Kristian, looking concerned. 'He could get run over if he gets onto the road. I don't want him to get run over.' I think that's probably the most words I've ever heard Kristian say in one go.

He is dressed in skater clothes, as always. He has on a pink shirt with the words VOLCOM STONE across the front, and the ubiquitous trucker cap, white and pink with streaks of black. The clothes are like a candy coating for something more complicated but way more fun. Right now, he basically looks like a smaller, cuter version of Brad. You'd almost say he looks like a girl – actually, that's a dumb thing to say, because he doesn't really, but there is something sort of girlish about him, delicate. He's just, well, pretty or something. He looks kind of compliant, like you could probably do all kinds of things to him and he wouldn't complain.

'I think he'll be right,' I say. Henry is still going nuts, jumping up and down, so excited he looks like he might be about to lose it completely.

Kristian pulls the dog away, struggling to contain him, and leads a reluctant Henry towards the sliding doors, motioning for me to follow.

The air is cooler inside the house; the Caldwells have the whole place airconditioned, which is absolutely necessary in weather like this. Henry dashes off, distracted by something else, his claws making a clicking noise against the polished floor as he hurries away. Kristian and I are alone now, standing in front of a big mirror. He stares at me, expectant, says nothing.

'So I brought you an eighth,' I tell him.

'What?'

Jesus, is he being deliberately vague or what?

'Drugs,' I tell him. 'Weed. I brought you some.'

'Oh yeah. That's really...yeah. You should, I mean, you can...Yeah. Come on.'

Kristian turns, leading me down the hallway towards the kitchen. I watch him as he walks ahead, noticing how skinny his arms are, his elbows. When we get to the kitchen, I lay the bag of weed down on the countertop. Kristian looks at it, then at me. I can hear noises coming from downstairs, muffled voices. I guess he must have a movie on or something. I almost ask him what it is, but I don't. He keeps looking at me, edgy, his eyes open wide. Something about his nervousness, his awkwardness, is a little exciting, and seeing him like this brings out something bad in me. I want to have some fun with Kristian. I want to either fuck him or hurt him badly and I'm not sure which. Possibly both.

'Your parents aren't around, right?' I ask.

'Nobody's here,' he says. 'Mum was here, but she's gone out. She saw this big spider by the pool this morning and she kind of lost it for a while. She had to lie down on the couch. She's gone shopping to calm herself down.'

'No shit.'

'I didn't see the spider but she said it was really big.'

'Yeah, those big ones are the worst.'

'I went out there to look for it. She made me because

she was really scared that it was going to, like, try and kill her if she went back out there. But I couldn't find it. She probably imagined it. Mum's always imagining weird shit.'

'What kind of shit?'

'I don't know. Like, she thought these people were trying to break into the house this one time.'

'Were they?'

'I don't think so. But she had the locks changed. It was freaky.'

A few seconds of silence pass between us. 'So...um, do you want a drink?' He motions towards the fridge.

'How did you get my number?' I ask, even though I'm already pretty certain that he took it from his brother. 'Just for interest's sake. I didn't know you had it.' I guess I'd like to know if he's going to lie, to see him wriggle his way out of it, if he does.

Kristian starts to turn red. 'Brad gave it to me.'

'Okay.'

'I mean, he didn't give it to me but his phone was lying around and your number was in there, so I took it. Well, I didn't take his *phone*, but you know what I mean, it was there, so I...yeah. I thought since you might...the weed and everything, I took your number. So I could call you.'

'Good,' I say. 'I'm glad we got that one cleared up.'

'Um, yeah, so...do you want a drink?' he asks again.

'I'm fine.'

He turns to the fridge, and I watch him half fill a glass with ice, then pour some grape juice in. There is a photograph stuck to the fridge – the family, Brad and Kristian and their parents standing on the deck of Mr Caldwell's boat. Mrs Caldwell has her arm around Brad's shoulders. Kristian looks younger. His hair is shorter and he has this goofy smile on his face. They have that 'family' look about them and it's essentially very innocent and very remote from what's going on now.

Kristian drains about half the glass then comes back over to me. He picks up the bag of weed then puts it down again. 'How much do you want for this?' he asks.

Oddly enough, the thought of that hadn't even occurred to me. 'Don't worry about it,' I tell him. 'It's free. It's a favour.'

'Really?' he asks, his expression even more confused than normal.

'Dude, you're Brad's brother. Your money's no good.'

'Thanks…That's really… I mean, that's awesome.'

'Listen,' I say, 'do you want to get fucked up?'

'Um, yeah. That sounds…good. But we'd better go up to my room. Dad's going to get pissed if he smells it in the house, but he doesn't go into my room.'

'Great,' I say.

'So, um, we should go up. Do you want to…?'

'Yeah,' I tell him. 'Brilliant.'

Kristian's room is on the third floor, up a narrow staircase. He leads me in and I shut the door behind me – I've never been in this part of the house before and it's a weird feeling. The room is basically filled with stuff – piles of Kristian's clothes lie all over the floor, there is a skateboard leaning against the wall, textbooks scattered around unopened and posters hung up at weird angles, the largest of which has the words GOOD CHARLOTTE written across the bottom in Gothic lettering. There is a big bed to one side, and Kristian drifts around for a while – nervous, opening windows, picking up some skateboarding magazine then putting it down again – before he goes over and sits down on it.

I walk across to the bed, and Kristian moves over a little to make room for me. When I sit, Kristian looks at me, then quickly looks away.

'Um,' he says. 'Liam?'

'What?'

He reaches across and touches my stomach, then thinks better of it and draws his hand back, and he actually starts apologising to me, telling me, 'I'm sorry dude, I didn't mean to... It's not like...'

To hell with it. Whatever the pretext, whatever reason the little fag invented to get me over here, this was always going to happen.

'You didn't really want that weed, did you?' I ask.

'I, um...'

When I lean across and kiss him, I can feel his heart beating pretty fast, and I can actually *feel* him melting in my arms. I push him back on the bed and anything else we might have been about to do that afternoon is forgotten about.

I start to get dressed, pull my boxers on and then my jeans. I remember balling my shirt up and tossing it somewhere and finding it again is basically a real nightmare. Eventually I track it down to the corner of the room, sitting with a pile of Kristian's clothes underneath a Tony Hawk poster. Something about seeing the poster unsettles me slightly, brings me back to reality and reminds me of who Kristian actually *is* and *where* the two of us are. I pull the shirt over my shoulders and try not to look around.

I would kind of like to leave now but when I turn around Kristian is sitting on the edge of the bed. He has pulled his boxer shorts on and is giving me this odd look as though he is expecting me to do something or say something. I run through a list of possibilities in my head – stuff along the lines of, *I don't know, it's been fun, I'll call you*, except I don't really want to say any of this stuff as he's Brad's little brother and I kind of don't want him to get upset and do anything irrational as that could destroy any number of friendships and, realistically, get me in a lot of fucking trouble, so this is basically a time for treading carefully.

I walk across to the bed and stand in front of him. I touch his stomach and then the bottom of his chin, bringing his face up so he's looking at me.

'Um,' Kristian asks, 'this is weird, but can I see you again? I mean, I'll see you again anyway, because of Brad and stuff, but can I...'

This is, of course, the moment I've been dreading. 'When do you want to see me?' I ask, as if being obtuse with him is going to be the way out of this.

Kristian's face kind of falls, and he says, 'I don't know,' and in that moment, looking at his face, I realise that

I'm actually feeling something for him. For a second it crosses my mind that Kristian really is all right – his face is nice-looking, innocent or something – and for a second the feeling gets the better of me and I tell him: 'To hell with it, I'm being a shithead...' He looks at me hopefully. 'Look... I guess... I mean, we can see each other again if you like.'

'You're over the house all the time...' he says. 'With...'

'This is different,' I tell him.

Kristian is silent for a few seconds. He picks up a can of deodorant which for some reason is lying on the bed and passes it from hand to hand.

'What's the matter?' I ask him.

He looks up at me. 'Don't...'

'Don't what?'

'Don't tell my brother, okay?'

This, of course, is when it strikes me that I still have the upper hand here. I realise I'm in the clear, at least for the moment.

'I won't tell Brad,' I say. 'Don't worry. This is between the two of us.'

'This' didn't actually boil down to much; some heavy petting followed by a sloppy but still fairly decent blow job, after which Kristian let me fuck him for about ten minutes, groaning, almost crying the whole time. Even so, I get the impression that what just happened might have been significant in some way to him.

Kristian smiles at me and we start to kiss again, and in a series of not exactly delicate motions I've pushed him back down on the bed, gotten up on my knees above him on the mattress – and he's smiling now, actually laughing, and he says 'Stop it' but I don't. The thought that I might really have fucked things up this time still lingers, but that's something I can worry about later.

I mean, it's not that I'm really into Kristian – that would make me a fag, which I'm not – but this is one of those times when you just have to go with it. We spend the whole afternoon together and in spite of Kristian being a dude and everything it feels, y'know...pretty good. Just don't get the wrong impression about it.

Six

Brunswick Street, ten-fifteen, and it's unusually crowded, even for a Friday night. I'm at one of the tables out on the mall, slightly bored, ignoring Brad – in so far as this is possible, as he's on his third or fourth Beck's and annoyingly talkative – and waiting around trying to figure out what we're going to do with the night. I'm nodding at Brad every so often, staring at the crowds of people walking by – pretty girls, punk girls, girls in tartan skirts, ravers on their way to Family, fags, white boys pretending to be black – and it's basically trucker caps and distressed denim as far as the eye can see. Bloc Party's 'Banquet' is blasting from somewhere behind me and it's all been done many times before but I'm on the edge of drunkenness myself so, thanks to that, as well as the fairly large spliff we consumed earlier, I'm capable of letting all this wash over me, capable of achieving my goal for the evening, which is basically *NOT LETTING BRAD KNOW I FUCKED HIS BROTHER*.

'...seriously, I think it could be for real with her,' Brad is saying.

'With who?' I ask when I realise that he's looking at me, waiting for a reply.

'With Isabel, dude. Like I've been telling you.'

Some guy walks past, giving off that drunken first-year kind of vibe, wearing a white Quiksilver shirt, carrying three beers and another drink that I can't identify. The table where his friends are sitting is just across from ours, and as he squeezes past he spills some beer on Brad, who looks for a second like he might be about to chew the guy out, but doesn't.

'It's mad. I mean, it's been ages but it doesn't really feel like any time at all...'

'You're sweet,' I tell him. 'It's the first six months, so you're still having crazy rabbit-sex all the time, and you haven't gotten bored of one another yet.'

'Dude... I don't really... It's more than that.'

'What do you mean?'

Brad actually looks embarrassed. 'Well, she's nice...'

'She's *nice*? You pussy. If you're married with kids this time next year, I'll whip your ass.'

Brad grins and takes a pretend swipe at me. 'Unlike you and Sara, you old married man.'

Weirdly enough, I hadn't even thought of that. 'That's different,' I tell him.

'I'll bet,' he says, still grinning. He holds his beer bottle up to the light and gives it this funny look, shaking it like he's trying to work out if there's any left in there. 'Crap,' he says, so I guess the answer must be in the negative. 'I'm out,' he says. 'You want another one?' My beer is still about half full but I nod anyway and Brad bounds up, heading inside to the bar.

I look across and try to make eye contact with the drunken first years at the next table but lose interest after a while. The Quiksilver guy kind of looks like Kristian. He has the same shaggy hair or something, similar sort of profile. Maybe he doesn't look that much like him. I guess I'm still thinking about Kristian for some reason. Anyway, to hell with it, none of this matters as I'm not a fag and I don't care what this guy looks like, so his resemblance to Brad's brother is irrelevant. I wonder what Brad would do if he found out I'd been with Kristian, and then try not to let it play on my mind.

Just then I see Zoe and Audrey approaching, but they haven't spotted me yet. They're walking down from the Belushi's end of the mall, in this loose, semi-drunken group with two other guys I don't recognise. One of the guys, who is wearing a tweed jacket covered in these badges even though it's like the middle of summer, is moving his hands as though he's in the middle of telling a story. Zoe seems to be listening, fascinated, and as they get closer, she bursts out laughing – doubles over and has to lean on the guy for support.

I call out to them as they walk past. Zoe sees me first, and opens her mouth wide in this expression of mock surprise. 'Ohmygod, Liam, it's you!' The group begins to converge on the table. 'Seriously, I'm so over this whole semester. Why the hell did I ever go back? I'm ready to jump off a cliff.' Zoe makes her way around a large potted plant. 'I need a drink or several, like, immediately.' She reaches for me, wrists out, and we hug. 'So, how are you? Can we sit here? Have you met everybody?'

I shrug and begin to say something but she launches into the introductions. 'Oh, of course you haven't. This is Audrey, who you know...' Audrey attacks me from the other side, kissing me on the cheek. 'This is Paul from uni.' She points to the guy in the tweed jacket who is squeezing behind her and he smiles in my direction. 'Paul's a sweetie and his ex-girlfriend is in a mental hospital but he's still kind of sensitive about that so try not to bring it up, okay? And this is Daniel.' Daniel nods at me, nonchalant, and takes a seat on the opposite side of the table.

Zoe is actually pretty good-looking tonight. She's wearing something low-cut and dark, too much eyeliner, but it's a look that works on her. Kind of like a cross between that singer Miss Kittin and the girl from *The Fifth Element* or something. 'Right!' she says authoritatively. 'I'm getting a drink now. Who else wants one?' She dashes off towards the bar before anyone can say anything, but the others begin shouting drink orders at her anyway.

Things have started to become slightly blurry, and it's a blurriness that I'm able to deal with, but I could do with a refresher nonetheless. Everyone at the table laughs at something, but I didn't hear what it was and this bothers me a bit. I don't know where the hell Brad has got to but he'd better have been kidnapped by terrorists or something like that because that's the only excuse I'll be prepared to deal with.

Jay was supposed to be coming out tonight and promised me that he'd have some whiz...The fag better be on his way. I already sent him a message earlier in evening, but as I sit here not really listening to the others I text him again.

dear fag where the fuck
are you?! need drugs come
into the valley now
liam

Finally I see Brad drifting back towards the table with Isabel and another girl I don't recognise. 'Check it out,' he says as he arrives and sets a bottle of Beck's down in front of me. 'Isabel came out tonight.'

'Hi, Liam,' she says.

'And this is...' Brad introduces Isabel's friend, whose name I don't catch, although she gives me this little wave and looks me up and down. Zoe is back from the bar too, and suddenly the table has gone from one to, like, eight and there aren't enough chairs. Brad steals one from this table of jocks and Audrey and Daniel decide to double up. When Brad suggests in a joking way that Isabel might like to sit on his knee, she agrees straightaway.

I look back at the table of drunken first-years. I wonder what it would take to talk the Quiksilver guy into letting me fuck him; if I pounded him really hard, would he complain, get upset, or would he just take it? How drunk would I have to be before I could do those things?

Audrey, who is a lot more drunk than I am, picks up

a coaster and throws it at me; I flick it back at her, grinning. My phone begins to vibrate, and when I look at it the 'message received' icon has popped up on the screen. Audrey makes some joke about how somebody loves me and Zoe says she bets a lot of people do, and I smile at the two of them before I check the message out.

> leaving jonathan's
> house, there soon,
> chill the fuck out.

I don't know who the hell Jonathan is or why Jay might be leaving his house, but this information seems secondary at this point in time. I tell the gang that he's on his way and it's kind of decided that after we finish our drinks we should head somewhere else. Daniel wants to check out the Empire but Zoe and Audrey insist that there's this place they know of further down Brunswick Street where we just *have* to go, and they know the guy on the door so they can probably even get us in for free. We argue the merits of both places and when we come to a decision I'm still not sure where we're going.

By the time we get to the club I realise I am actually pretty drunk. As we get in the line, there are still crowds of people walking up the mall – girls who look seriously underage; a group of ravers, many of whom seem to be on pills already; a group of guys I think I recognise from uni. The line moves slowly forward. Isabel starts to laugh at some joke Brad has just told her and I grit my teeth, listening to the conversation that a group of obnoxiously fashionable twelve year olds is having behind us in the line.

'We should be nice to him,' a girl is saying. 'He has, y'know...a problem.'

'A problem?' her friend asks.

'Let's just say it has to do with the H-word.'

'Homosexual?'

'...Heroin,' she whispers, really conspiratorial.

'Please,' says someone else. 'Adrian is so dumb, he'd try to cook it up with a plastic spoon.' They all begin to laugh at this.

After what seems like a very long wait, we've made it to the head of the line. Zoe is attempting to talk her way around the door bitch, but things are not going according to plan. Apparently her friend isn't working tonight. 'But Hamish *always* lets us in,' I hear her saying – a last resort if ever there was one. As she continues to negotiate, I feel a hand on my shoulder. Jay has finally arrived. 'What's happening?' he asks me. I tell him not much, and when I introduce him around the group, he and Paul seem to size one another up and I wonder if the two of them have met before.

It looks as though negotiations have failed and we're going to have to pay our way in – an irritation, but a minor one. When I present my wrist to the girl so she can stamp it, I notice that there is another stamp on there already. I think back, trying to remember where it might have come from. The stamp may be left over from last night, or possibly even earlier, I have no recollection, but seeing it there reminds me of the morning Sara left, or, more specifically, of the fucking evil hangover I'm going to have tomorrow.

We have to climb up three extremely narrow flights of stairs to get into the club. The walls in the stairwell are painted red, plastered all over with posters for bands, movies, club nights. *Love & Roxy. The Distillers. Bright Like Neon Love.* As we get to the top of the second flight of stairs, Scarlett Johanssen's face is staring down at me from one of the larger posters, the words *Lost In Translation* beneath it. I turn to Jay, who is walking up behind me. 'Do you...?' I ask him.

'Yes.'

'Should we...?'

'Right away,' he says. 'Anything that might make this night halfway salvageable.'

The distorted echo of music that we've been hearing on the stairs resolves itself into Interpol's 'Say Hello to the Angels' as we walk into the club itself. The ambience inside is kind of indie strip-club meets an eighties *Miami Vice* set – lots of glass and blue lights, as well as an actual catwalk. The gang start to make their way across the mostly deserted dance floor, staking out a place on some couches in the far corner.

'We have to do, um...something,' I tell Zoe. 'Jay and I have to talk. I'll meet you over there.'

She gives me this look, like *you're a bad liar*, shakes her head, but she's grinning. 'Okay, we'll save a place for you.'

'Great.'

'Have fun,' she says.

I almost ask what she means by that but it's not even worth it. The bathroom is down the end of this narrow hallway; a guy and a girl are making out fairly strenuously, and we have to squeeze past them to get inside.

'After this I need a drink,' I tell Jay.

'After this I plan to not stop drinking,' he says.

The bathroom is basically pretty gross; it has these tiles that don't even bear thinking about and these harsh fluorescent lights that really make you aware of *exactly* where you are. Both of the stalls, it turns out, are occupied, so it seems we're going to have to wait this one out. This extremely annoying guy – ripped shirt with a print of Sid Vicious – I mean, *Jesus*, punk is rolling in its grave as we speak – is standing over by the mirrors, yelling very loudly into his phone, trying to convince the person on the other end to come out. 'Where are you? Where? I can't... I can't *hear* you.'

Jay sighs heavily. 'To hell with this,' he says. 'To hell with all of this.' Then, seemingly unprompted: 'I broke up with that Travis guy.'

'I didn't realise you were going out with that Travis guy.'

If I remember right, Travis was the Fine Arts student. 'It was only for, like, two weeks or so,' Jay says. 'He was cute, but like, *really* bad with the basics. I mean, really bad – he acted like he'd never been to bed with anyone before. It was terrible. And I was like, okay, maybe I can fix him up, look at him as a work in progress or something... Didn't work. The guy was a lost cause. Sad really. He was cute.'

The guy in the Sid Vicious shirt is still howling into his phone, oblivious to everything else around him. 'Come to the Valley...' he's saying. 'I got a new piercing...Yeah, but I'll only show you if you come in...The Valley...The *VAL-LEY.*' The conversation continues like this, as though on an endless loop.

Jay is becoming increasingly agitated, bouncing up and down on the balls of his feet and shooting the guy these extremely hostile looks. 'Jesus,' he says through gritted teeth. 'It's bad enough as it is *waiting for a bathroom stall*, this guy is *not* making it any easier for me...'

While this has been going on, I've been thinking about how Kristian called me a few days ago, asking if I wanted to hang out. That's the way the little fag put it...*hang out.* I told him I was busy and he acted all nonchalant, told me that was fine, that he didn't really care.

'We should just do it here.'

'Isn't that kind of gross?'

'Isn't doing it in a bathroom stall kind of gross?'

'But it's private. *Shit!*' Jay looks over at the phone freak. 'I want to kill this guy. Sid Vicious... I mean, Jesus. If he knew it was his destiny to wind up as a fashion accessory on this piece of Valley trash...'

'...he'd have done himself in a lot sooner. What is *tak-ing* them so long?' I glance across at the stalls again.

Finally, movement. Zoe's friend Paul – though I have no idea how he could *possibly* have got in here ahead of us – emerges from the further of the two. He nods at us and brushes some hair out of his face before looking away again.

'Is this going to look suspicious?' I ask, not really caring if it does as Jay and I brush past Paul.

Jay mutters something under his breath as I close the door behind us.

'What?' I ask him as he fishes around in his pocket for the baggie.

'I said did you have to?'

'Did I have to what?'

'People saw us coming in. It's going to look, Jesus...' Jay finds the baggie, holding it up for my inspection. Up close, the yellowy powder inside actually looks sort of disgusting. 'It's going to look dodgy if we're, dammit...' The small ziploc bag still refuses to give. '...if we're in here for too long.'

'Naw,' I tell him. 'People will just assume we're having sex.'

Jay looks up at me for a second, not amused.

'What's the problem?' I ask. 'I thought all gay guys did it in bathrooms.'

'First of all,' he says, and then pauses, distracted for a second by fidgeting with the baggie, which he can't seem to get open, 'I'm providing the drugs so you can drop that pretend tough-guy bullshit. Secondly, the problem is...' He drops the bag, leans down to pick it up. 'Jesus, I hate to think what's been on the floor in here. The problem is Paul...You saw him coming out of here before?'

'So?'

'So he's really cute... And he's friends with Zoe, and

she told me he's just broken up with someone.'

'So?'

'So I don't want him to think I'm, y'know, already here with somebody else.'

'Has that ever been a problem with you before?'

'That's *not* the... Ohmygod, *finally*,' he mutters as the baggie comes open. 'What was I saying? Oh yeah, that's *not* the point. I think I might have a shot with him. I'm cute. I can help him through these troubled times. But not if he thinks I'm...'

'...the kind of guy who'd be fucking someone in a bathroom stall?'

'That's the essence of it, yeah.'

'Well, if that's the case, then let's try to, y'know...' I look down at the baggie then back up at him, '...expedite matters a little.'

He dips a finger in the baggie, works it around a little bit then raises it to his lips. 'It's really...' His eyes widen. 'Shit. I'm wide awake all of a sudden. It's really good.' He dips his finger in the baggie again and then holds it out to me. 'Jesus, you need to do some of this right away.'

'Umm...'

'What?' He looks down at his finger. 'Do you have a problem with me sticking this in your mouth?'

'Yes. No. Not really. Jesus. I don't know. Yes.'

Jay huffs at me, shakes his head. 'You're such a fucking girl, Liam.' At this point Jay basically forces his finger into my mouth and moves it across my tongue before he starts to rub it across my gums. At first it's a jolting kind

142

of a feeling, a bitter taste, and then...

'Um, you can stop sucking my finger now,' Jay says, grinning.

'I *wasn't*. You're a homosexual.'

'We could discuss this all night. Let's just do some more of this shit and get out of here.'

When we open the door of the stall the guy in the Sid Vicious shirt, finally off the phone, smirks at us.

'That guy,' Jay says through gritted teeth. 'I mean, seriously, what's with the attitude?' We push past the couple, who are still kissing in the hallway. 'If I see him again, I'm going to kill him. Who the fuck does he think he is, with that look?'

'I think you need to just forget about it.'

'Fuck it. As a matter of fact...' Jay turns and makes like he's about to go back into the bathroom and have words with the guy, and I actually have to grab him and tell him, 'You wanna try and chill the fuck out?'

The club is dark and seems to be a lot more crowded now. Some movie is playing on a big screen – Michael J Fox leaving a nightclub at dawn, trying and failing to hail a taxi cab. The group has expanded since we left, and they've formed a kind of circle by pulling two of the couches and various cubes of dark-coloured cushion together. As we approach, Zoe looks me over again, still with that same grin on her face, and motions towards a space on the couch next to her.

I look across at Brad and Isabel, who are getting very familiar on the other couch. She is talking to someone else, but his hand is slowly making its way towards her

143

thigh, and when it gets there, she doesn't remove it. Jay and Paul are talking at one another very rapidly and the grin on Jay's face seems slightly forced, slightly too cheerful, and I'd sort of like to hear what they're saying but the music obliterates everything.

The DJ segues from the Rapture's 'House Of Jealous Lovers' to Madonna's 'Like a Prayer' and many more people begin flocking to the dance floor. Zoe asks me if I'd like to dance with her, I tell her that I don't know, that basically life seems very confusing to me right now, and she tells me she knows exactly what I mean.

The night gradually becomes a sped-up blur. I drink a lot more, get into a long and pointless conversation with Daniel, and do in fact spend some time dancing with Zoe, who is flirting quite openly with me. Jay and I do some more whiz, snorting up bumps of the stuff, and later we have a mostly incomprehensible exchange because it's difficult to concentrate on what we're saying as the whiz is starting to run low and we've both basically been reduced to fiends at this point and are eyeing off the rest of the stuff. I ask him what he thinks of Brad's brother – if he's cute, if he's fuckable, from a fag's perspective – and Jay gives me this funny look and asks what the hell I'm talking about, and I tell him nothing, forget it. I tell him he should do the rest of the whiz as he's the one who provided it after all, and he seems amenable to this idea, and pretty soon, the conversation is forgotten.

Some time much later in the evening I'm feeling somewhat dazed and drifting back from the bar when I spot Jay making out fairly energetically with the guy in the Sid Vicious shirt. Jesus, I think, what the fuck is the world coming to? I watch them for a while, but it all seems like too much to deal with so I leave the fags to it, wondering if the guy is going to show Jay his piercing later. On the screen Michael J Fox is chasing a girl, a model, down the length of a catwalk – I watch this for a while then head back to the couches where Zoe gives me a fairly penetrating look and I don't look away.

Seven

Lachie has been in a bit of a slump ever since being trashed by that Anna girl a week ago – she made the inevitable 'it's not you, it's me' declaration, told him that he was a wonderful guy, truly, she just wasn't ready to be with someone so...intense. That's the way Lachie, whose palm is still bandaged up, told the story to us anyway. He didn't take it very well – Callum told us that, a few nights ago, the big guy called him up and was actually *crying* on the phone – so, accordingly, we've made an executive decision to take him out for some drinks and some laughs and maybe get him to cheer the fuck up. There have been signs all along Coronation Drive this week advertising the first heat of the Miss Regatta contest for tonight, and so we figured, not without reason, that a blatant display of extremely dumb babes in extremely skimpy clothes would be just the thing to cheer Lachie up.

The Regatta is one of those places that have kind of been here forever – I mean, my dad and Brad's used to go here when they were at UQ, and though Dad likes to complain that, after so many remodellings and renovations, the place now resembles any other trendy bar in any other city, I still think the place is all right. Our dads – Brad's, Lachie's and mine – took us to lunch at the Boatshed, the restaurant out the side, the week before we graduated from high school. They spent all afternoon drinking Penfolds, making a big deal out of 'surreptitiously' sneaking a few glasses our way, and at one point it looked as though Mr Caldwell was getting ready to make a speech. The theme of the afternoon was, essentially, that we were about to enter into some big rite of passage, the next stage of our manhood or something – I don't know how much of the sentiment rubbed off, but the following year, for reasons that may or may not have had anything to do with that lunch, the place became one of our regular hangouts too.

Being a Friday night, the main bar is crowded; there are lots of other UQ and ex-UQ guys here, and everybody is preparing for a weekend of getting trashed, recovering and then getting trashed again. Most of the guys here – collars up, biceps bulging – are already pretty drunk, even though it's only early in the night, but, then again, many of them probably started at around lunchtime, so it's understandable. Basically, it's crowds of five and six guys – college boys, jocks, some but by no means all of them with an extra girl or two – admiring the cut of each other's jibs and getting smashed on imported beers with wedges of lime in the top. Pastel-coloured polo shirts and painstakingly styled hair are pretty much the order of the day – as Sara once said to me, 'It used to be that you could judge a man by the quality of his soul, now you judge him by the price of his haircut.'

The atmosphere inside is pretty relaxed, but you get the sense that it might not take all that much – saying the wrong thing, bumping into the wrong person on the way to the bar – to tip the feeling of good-natured camaraderie into violence of some sort. We came within mere inches of getting into a punch-up in the car park when we arrived, the result of some general carelessness on Lachie's part, but also a pretty worrying indicator of where the night might be heading.

Lachie finished uni just before six and picked us all up from Brad's house soon after. He seemed to have something on his mind as he drove us back towards Toowong – he was tailgating cars that weren't even going that slowly, overtaking randomly and gunning it to ninety and a hundred in sixty zones. He wasn't driving any more recklessly than any of us normally would, but there seemed to be an extra element in it today, something more worrying. At one point he veered out into the left lane, coming within inches of clipping a silver four-wheel-drive and forcing the woman in it to slam on her brakes. Callum said something like 'Dude, what was that?', but Lachie snapped back, 'I know what I'm doing, okay?' and after that, the subject was pretty much dropped.

Dropped, that is, until we made it to our destination, where the situation very nearly went to shit all over again. The parking lot behind the Regatta is a treacherous, forbidding dust bowl at the best of times, but if you can find a space in there any time from late afternoon onwards, you're doing pretty well. As we pulled in from the street, Lachie turned so quickly and sharply that he scraped the undercarriage of the blue Subaru on the raised driveway, cursing under his breath as he did so. We circled the parking lot, manoeuvring around spaces that had already been taken up, cars parked at odd, random angles.

'This is fucked, dude,' he said to none of us in particular. 'We're never gonna find a park in here.'

'Chill. We'll be fine.'

'No, we won't. *Learn to fucking park, dickhead!*' he yelled at a white Holden that seemed to be taking up two spaces.

'Maybe we can just park on the street...' suggested Brad.

'Fuck that, I don't wanna walk.'

'Hey, there we go, check it out!' All heads in the car turned to Callum, who was pointing to the far corner of the dust bowl, a miraculously vacant spot, one that we must have somehow missed the first time around.

As Lachie approached the space, however, we discovered that some girls in a small Japanese car had noticed it too and were hastening towards it from the opposite direction.

'I don't fucking think so,' Lachie said, and planted his foot and jerked the wheel to the right. At the end of what had suddenly turned into a fairly tense race, Lachie was victorious. He only just squeezed into the space though, which was a lot narrower than it looked, and in the process of swerving he nearly ran over some dude who was getting out of a bright green Holden ute a few cars away. I saw the guy duck out of the way, cursing, and all I could think as Lachie corrected, backing out of the park and then inching in again at a better angle, was: *This is going to be fucking trouble*.

The girls in the Japanese car drove past us, blowing their horn, Callum waved at them as they went. 'The one in the passenger seat was hot.'

'I don't think they like us very much,' I told him.

'Fuck it. I'll buy 'em a drink.'

'We stole their parking space.'

'It's *our* parking space,' Lachie cut in.

'I'll buy 'em two,' said Callum.

As we were piling out of Lachie's car, the dude from the green Holden approached with one of his mates – a large guy in pluggers, sporting a pair of eyebrows so indistinct that they were practically joined – in tow. The dude still looked remarkably pissed off; he had Lachie in his sights, and I had the distinct feeling that this was almost definitely not going to end well.

'What the fuck, mate?' said the dude from the Holden, whose sandy blond hair was flopping down over his forehead.

'Are you talking to me?' asked Lachie. 'You talking to me, mate?'

Yeah, right, I thought, *I'm pretty sure they've seen that movie too*.

'Yeah, I'm talking to you, mate,' said the blond dude. 'You could've killed me back there. Run me over. What the fuck were ya doing?'

Lachie took a step forward, like he was getting ready for a scrap, but it was way too early in the evening and we were still nowhere near drunk enough to entertain the possibility of an actual real-life punch-up.

Callum stepped in, talking to the dude directly in an attempt to keep the peace. 'We're sorry, mate, we spotted this park over here and we didn't even see ya. You know how it is...' The dude gave him a look that pretty much confirmed he wasn't going to be sold on our bullshit that easily.

'Buy you a beer, okay?' Brad said. 'How about that? When we get inside, we'll buy you guys a round, we'll forget about the whole thing.'

The blond guy and his friend looked briefly at each other, and I got the sense that the decision – were they going to act like men and attempt to beat the shit out of us, or were they just going to take the easy way out – rested heavily on that momentary glance. The dude and his friend, not drunk enough to do anything truly stupid yet, backed down, going for the safe option.

Brad promised the two dudes that we'd find them later that night, buy a round for them. Satisfied with this proposition, the two of them disappeared in the direction of the Regatta. Lachie, as we dragged him into the bar a few minutes later, was still smouldering, but now he was angry with *us* for not letting him draw some blood.

'Fuck that,' he kept saying. 'Those guys were getting in out faces... They were *begging* for a fight. Why didn't you let me...'

'Because,' I told him, 'those guys were tradies. They work on building sites and shit all day. If we'd let them at you, they would've fucking flattened you.'

'Hey, I work out. I still *row*, for fuck's sake... I could've held my own...'

'You're holding it right now, dickhead. Let's get you a drink, come on. You'll feel better.'

So Lachie finally, and grudgingly, gave up on the urge to fight for his territory, or if not give up on it, at least defer it until later. Now, standing at the bar, the situation feels like it's cooled off, if only a little. It takes us a long time to get served, but eventually this tall beefy guy in a black shirt asks us what we want; we each order a Hahn Premium except for Lachie, who orders two, and then make our way back through the crowd to try to stake out a table.

Eventually we find a spot near the DJ booth – it's near the back of the bar, right next to a big steel column, but it has a good view of the catwalk on which the girls of the Regatta will presumably be strutting their respective stuff fairly soon. We've barely even made it to the table when Lachie has finished off his first beer, placing it down on the tabletop more firmly than is probably nec-essary, to start work on the second. Brad looks across the table at me, questioning, and I shrug – *Nothing I can do about it*. 'I could've taken those faggots,' says Lachie, but really, he's talking to himself now, so we ignore him.

Lachie downs roughly two Hahns to every one of ours, alternating between moments of aggressive good cheer – hugging us, telling us what great mates we are – and sulky silence – brooding at us all from behind his drink. Every time a hot girl walks by, he enthuses about the size of her rack or fullness of her lips, only to switch, midsentence, to a resentful rant about Anna and her refusal to 'give it up'. As the night wears on, it gets harder to hear what he's saying – partly because it's so crowded and partly because the music is blasting so loud – but that doesn't matter so much, because the first round of Miss Regatta is starting soon, so all we really need to do for the rest of the night is drink and point.

When Lachie slams down yet another empty beer bottle on the table, I consider telling him that it might be time to slow down, have a drink of water or something, but I really don't feel like getting into anything like that right now. As he stalks off to the bar, I shout at him to get me another drink too, but it's doubtful whether or not he hears me.

'What the fuck's his problem?' yells Callum from across the table.

I shake my head. 'He's depressed,' I yell back. 'He wants to get trashed. Just let him go.'

'Even if we manage to *locate* some pussy for him tonight – the odds of which are looking increasingly slim here – he's not going to get any the state that he's in.'

'He'll be fine.'

Callum shakes his head. 'I'm not looking after him if he chucks.'

An R'n'B song called 'Milkshake' starts to play over the sound system and, as Kelis leers knowingly at us from the video screens above, guys, drunk and horny, grab girls and start to dance, crotches pressed into backs, all but dry-humping in full view of everyone.

'This song's about blow jobs,' I yell to nobody in particular.

Just as Lachlan is returning to the table the first of the Miss Regatta heats is starting – conversations all over the bar are dying down, just the odd burst of drunken laughter here and there as everyone's attention turns to the cordoned-off area at the back. After some half-hearted encouragement and a series of weak innuendos from the female announcer, the first girl of the night, Renee, takes to the catwalk, and some breathy electro song begins to play as an accompaniment. A personal trainer from Kenmore, Renee – so we are told – listens to both R'n'B and pop music and is single but waiting for that special someone to come along. Her dream is to travel to Europe.

'Fuck...this bimbo seems too dumb to live...' I hear Callum mutter.

'Maybe she has a PhD in biotech.'

'Maybe you're a shithead.'

Renee reaches the end of the catwalk and poses for the crowd, including several polo-shirted dudes near the front who actually seem to be *baying* for her, smiles in a way that's difficult to decipher entirely, and then exits. The announcer, this entirely too perky blonde with the air of a rejected reality TV contestant, asks the audience to cheer if they like what they've seen, and the approval of all the guys in the place is registered accordingly.

And so it goes throughout the evening.

'That third one was like a fucking vacuum...' someone, I think Lachie, says. 'I mean, there was literally nothing there.'

'She was hot though.'

'She was hot? I'd be surprised if that bitch even knew how to tie her shoes.'

'I'd tie her shoes for her.'

'You'd stick it in anything.'

Two chicks and another beer later, I realise firstly that I'm more drunk than I thought, and secondly that I need to piss very badly. Excusing myself from the table, I push my way through various jocks – the combined smells of sweat, deodorant and melting hair product is almost overpowering this time of the night – and make for the bathroom.

The men's room on this floor is all glass and chrome, and so dark inside it's difficult to make your way around without bumping into any number of drunk and voluminously pissed-off dudes. The outer edge of the room is all urinals, and one-way mirrors allow you to see the people outside on the terrace. It's pretty wrong when you think about it, but certainly makes for an interesting experience while you're in here.

As I stumble my way to the one available spot at the urinals, I realise, too late, that the guy standing next to me is in fact the blond dude from the car park, the one who Lachie nearly ran over several hours and who-the-fuck-knows how many beers ago. Once I've gotten comfortable, I turn to look the dude over. At precisely the same time, the dude turns to look at me. He gives me a smile that is neither friendly nor threatening, and nods his head. I make the same gesture.

'How're those beers comin' along?' he asks.

'On the way,' I tell him, and I guess we leave it there. I start to feel hot and kind of uncomfortable. I take another quick look at the dude, who is in fact taller than I realised before, better built. Something about the blankness of his expression as he stares straight ahead makes me wonder, if this dude told me to go out to the car park with him, if he told me to get in the cab of his ute and then locked the doors as he got in, would I go along with it?

Suddenly very aware of how drunk I am, and reprimanding myself for thinking about this shit, I zip up quickly and retreat. The sink – one corner of a free-standing, octagonal island – is like something out of a nightmare. Even though I've been here many times before, when I try to remember how you use the fucking thing – it involves a complex set of manoeuvres, pushing on a concealed panel down near the floor – my mind goes blank. As I'm waving my hands uselessly under the tap, waiting for water that doesn't – is never going to – come, I see the blond dude approaching again.

'Here we go, chief,' he says, reaching down to push the panel in for me. 'Not as hard as it looks.'

My shirt and arms are splashed by a torrent of water from the tap. 'Don't you and your mates forget those beers,' he says as I'm leaving.

'Wouldn't dream of it,' I tell him.

By the time I get back outside, the girls of the Regatta have taken a break from displaying their assets, and about a hundred people are pushing their way towards the bar. Moving in the opposite direction, trying not to think about the dude from the bathroom, I make it back to the table. When I get there, Brad is guarding it.

'Miss anything? Any hot snatch?' I ask, though he seems confused. 'The contest...' I add.

'Ohh,' he says. 'Right. No, not really. Umm... A lot of the girls have been saying that the White Stripes are their favourite band, though.'

'Right,' I nod. 'Weird.'

'Yeah. Lachie and Callum went to the bar. Lachie's pretty fucked up.'

'Tonight, or in general?'

'He called Anna before – from his mobile. He wanted to tell her he was over her or something, but I don't know that the message got across.'

'Really?' I say, though it's not exactly a question.

'He was repeating himself a lot. I think he started to cry. It was hard to tell though. By then he'd just started apologising a lot.'

I am wondering what it is that I'm meant to do with this information when Lachie and Callum return to the table. Each of them is carrying a pair of Hahn Premiums, and Lachie, when he spots me, yells my name, the manic grin on his face a little too large to be entirely genuine. 'Where did ya go, Liam?' he asks. 'We've been looking for ya.'

'Bathroom,' I say. 'I was getting a blow job courtesy

of Renee from Kenmore. That for me?' I point to the beer.

Lachie tells me that the beer is indeed for me, but refuses to hand it over until he makes sure that I *really understand* what a *good friend* I am and just *how much* he loves me, loves all of us, though not in a faggy way, just in general, and tells us several times how he could never have asked for a better bunch of friends. When I tell Lachie that I love him too, he starts to get stand-offish, questioning whether I really *mean* what I'm saying, or if I'm just saying it because I think it might be what he wants to hear. Noting the feeling of circularity in the conversation, I do my best to change the subject.

'Hey,' I say to him in what I hope is my most convincingly jovial tone of voice, 'I saw that dude again.'

'What dude?'

'From before? Dude with the green Holden?' Lachie says nothing, so I continue. 'Says we still owe him that round of drinks.'

It's when I say this that the shit completely hits the fan.

The last time I saw Lachie's composure deteriorate this quickly was that night on schoolies week when we decided it might be fun to do tequila shots through our eyeballs, although, really, that has nothing on this. Seconds after cursing us all out for not standing our ground against 'those fucking fags', Lachie's head is in his hands and he is crying – sobbing, like a little kid might do, his shoulders moving up and down with every intake of breath. I look to Callum and Brad for help but the two of them just stare back at me, their incredulous expressions saying, *I don't know, you fucking deal with it.*

Before any of us has time to comfort him, to put a hand on his shoulder, tell him it's probably time to go, Lachie has become animated again. He snaps, red-faced, to attention, and takes a step back from the table, his fists and his teeth both clenched.

'I could have taken those guys but you wouldn't let me... I'm a fucken joke to you...to everybody...'

'Dude...' I say cautiously.

'No! Don't fucken... Don't talk to me about that... You all think...'

The expression on Lachie's face says he's about to take a swing at me, and I raise my fists instinctively as he raises his. The bandages on his right hand make him look like a boxer of some sort, marking, in a strange way, the increasing seriousness of this endeavour, and I wait for the first blow, but it doesn't come. As if in slow motion, Lachie turns, shivering, and sets his sights on the big steel column instead.

We all realise at roughly the same time what he is going to do.

'Lachie,' I say, 'your hand, don't...' If he hears me, though, it's already too late.

Minutes later we are sitting on the wet grass in front of those new sets of apartment buildings; my hand is around Lachie's shoulders, and Lachie himself is still crying, shivering, and apologising for what went down in the bar. It all happened pretty quickly, but I can still see it in flashes – Lachie punching the column two and then three times, his teeth clenched and this expression on his face that I've never seen before; people in the bar clearing a circle around us, and freaked-out staff members trying to appear helpful; the cuts on his hand all opening up again, and someone wrapping them up with paper towels.

He's way too fucked-up to drive home – that much is pretty clear – so as the guys debate the merits of walking to the city versus calling a cab, I sit and try to talk some sense into him.

'You could have hurt yourself in there, bro,' I say to him.

'Nobody...You don't fucking...You don't understand,' he says. The closest he's come to completing an entire sentence in several minutes.

'It's fine, Lachie,' I say. 'We're here for you.' Lachie manages to stop sobbing for a second and actually glares at me, probably as aware as I am of how meaningless this sounds. 'You know what I mean, mate... Don't go doing stuff like punching walls. You can talk to us.'

As I say this, I hear the sound of Callum, a few drinks too many inside him, vomiting not so discreetly into some bushes.

'Even him,' I say. 'It's okay, dude.'

'It's just...' Lachie says after a big intake of breath. 'It's just...fuck it. I'm fine. What say we...what say we just go out and...' He stops for a second, dizzy. 'What say we go out and keep...drinking? Fellas?'

Brad, who is listening, shrugs. 'Walk might do him good.'

'I'm... It's nothing, guys... I'm *fine*,' Lachie says.

'Better than him,' I say, motioning towards Callum, who is still leaning over the bush, retching loudly.

'Let's do it,' Lachie says.

As we stumble back along Coronation Drive, even with the lights of the city in the distance and the cars that pass by every few seconds, the night starts to seem a little darker.

It's a Friday afternoon, the uneasiness of that night has moved into the category of 'stuff we can laugh off because we were drunk at the time', and Brad and I are walking into the General Pants store on Queen Street. Brad saw some new Industrie polo shirt on a guy at uni today and decided that he really wanted to find one for himself. So a mission into the city was declared. As we enter, some skinny blond dude in thongs and a wife-beater greets us a little too enthusiastically, asks us how we're doing, and we nod back as we enter.

Some punk-pop song I don't recognise is blasting over the sound system – the singer, a dude with a nasally voice, is describing his *feelings* about being dumped by some girl, and the whole thing is bearable only because of where we are. Brad and I look around, and though we don't find the shirt that he was looking for, he finds two others that he wants nevertheless. When we head up to the counter so he can pay, the blonde girl who is meant to be serving is leaning up against the counter, flipping through a magazine and looking what could essentially be described as oblivious, and it takes us a moment to get her attention.

'Sorry,' she says slowly, giggling, 'I didn't see... Brad?' she asks, suddenly aware. 'Is that you?'

'Kelly?' he asks, mildly confused.

'Brad, you sexy motherfucker! How are you?' The girl's face breaks into a big grin and she leans across the counter to plant a kiss on his cheek.

It takes me a moment to realise that the girl behind the counter is, in fact, Kelly Ashe, an ex-girlfriend of Brad's from about three years ago. She looks different now – her hair is longer and looks as though it has been lightened, and her breasts seem to be a lot bigger than they were, though perhaps this is because I've never seen her in anything this low-cut.

'...and Liam!' she gushes. 'I remember you! Ohmygod, you guys are looking so good! What are you up to?'

'I dunno,' Brad says, grinning. 'Hanging out. I'm out at UQ now, second-year business. Liam's out there too.'

'Ohmygod, that's awesome!' Kelly says. 'That's such a cool thing to be doing! I'm doing this event management course. It's pretty dull but my dad says I have to do it or I can't keep my car.'

'That's too bad,' says Brad.

'Yeah, but the people there are cool. There's this guy there who thinks he can get me a job in Sydney...'

'That sounds good.'

'I guess... Wow, it is *so* weird to see you again! I guess you have a *girlfriend* now...'

'Yeah,' Brad says. 'Isabel. She's pretty nice actually.

What about you?'

'You mean, do *I* have a girlfriend?' Kelly laughs a little too loudly at her own joke. 'No. Haha. No. But I am seeing this guy – Benjamin. He works at this club down the coast but he wants to move here soon...'

While Kelly and Brad continue catching up, I wander off, walking around the store in something of a daze. The music has changed to electro-house, with a bored-sounding girl speak-singing about nothing in particular – the keyboard riff from the song that's playing is, I'm pretty sure, ripped off from an older and better song, but I can't think what it is, and I guess it doesn't really matter. I flick boredly through a rack of shirts with slogans like WILL GIVE HEAD FOR DRUGS and SUCK IT, FAGGOT and I WILL BE YOUR SEX SLAVE emblazoned across the front in bold letters. I'd consider buying one of these but I have one very similar already.

I go back to find Brad, who is still talking to Kelly, and looks as though he might be keen to make a move. 'It's been awesome seeing you again,' he tells her. 'Really great, and you still look...yeah, I mean, wow.'

'Oh, Brad,' she says. 'You're such a sweetie. We should all go out sometime! We should go out for drinks. I can meet your new girlfriend and stuff and it'll be awesome!'

'Yeah, totally.'

'I'm out in the city like all the time,' she says. 'You should call me!'

'I will,' Brad says as we beat a retreat.

'Don't just *say* that,' Kelly laughs. 'Call me!' She holds her hand up to her ear, miming a telephone and mouthing the words 'call me' again.

'You bet I will,' says Brad, laughing along with her, and then we are gone, out into the street.

'Still fucking crazy,' he says to me, grinning.

'Yeah, but she's hot though.'

'I wish she'd been that hot when we were dating.' We both laugh.

'I don't remember her tits being that big.'

'They *weren't*. I don't know what the fuck's...' Brad stops talking for a second, drops his jaw like he's suddenly remembered something. 'Oh shit,' he says.

'What is it?'

'Shit. I was meant to get these... Dammit. These tickets. For Isabel. I completely forgot.'

'What tickets?'

'Ohhh shit. There's this band Isabel likes, this girl-band called...fucking, Attack Of The Tiger Woman or something...'

'Le Tigre?'

'That's the one. They're coming next month and Isabel *really* wants these tickets for her birthday. She told me that everywhere in the city is sold out except for this one record store.'

'Really?'

'Yeah. Um, some place on Elizabeth Street. I don't remember, but I have to go there and find these tickets before they sell out or Isabel's going to kill me.'

'Come on then,' I say. 'If your dick's on the line, we'd better get moving.'

We walk down the mall towards Albert Street, negotiating our way through the crowds of kids, occasionally bumping elbows or shoulders as we pass. This being a Friday afternoon, the city is infested with groups of little emo and skate fags. I keep looking around, half-expecting to see Kristian, although why I'm thinking of him now I'm not so sure.

Eventually Brad and I get to the record store, which turns out to be below street level. The place has a strange smell – like indie rock, old carpet and failure – which becomes increasingly overpowering as we descend a narrow staircase plastered with flyers for bands – I Killed the Prom Queen, Funeral For a Friend, and the Postal Service – most of which I've never heard of.

The place is just as dingy inside as the staircase and the smell suggested, perhaps even more so. The guy behind the counter – twenty-one, heavily tattooed, worst case of emo hair I've seen outside of a Jimmy Eat World video – looks us over as we enter, passing some sort of silent judgment.

'What the fuck's his problem?' Brad mutters to me.

His problem, of course, is that Brad and I are both wearing polo shirts, and the collars on those polo shirts are turned up. 'Because we look like jocks and we're invading his territory,' I say. 'He resents us because we're the kind of guys who used to whip his arse in grade six, and given half a chance we'd still be able to whip his skinny arse today, and he's fully aware of that fact.'

Brad laughs. 'You're always thinking about this stuff, Liam.'

'No, I'm not.'

'What was the name of that band again?'

'Le Tigre, shithead.'

'Right. Wish me luck with this fag.'

'Luck.'

Brad goes off to negotiate about tickets with the tattooed, cooler-than-thou guy at the counter while I stand around, browsing through the racks, thinking I might have a look through their vinyl, which is down towards the back of the store. There are various groups of emo and skate fags milling around in here – the city is their biggest hangout, and record stores are their favourite places in the city, so it figures – and I try to avoid them as I walk around. One group in particular is standing near a display of T-shirts, snickering.

'...she drank so much that she completely passed out,' one of them is saying, 'so Joseph decided to have a little fun with her.'

'No way,' another one cuts in. 'I know him, he's a faggot.'

'How do you know that? Did he suck your dick?'

'Did you suck his?'

'Don't be so fucking retarded, guys...'

As I brush past the group, trying to avoid touching any of them, my eyes lock on those of a gangly, scruffy-looking kid in a New York Dolls shirt, with chequerboard-patterned Cons and a vaguely apprehensive look on his face. Of all the fucking record stores in all the fucking towns in all the fucking world, Brad's brother had to walk into this one.

Though he makes no attempt to acknowledge my

presence, Kristian keeps staring at me as I pass. His friends don't seem to notice – still wrapped up in whatever twisted conversation they were having – and I make my way towards the vinyl. I avert my eyes from Kristian, but I can still feel him looking at me, and sure enough, when I look up again, he has broken away from the group and is walking towards me.

I duck, surreptitiously, behind a cardboard cut-out of Freddy Kruger, and he follows me.

'So...' I say to the little fag, nodding my head slowly.

'Hi, Liam.'

'Hi.'

Kristian is making an effort to glower at me, but his expression, while it's probably meant to look threatening, is actually more than a little on the funny side. Although the fag is clearly trying to do the tough-guy thing, I start to suspect that if I wanted to fuck him again, talking him into it wouldn't be difficult. Although why I would have messed around with Brad's brother the first time, let alone why I would want to do it again, is beyond me.

I breathe out heavily, steel myself for the inevitable conversation. 'So...what have you been...doing?' I ask. 'With yourself. What have you been up to?'

He shrugs. 'This,' he says, motioning towards his friends. 'Playing video games. I don't know.'

'Great.'

'This week has been kind of fucked up, actually,' he says.

'How so?'

'Well, there's this friend of mine, Josh, who's the

guitarist in Bad Day Dying, but he also plays guitar with Another Day Dying...' He pauses, looks at me as though he's trying to detect a flicker of interest on my part. I nod my head for him to go on. 'So last weekend, Another Day Dying were doing a benefit show at this club in the Valley with Die Another Day, but James, who plays bass in Bad Day Dying, got confused because he thought that *he* was meant to be playing that night so he showed up early, ready to go, and when the bass player from Another Day Dying saw James there with his bass and everything, he thought he was being kicked out of the band, so he got really upset with everyone and blurted out that he'd gotten a blow job from the singer of Bad Day Dying's girlfriend...'

Kristian pauses for a second to catch his breath,

'Anyway, word got back to the singer of Bad Day Dying – who was also there at the show – and he went to beat up the bass player from Another Day Dying, but accidentally beat up the drummer from Die Another Day instead because I guess the two of them look pretty similar. So now no one's talking to anybody and it really sucks.'

When I realise that he's finished talking, I stare at him, not sure what the hell I'm supposed to say to that. It may in fact be the longest statement Kristian has ever made, and I wonder if the little fucker is not feeling a bit nervous. 'That's too bad,' I tell him. 'Really, that's...wow.'

'So there's been that,' he says, 'and I ran out of weed again. I mean, I didn't get through it all on my own. I had, um, *help*' – he emphasises the word help, like I'm meant to be curious about who he's been smoking weed with, which I'm *not* – 'but...it's gone.'

'That's too bad.'

'I thought about calling, y'know...to ask for more, but...'

'Why didn't you?'

He stares at me, confused almost. 'I didn't think...'

'Kristian, you know you can always call me when you need something,' I say, trying to sound sincere but perhaps not doing a very god job of it. 'I'm...more than happy to help out.' If this is not the most meaningless string of words I've ever uttered, it's almost definitely in the top ten.

'So I guess you're out with Brad this afternoon...' he says, looking at me expectantly.

'Sorry?'

'With Brad. My brother.'

I nod.

'He doesn't know...'

'What?'

'In case you were...y'know, worried...about him finding out. My brother doesn't know. What happened between us.'

Kristian begins to fidget, tugging at the edge of a poster that someone has glued to the wall, a photocopied flyer for some local emo band featuring pictures of several mopey-looking guys with dyed-black hair and Cons. I stare at him, say nothing.

'What are you getting at?' I ask him.

'Nothing,' he says, staring down at his shoes. 'I'm just

saying, I don't plan on telling him what we did, and I guess you don't plan on telling him either...'

'You think?'

'...so I guess we're okay. You don't have to worry, I mean...'

The little faggot seems innocent enough, but there's an edge to his voice, something that suggests he might even be attempting to make a threat of some sort.

'Do you wanna go somewhere?' he asks me when it becomes apparent that I'm not going to say anything else.

'What do you mean?' I ask.

'Somewhere we can talk... I mean,' he looks over, nervously, towards his friends, who are laughing at something they've found in one of the racks, stamping their feet, '...those guys are here. And Brad. I mean...they'll probably see us here. Which might be weird, you know, for the two of us to be...'

'What do we have to talk about?' I ask, cutting him off.

He shrugs, helpless. 'I've been thinking about you a lot, since what happened, and I mean...'

'Fine,' I tell him. 'I'll talk to Brad. I'll tell him... Fuck it, I don't know.'

For the first time since we've been talking, Kristian's expression actually breaks out into what looks like it might be the beginning of a grin. 'Great. How about I meet you outside Borders in ten minutes?'

'Outside where?'

'Borders...' he says. 'The big bookshop? Down the street?'

'Right,' I say, not sure if the little fag is patronising me or not. 'I've never been in there.'

'I guess not.'

When I told Kristian I'd be taking him home, he didn't argue. I kick off my shoes and lie flat on the bed. Looking nervous but maybe excited at the same time, Kristian gets on there with me. He sits on my thighs and stares at me for a while; puts a hand on my chest and then takes it away.

Eventually, after some urging on my part, he gets down on all fours, crouching down over me. He brushes my crotch with his hand on the way past and looks sort of embarrassed but pleased with himself at the same time. He lowers himself so his forehead is touching mine and I reach up to grab his waist, which is firm and feels skinnier than it looks. The little fucker, suddenly very animated, leans down so he can kiss me, and I let him. He's a bad kisser, sloppy and way too enthusiastic, but that in itself is kind of hot.

He lowers himself so he is lying on top of me – he is wearing only boxers and I can feel his dick hard against my stomach; he is aware of this too and seems to laugh and flinch at the same time, and I really can't tell if this is cute or pathetic. I take him by the shoulders and manoeuvre him down until his face is closer to my crotch. I work my way out of my jeans and make him lick my dick up and down for a while, groaning, my fingers in his hair, and then lie with my feet wide apart and watch as Kristian gives me an awkward but determined blow job. He's not doing it right and I'm not really feeling anything, but equally so, I don't want him to stop, so I'm saying the right things to him like 'come on' and 'yeah' and 'yeah, come on, suck it', and saying these things seems to encourage him, makes him go faster, which is good.

He keeps doing this for a while and it doesn't feel like I'm close to finishing but I don't really want to do that yet anyway. Overcome with something I really can't explain, I lift Kristian's head, tell him that was good, that was great, then push him backwards by the shoulders so he's lying flat on the bed and raise myself so I'm on top of him. I kiss him all the way down his chest and underneath his arms, stopping for a while on his stomach, then pulling down his boxers, enjoying the way he squirms and the noises he makes as I kiss the insides of his thighs, and finally as I put his dick in my mouth and move up and down on it, making him groan even louder, which in turn makes me want to go even harder.

After a while I sit back up and tell him I'm going to fuck him now. If Kristian was somewhat nervous and cautious before, the little fucker has really come alive now, pleading with me to do it, telling me yeah, telling me over and over that he wants me to fuck him so bad. I fish around for the condom in my jeans pocket while working on him with the other hand, getting him ready, which makes him breathe even harder, and when I slide into him his whole body stiffens for a second and then relaxes, and he groans once, twice, telling me to go slower, not to go so fast, and I nod, out of breath, apologising, telling him I won't hurt him, that it will be fine, telling him over and over how hot he is, how hot he looks, and when I grab him by the ankles and lift his feet over my head he seems to lose it completely and comes once, twice, panting for air, and I keep fucking him, kissing his calves, his feet, and when I finally finish I'm still hot as hell and when I ask him if I can go again, he tells me I can do whatever I want.

Thinking about it later, I realise part of the reason I like to be with guys like Kristian is that you can talk them into doing *anything*. Most of the time it doesn't even take that much convincing. I don't know if it makes me a fag, but...

Eight

It's another Friday night and Chloë sends me a message telling me that she and some friends are going to Brut and that I absolutely have to meet them there. I'm fairly dubious at first – Brut is a bar that has just opened on James Street, one of those ridiculously, nauseatingly hip places where twenty-something bankers go to suck one another's dicks and pat each other on the back for being so damned successful. I call Brad from work to ask if he's interested. Isabel, who is with him, says that she's been hoping to check the place out for a while and Brad, eager to fall into line, agrees that it might be a okay, it might be fun.

When we get to Brut, the place is already crowded, even though it's still pretty early. Chloë arrives at the same time as we do – she's with Annabelle, the model, who was kicked out of the hotel in Melbourne last week. Chloë, who is pretending to be completely shocked and saddened by the whole thing, is, of course, delighted.

There are lots of people on the terrace, but we manage to find a table and we annex it as quickly as possible. There is a bench that Brad and Isabel sit on, the rest of us have to grab these perspex cube things that I guess you're meant to sit on. The cubes are incredibly uncomfortable – the kind of thing you see in those ludicrously hip architecture magazines but never think you'll actually encounter in real life. My cube is purple. Chloë's is white.

Chloë crosses her legs under her, shifting her weight around trying to find a comfortable position, but I know that she is destined to lose this game – *there is no comfortable position*. I watch her, amused, out of the corner of my eye; after a while she sees me watching her and settles, huffily, into what must be an extremely awkward pose. She lights a cigarette, refusing to give away any hint of discomfort. Refusing to let me have the satisfaction. The cube has won this round.

I listen, half-interested, while Annabelle tells us about her time in the hotel. She goes into detail about all the other models and their respective eating disorders, tells us how weird it was to have the cameras following them around all the time, says she felt 'like, totally invaded by it'. She alludes to something that one of the boys did with one of the girls and another of the boys on their first night in the hotel, tells us that the producer of the show was also sleeping with one of the models, the girl who will probably go on to win.

Sometime later, most of the way through my second Corona, I look up and see these three painfully hip-looking guys approaching; Chloë looks up too and when she sees them, she yells out: 'Ohmygod! My boys are here!'

Annabelle squeals, joins Chloë as she jumps up to hug them. The guys are basically all distressed denim and Tsubi and are too cool for words. Two of the guys – a blond with hair over one eye and a guy in an I FUCKED PARIS HILTON shirt – I don't recognise. The third guy is Edward who, unfortunately, I do.

Edward is a model and sometime actor, in case I even need to point that out. He went to school with me, and we were friends for a while but more or less stopped hanging out some time ago. Edward was once in an advertising campaign for an energy drink called Lucid. The ads showed him leaning back on his elbows – ripped jeans, barefoot, total crotch shot – with the blue and red can positioned somewhat suggestively between his thighs. The words GET LUCID ran in Gothic lettering across the bottom. This was in our last year of school, shortly before he dropped out. That fucking ad was everywhere. At that stage Edward was pulling fifteen bongs a day in order to function. He was later diagnosed as clinically depressed but kept smoking weed anyway. We used to joke that he was the poster boy for lucid. I don't think he ever got it.

I had no idea that Chloë knew Edward, but I guess it doesn't surprise me – he's spoiled and good-looking and completely shallow, so basically he fits all the criteria. It would make no sense if Chloë *didn't* know Edward. Anyway, we haven't seen each other for a while. Not since that fateful party two years ago, a night I had actually forgotten about until just now, a night I'd still rather not think about.

'Dudes!' Edward says, approaching us with this stupid grin on his face. 'What's happening?'

'Motherfucker!' says Brad, who is obviously happier to see Edward than I am. 'It's been ages!' At this point, Brad stands, and the two of them trade one of those handshakes.

When Edward comes around to me, I don't offer my hand, don't stand up, and he doesn't seem to mind. I look him in the eye instead, and nod meaningfully. My legs are reasonably wide apart, his posture is basically defensive, and something passes between us, some primitive male signalling thing that began back in the days when we all lived in caves or some shit, and whatever's meant to be understood is understood.

'Liam Kelly,' Edward says. 'I haven't seen you for...not for two years or something. Not since...hell, not since that party at your house.'

'It was my brother's house back then.'

'Right...' he says, still grinning, but there's a definite edge to it, and I get the vaguely sickening feeling I know where all this trip-down-memory-lane shit is headed. 'That was a crazy night. We all got pretty fucked up. I was with that girl – whatever her name was, shit, I can't even think – and you were with –'

'I was with Sara,' I tell him.

'Yeah, but she wasn't there that night... Oh man, *who* was it you hooked up with at that party?'

'I don't think I hooked up with anybody.'

'Come on, dude,' he continues. 'You dog. I know you disappeared pretty early that night.'

Right now, I would really like to punch the fucker's face in, but I resist. 'I was pretty drunk. I passed out in my brother's room. By myself.'

'Are you sure about that?' he asks, laughing.

'Completely sure.'

'Because I thought you were –'

'I wasn't. Whatever you thought I was doing I wasn't. I was passed out. I was shitfaced.' The others are all staring at me now. 'Anyway,' I tell Edward, 'I'm still with Sara. In case you were, y'know, wondering about that.'

'That's awesome, dude,' he says tonelessly. 'That rocks my socks off.'

I finish the rest of my beer as Edward and the other two guys, who are introduced to me but whose names I immediately forget, pull up some more of the cubes and join the group. Edward is telling us about a part that he's up for in some new courtroom drama series. If he gets it, he'll be playing the troubled but sensitive son of a newly-single barrister in inner-city Melbourne. Someone asks who's playing the part of the barrister. Edward smirks, claims a little too smugly that he's not allowed to say, but insists that we'll all know who she is. *Right.* Chloë is leaning in to hear him speak, smiling – I think she's actually attracted to this fucking moron. I'm not sure what annoys me more, Chloë's interest in Edward, or the fact that Edward actually is quite good-looking.

During the conversation, I get a phone call from Kristian, which I ignore. The two of us hooked up again last week; he and a bunch of his skate fag friends came by Metro one afternoon, checking things out, and he came back later, alone, asking if I could give him a lift home. Something about the way the little fag looked that afternoon made it impossible for me to say no, so, in spite of my better judgment, I drove him back to his house, where we went down on one another by the pool and then had sex for two hours in his room. The little fag kept holding onto my wrists, telling me not to stop, to keep going, and I fucked him over and over as he bit his lip, breathed out hard, and I eventually came twice, then the two of us got fucked up and watched *Finding Nemo* on DVD.

I stand, tell people I'm heading for the bar. In circumstances like these another beer will be absolutely necessary. Edward asks me, since I'm going, if I'll get him a Corona. He makes no attempt to offer me any money and I don't ask for any. I nod, do a pretty convincing job of concealing my fucking rage. It's not that I can't afford the beer, it's the fact that a fuckstain like Edward would presume to ask me for one in the first place. When I get back, I'll tell him that I've forgotten.

The interior of Brut is ridiculously opulent, like something cribbed from *Architectural Digest*. Light-fittings that hang down like jellyfish tentacles, couches that totally fuck with your preconceptions about what a couch should be. Tasteful French house music rising over the noises of conversation and drinks being set down. A colour scheme that incorporates a great deal of white. It's also extremely crowded – groups of three and four guys in suits, pretty girls in pairs, some a lot more drunk than others, guys checking girls out, girls pretending not to notice, all of them trying to jostle their way to or from the bar. I'm already a little unsteady on my feet as I make my way there, maybe a little more drunk than I thought.

When I finally make it to the bar, a dark-haired guy who is not wholly unattractive – tall, Roman nose – looks me over. He only does it quickly, only for about a second before turning back to his girlfriend, but something about the look makes me feel...not excited, but something, and I get a weird feeling I know what he might have been thinking, a suspicion that's confirmed when he turns to look at me a second time, and I realise I've played this game before, it's easy, and maybe it's all the beer I've drunk, maybe not, but all of this makes me think of that night those couple of months ago at that place on Brunswick Street, the boy in the Von Dutch shirt who'd broken away from his group of friends, who'd walked past us as we were settling down in the booth trying to work out whose drink was whose. Then later Sara asking where I'd been for half an hour, me trying to come up with a plausible explanation and Sara, stupidly, believing me. I wonder if this guy at the bar would let me do the things the boy in the Von Dutch shirt let me do that night. I think about the things he might make me do, then I realise I'm being a fag so I stop.

There are two guys working behind the bar, and about twenty people waiting. One of the bartenders is down on his hands and knees and seems to be looking for something underneath the bar, but he stays there for a really long time, and after a while I start to suspect that he might actually be *hiding* down there, in the throes of some kind of bartender breakdown. Existential crisis? Ex-girlfriend sighting? I don't want to know. The other bartender, this floppy-haired metrosexual, ignores everyone comprehensively, flirting with a blonde girl in a backless dress and taking about half an hour to pour her cocktail. I want a beer and it's taking an irritating amount of time to materialise, but I'd rather be here than out there at the table. I wonder if they're talking about me.

When I turn to see if I can spot where my friends are sitting, I notice a guy I vaguely recognise by the window. I wouldn't even have seen him, except that he seems to be looking at me, gesturing and saying something to a girl nearby. I try to ignore him, tell myself he's probably looking at someone else, so I turn away, but when I turn back to make sure, he's still looking at me. Judging by the way he's dressed, he must have been at some kind of black-tie party earlier in the night, but here at the bar, the look has more or less come apart. His bow tie is undone, sleeves rolled up, jacket no longer in evidence. He's clearly drunk, more than a little sweaty, and is now trying to convince the girl, still ignoring him, to look in my direction. I try to work out where I've seen this person – maybe he's a friend of my dad's or my brother's – but whoever he is, he definitely seems to recognise me. I'm seriously not in the mood for one of those 'How the hell are you? I've known you since you were *this big*' conversations tonight.

The bartender who was hiding before has finally

181

emerged and turns his attention to me. I order a Corona, and wonder how many more beers it's going to take before this evening becomes even halfway bearable. This boy – blond, distracted-looking, possibly stoned – carrying a tray of empty glasses veers into my path as I turn away from the bar, and when I swerve to avoid him, I bump into an older woman in a little black dress. As I apologise, she looks at me strangely, then touches my arm and actually smiles. I know why she's smiling. I'm dressed all wrong for this place – in a room full of cocktail dresses and Country Road suits, I'm in a trucker cap and denim, a fact that has really sunk in now I'm inside. But that's okay, because the crowd seems to have accepted me. I get the feeling that I probably remind them of their little brother. I probably look to them like the first step in a progression that will one day lead to exactly where they are; one day I'll be doing the same things and I'll be dressed exactly the same way.

I'm attempting to sidestep a group of suits – drunk, gesturing expansively – when I feel a heavy, sweaty paw on my shoulder. I try to convince myself I've imagined it, keep walking, but the grip tightens, and I hear a voice slur what is unmistakably my name.

'Liam!'

I turn around slowly. The drunken guy from before, the guy who was gesturing at me, has come over, dragging his girlfriend along with him. The girl – brunette, tall, looking kind of like that model, whatever her name is – is clutching a glass of champagne, her knuckles white.

'Umm...' I hesitate. I really don't want to commit myself to anything. There's still a reasonable chance I could get out it this.

'Mate! It's...' *hiccup* '...it's Liam, isn't it?' When I show no signs of recognition, the guy's face breaks into this ludicrous grin. 'Max!' he says. 'Max Pearson. You don't remember me at all, do you?'

I vaguely recall a Max, a guy who went to school with Euan, the older of my two brothers. This Max guy and Euan played rugby together or something like that, and I remember him coming around to the house a couple of times. My parents probably thought he was a charming young man. They thought that about all of Euan's friends. Whenever they were around for a party or anything like that, my dad would get into the Scotch and take them aside for these little talks, tell them they were destined for great things, and how much he'd love to be their age again, and... Jesus, you get the idea. It was sickening. My parents always look at my friends like they're going to stain the furniture, or pull out a nice big bag of drugs and start snorting them off the coffee table.

'You're old enough to be out drinking already?' this Max guy asks, patting me on the back, friendly in a slightly aggressive sort of a way. 'The last time I saw you you were...twelve? You're still twelve, aren't you?'

I shake my head. 'I'm at uni now,' is all I can think to say.

'This is Katie,' he says, motioning towards the girl. Katie is trying as hard as she can to ignore him, scanning the room for possible escape routes. Drunk, oblivious,

Max puts his arm around her shoulders and pulls her in an uncomfortable embrace that causes her to visibly squirm. I smile at her, this *Alcoholics...what can you do?* kind of a smile, which she ignores.

'Katie, this is...this is Liam. This fine young fellow is Euan Kelly's little brother.'

Katie seems to become alert at the mention of my brother's name. For a second her gaze actually fixes on me. Confused maybe, or at least interested.

'Hello, Liam.' It actually looks like she flashes me a funny half-smile, but it's gone before I can make up my mind.

'... But I think we've caught him out,' Max continues, unstoppable. 'He's not old enough to be out this late... He's...twelve, aren't you, Eu-umm-*Liamm*?'

'Yes, I am, and my parents are worried sick that I'm out drinking and gadding about, so if you'll excuse me...'

'I think you're *scaring* him, Max.' Katie looks pointedly at him when she says this. 'I think you need to set him free so he can run with his own kind. I'll bet he doesn't want to stay in here with us oldies do you, Liam?'

Not with him. I stop myself before I say this.

'No, he wants to catch up, have a drink, don't you, Liam? Did you say you were at university?'

'He did,' says Katie. 'Some time back.'

'That's great. That's *fantastic*. You need to go to school. You kids are the future. What is it that you're studying?'

'Business.'

She raises an eyebrow. 'You're a Kelly after all.'

'Thanks.'

'Listen,' Max says. 'I'm heading to the bar. What are you drinking, Liam?'

'I'm fine,' I tell him, motioning towards the Corona. 'Just got one.'

'Don't be like that. Look, it's nearly empty.'

It's clearly not. I've barely even taken a sip yet. I don't know what to say to this. 'No, man...um, Max. I'm good, really.'

Something about my refusal seems to sadden him. 'Come on, you're a teenager. What do teenage boys do if not...' *hiccup* '...drink beer? When I –'

He seems to be veering dangerously towards some misty-eyed 'when I was your age' tangent – the look on Katie's face confirms this – so I cut him off, hold my drink up for his inspection and tell him: 'Seriously, I'm good.'

Confused, he stops. 'Are you... Are you saying no to a beer?' His voice takes on a harder quality. He's leaning in close, staring at me over his glasses in a way that could, if it wasn't so pathetic, be interpreted as threatening.

I don't want to push it any more. 'Man, you know what, that would be...great. A beer would be *great*. Corona?'

Max sways a bit, uncertain, then his expression breaks into a massive grin. 'Corona!' he shouts. His menace is dissolved now, in its place a ferocious good cheer. 'One Corona coming up!' He slaps me on the back, then pulls me into a bear hug. Actually, I might need another beer now, since I seem to have spilled a fair bit of this one on Max's shoes. He doesn't notice, instead turning his attention to the crowded bar. This young couple – a guy in a suit, Asian girlfriend, not bad looking, red strapless dress – have been waiting since I was there previously, but Max attempts to cut in on them anyway. He presses himself against the bar and starts yelling for the bartender, waving a twenty in the air. People are turning to look. The young couple is staring at him, outraged. Katie, mortified, can only shake her head.

'So...' I begin in an attempt to break the near-arctic silence. 'You're a friend of my brother's?'

The mention of Euan cheers her up again. 'Of course! Euan? We went to uni together, business school, back in... Oh god, that seems like so long ago.' She touches my arm when she says this. 'We had so much fun together... All of us, I mean, all our friends used to have fun. And Euan...'

'That's...weird.'

'Why's that weird?' She giggles, perhaps more drunk than I thought.

'It's...well. Euan. *Fun* isn't exactly the first word that leaps to mind.'

'Oh, he was. I...' She clears her throat. 'But I haven't seen him for years, not since... God, since before he went to London.'

'He's back now,' I say.

'Really? Euan?' For a second an expression of genuine surprise – maybe even confusion – flickers across her face. When her composure returns, her laughter seems a little too exaggerated. 'And he hasn't even called me to ask how I am. The scoundrel!'

'He's only been back for...' *Two months.* '...a couple of

weeks. He's in Melbourne, actually, and I think he's been pretty busy. New job, new apartment. You know what it's like…'

'I'll bet he's brought back some gorgeous stick insect too…'

'I wouldn't say she's a stick insect,' I say, thinking of the pictures Euan sent me of his girlfriend, the email with the subject line WHAT A BABE. 'Cigarette maybe.'

'Oh. Oh! That's funny!' She laughs again, reaches over and messes up my hair a little. 'You're a funny boy, Liam.'

'…Thanks.'

'Well… Tell Euan I said hello. Tell him to call me – the bastard – so we can catch up. I'd *love* to see him again. You should come along too! Bring your girlfriend if you like…'

She gives me a significant look when she says this last part. I don't know why, but a smile creeps across my face when I tell her: 'My girlfriend's in Europe.'

'Oh…really? That's terrible.' Katie's smile deepens. 'Aren't girls terrible? The way we just run off and leave you…' Silence. We both look down at the champagne glass in her hand, then back up at each other. 'You should come along anyway, Liam! You never know…'

Is it possible that this woman is actually cracking onto me? I'm on the verge of cranking out the line about Sara and me being faithful to one another when our conversation is interrupted by shouts, hoarse above the music and the background chatter. It's Max's voice. Oh God. '…a Corona with lime for the fine young fellow here!'

He's motioning expansively in my direction, and half the people within hearing range have turned to look. The young couple are eyeing me with contempt, and the floppy-haired bartender is actually smirking.

I turn away. 'So,' I say. 'Euan.'

'He was always so nice...' she says, shaking her head. 'Such a gentleman.'

I stifle a snort, taking another sip of my beer instead. Katie drains her champagne, looks off to an indeterminate point in the distance, saying nothing. Max returns with the second Corona, places it in my left hand. I am now holding two beers.

'Cheers, Liam,' he says, clinking bottles with me. 'Here's to studying hard.'

'...and absent friends,' says Katie, waving her empty champagne glass at both of us.

'Well, it's been fun,' I tell them. 'Thanks for the beer. I'd better be getting back – I'll tell my brother you said hello.'

'Do,' says Katie.

'It would be great to catch up with old...' Max trails off, staring down at his beer like he has no idea where it came from.

'Euan,' Katie and I both say at the same time.

'That's the one!'

Nine

I understand instinctively that something is wrong when I wake up in the dark to the sound of my phone ringing. I've been having a dream in which I'm trapped in a big hotel where every room looks the same, and it takes me a while to realise where I am. The angles of my bedroom – the stack of old *Wakeboarder* magazines and the panel of lights on my iMac – seem unfamiliar and threatening at this hour of the morning. I stumble across to the desk, my head too fuzzy to even curse when I trip over a discarded pair of jeans, and reach for the phone.

A number I don't recognise is flashing on the blue LCD display, but the code is international, which can only mean Sara. I let the phone keep ringing for a while – as if doing so might somehow abate the growing sense of dread – but my 'Mr Brightside' ringtone starts to sound so ridiculous in the darkened room that I answer.

'Hello?'

'Liam?' Sara says immediately. 'Liam, is that you?' She sounds frightened, out of breath.

'It's me, babe,' I say. 'What's wrong? What's happening? Are you okay?' The three questions run together as one in my half-asleep state.

'Oh God,' she says breathing out heavily. 'Liam, I don't know what the fuck's going on.'

'What?' I ask again, panic working its way up my neck. 'What is it?'

Sara breathes heavily, in and out, and the sound of that makes me aware of the silence in my bedroom. The montage I'm seeing of blown-up train carriages, smoke pouring from underground stations, and dazed, bleeding tourists fills up the rest of the space in my mind.

'What happened?' I ask again.

'I don't know,' she says again. 'I've been robbed... I mean, I think I've been robbed or something, I don't even know, but my money... I mean, my money, the whole lot of it's gone.'

It takes a second to process this information. 'What?' I keep asking. 'Who... I mean, who did it to you? Are you... Fuck, are you hurt? Are you okay? Where are...'

'Liam,' she cuts in, breathing quickly, 'Liam, *I don't know*, I can't answer all these questions, I don't know what to do.'

'Where are you?' I ask again, because it's the only question I can think of.

'I'm in... I'm in some police station. They're letting me use the phone.'

'Where are you though? What city?'

'I'm in... Jesus. I'm in Berlin,' she says, and then starts to cry.

The first thing I think is that this is my fault. It's my fault that this has happened, for not going over there with Sara. For not being there with her. I feel myself start to sweat. This is what everyone is going to say. Everyone is going to know that I wasn't there for her, that this failure reflects on me as a boyfriend and pro- tector, and...

'What happened?' I ask again. 'Tell me everything.'

'Charlotte – my friend, who's over here – we went to lunch today, and afterwards, I went to pay the bill but I couldn't find my card anywhere. I looked through my bag – the Louis Vuitton – and through everything but I couldn't find it...'

'I don't understand,' I say, 'how did...?'

'Charlotte had cash so she paid the bill, but I was still really... I was worried and I called my bank to check the balance on the account...and there was nothing there. There were like forty-three cents or something in my account, I don't know what the fuck...'

At this point Sara loses it and starts to cry again. This whole time I've been pacing my room, sitting down on my bed and then standing up again, running my fingers through my hair, this feeling of powerlessness that Sara is on the other side of the world and something is wrong and there is absolutely nothing I can do to help. I try to think of how much money I have, wonder if I can transfer any to her this late at night, but as I'm about to suggest this, Sara starts talking again, this weird note of hysteria in her voice.

'I didn't know what the fuck I was meant to do,' she says. 'I tried... Oh fuck, I've tried talking to an operator but it's outside of office hours and I can't get anybody there to help me...there's only this man at the currency exchange place and he's no help because he doesn't even speak *English*, Liam, and I can't even remember any of my German, and I just don't know what the fuck I'm meant to do...'

'Have you tried –'

'I've tried calling Dad, I've called him like a hundred times, but it goes straight to his voicemail and I can't even *get on* to anybody at the house... I just... Fuck, what if I'm stuck here? I don't even know what happened and I don't know what the fuck I'm meant to do.'

'Are you sure about the account?' I ask.

'Yes, I'm sure,' she says. 'I've checked it and I've checked it and all my money is *gone*. Oh Jesus, I had thousands of dollars in there, everything, and now there's nothing there...'

There is a photo of Sara and me before our high school formal which I keep in a frame on my desk, and I pick it up and stare at it in the half-light, although I basically already know the image by heart. The smile on Sara's face and the cheesy grin on mine; my Hugo Boss suit and the pink spaghetti-strap dress that showed off her shoulders and her breasts. We look like one of those couples who are meant to be together.

'How could anyone...?'

'I've heard of this happening before. A friend of a friend was in Europe last year and she had this happen to her. They watch you...when you go to a cash machine, they watch you taking money out, and...'

'Who does?'

'The thieves, whoever, I don't fucking know – they

watch you through a telescope or something, and memorise your PIN – then they follow you and steal the card from you when you're not looking, and they empty your account...'

All of this is said in a rush. It's hard to follow what Sara is saying, and she's starting to repeat herself.

'Do you need money? What can I do? What can I...?'

'I'll have to... I'll call Dad again. I'll keep trying. He'll have to be there. I'll tell him what happened and he'll transfer me some money.'

'What about the police?'

'What about them?'

'Are they helping you? I mean, are they trying to find the guy...?'

'They can't do anything. Nobody knows –'

'That's bullshit! I can't believe they won't at least try to –'

'*Nobody knows* who did it, Liam. I didn't see the guy who did it. It could have been anyone. I just...' There is silence on the line for a few seconds. 'I'll be okay, Liam. I'll get my dad to transfer me the money, it's just that I... I really miss you right now.'

'Jesus, Sara, if I can do anything...'

'It's okay, Liam... I'll be fine. I'm just... I'm just feeling very lonely right now, and I just... I just keep wishing you were here. I really want to be with you right now.'

'I really miss you, Sara,' I say.

'I'm sorry, I know it's really late at night for you, but can you just keep talking to me? I really want to hear the sound of your voice right now...'

So I do what any boyfriend would do – I talk to Sara through the night, talk about anything and everything. I tell her stories about what her friends have been doing – about Brad and Isabel – and remind her of the things we used to do together, the drives to the airport and the stupid stuff her brother and his friends would always do at parties. I ask her questions about Europe – safe questions, about the food, about her friends and how crazy German people are, and tell her, whenever she sounds like she's about to cry, that everything will be okay.

After about an hour or so – when I can actually see the beginnings of the sunrise outside my window – I start to hear beeping noises on the line.

'Ohmygod,' Sara says, 'I think that's my dad calling, I really have to go. I love you so much, Liam.' I tell Sara how much I love her and she hangs up. I go back to bed but I don't really sleep – I stare at the ceiling for an hour or more, until my room is filled up with morning sun.

Sara calls back to tell me that she has finally spoken to her dad, who is transferring more money into her account later today. The first thing she has to do, she says, is call the bank and change all of her PINs, but she wanted to talk to me first, to apologise for losing it, for the way she must have sounded before. I tell her not to worry, but she interrupts.

'I don't know how well I thought this through.'

'What do you mean?'

'Coming here, to Europe, alone... Maybe I should have waited. You know, until you were ready. We could have come together.'

'I'm sorry,' I tell her. There are a few seconds of silence on the line.

'For what?'

'For everything. I don't know.'

'Listen,' she says, 'it's late here, I really have to go, but... I love you, Liam. You know that, don't you?'

'Of course I do,' I tell her. 'I love you too.'

I'm not sure what it is that passes between us, but I have never felt as close to Sara – or as remote from her – as I do right now.

Plastic teddy bears painted to look like robots. Ripped shirts with prints of The Ramones and Siouxsie Sioux on them that sell for a hundred and eighty dollars. Anarchist badges. Original Converse sneakers. Death Disco compilations. Tsubi. Industrie. Mooks. These are some of the things that pass through my field of vision today at Metro. It's a Wednesday, so the place is basically deserted. The only people hanging around in the shopping mall seem to be around my age, kids who have finished school or uni for the day or who have just decided to skip it. People walking around, trying things on and taking them off, flirting, laughing, deciding what movie to see, blindly spending money. I'm still thinking of Sara's phone call from this morning, relieved that she's okay, but the idea that I wasn't there, that I couldn't help, still bothers me.

I'm working with Jay this afternoon. He's in a shitty

mood, in the midst of another break-up, his second or third this month, this time with an advertising student called Fischer. I didn't even know that the two of them were going out, but Jay insists that Fischer spent most of the weekend over at the house. I may have even met the guy, but I doubt it would have registered, and I probably wouldn't have cared anyway. There were times, late at night, when I heard loud music coming from under Jay's door – Peaches, singing 'Fuck the Pain Away' – but it's pretty normal for Jay to be listening to that stuff, I think it actually helps him sleep, so I didn't think anything more of it.

Right now, Jay is on a rant, and trying to stop him would be pointless. 'There are essentially... Okay...gay guys, or, like, ones my age...Actually, no, scratch that, just in general, they're all...they can essentially be divided into two categories.'

I'm leaning on the counter, playing around with a leather cuff, doing the studs up then undoing them again, sometimes in the right order and sometimes trying to make them overlap. All I need to do is nod and let Jay continue with the story.

'One,' he says, 'you've got guys who are really great fucks, and these guys are either too dumb to string a sentence together, or too arrogant to be into anyone but themselves. Then two, you've got quote-unquote *sweet guys* – as in, *you've got to meet this friend of mine, he's really sweet*. Believe me, the fucker's *not*. These guys are either damaged goods, in which case you have to fucking wade your way through all their emotional problems and hold their hand while they take pills and cry about how their father never loved them or how they lost their virginity to some dude who videotaped the whole thing and put it on the internet and it was so awful it scarred them for life. Or they just can't get it up.'

'You certainly do it tough,' I say.

'Shut up. Just because you're my token straight friend, I'm not sparing you this.'

'You have lots of straight friends.'

'You know what I mean. I was with this one guy last year. Nicolas, his name was. Nicki for short. He was from France, over here on some kind of exchange program or other – I don't know, it doesn't matter – but the point is that Nicki was dumb. I mean, really dumb. The first time I saw him this didn't even occur to me. I met him out at Family this one night, in the queue to get in, and I thought he was kind of hot and he made it clear that he felt the same about me, and blah blah blah, we end up going back to this house he lives in, in Paddington.'

I'm not really interested – still dwelling on Sara, replaying various awful 'what if?' scenarios in my head – but I nod anyway.

'Point being, I was so into him – I still can't believe it's *possible* to be so into a person – because, physically at least, Nicki was perfect. I mean, he had these deep brown eyes and this amazing body, and he used to wear this little leather thing around his neck. He told me he got it…I don't know, backpacking through India with an old boyfriend or something, but that's not really relevant right now. The only thing you have to understand is how attracted to Nicki I was...'

'I get it,' I tell him.

'Sorry, I'm going on. But you have to understand, I've *never* been as physically attracted to another human being as I was to Nicki. So yeah. It's the next morning and all the drugs have worn off and once we wake up we actually have to start making conversation with each other... And I started to realise gradually that even though his English was okay, even taking the language barrier into account, there was... Absolutely. Nothing. There.'

The conversation is put on hold when a girl comes in looking for a shirt for her boyfriend; we show her about five or six before she settles on one she likes, light blue, with the outline of a sportscar on it in orange, and it's all basically too eighties for words but not in a bad way.

'Anyway, as I was saying, Nicki was *gorgeous*, but he was *stupid*. I mean, like, incredibly, astonishingly stupid. I mean, this one time, somebody was talking about the Second World War, and he asked me if Hitler was dead. And this was, like, *last year*.'

'That's pretty fucked up,' I say.

'You're not wrong. So I started playing these little games with him. Testing him. Experimenting on him or something. I knew how into me he was, and I guess I kind of used that to my advantage. I don't consider myself a nasty person. I'm not mean or anything, not normally. I'm fairly considerate. But there was something in Nicki that just...awoke this real fucking bastard in me. He was so dumb and trusting – like a puppy dog or something – it's like there was a really big part of his... Let's just say he was willing to do stuff, willing to, like, surrender without even knowing it or thinking about it. It sounds...it's difficult to explain, but I used to try and test the limits of that. See how far I could get him to go, get him to, like, follow my commands and shit. I'd say something to him like, *We're going to play a game, okay, and it's the kind of game where you have to do whatever I say.'*

I nod, slightly dumbfounded. Jay goes on rants like this from time to time. I never know quite where they're heading, but it's best just to ride them out.

'What really got to me was the fact that he never seemed...like, he never seemed to know any better than to follow my commands. He just used to obey me blindly. I made him into, like, my slave, I guess.'

'So how long did it last?' I ask.

'A month, maybe six weeks. Probably not that long. We broke up. I really couldn't take it after a while...' He trails off.

'What's the point of all this?'

'The point is, Liam, that people are terrible. People are fucked up, and *you* become fucked up without even realising it.'

'Okay.'

'You're lucky that you have Sara.'

'What?' I ask him, caught off guard.

'You're lucky that you have someone to be with. That you don't have to deal with all the terrible things that are out there.'

I grunt, thinking again about Sara, about my failure

to protect her as she makes her way, alone, through the world. Everyone will find out about this, will know that I am less of a boyfriend; less of a man.

A customer comes in, and then another, and by the time Jay and I are done dealing with them, the topic is essentially forgotten and we move on to other things. When I check my phone, I have a text message from Sara – it's night and she is out drinking with that friend of hers – the money her dad transferred having come through – but she wants to tell me again how much she misses me, and thank me for helping her through the worst of it earlier. I reply and tell her the same, and keep wondering what it was that Jay meant.

I finish work early, around four or so, and Brad comes to meet me after his last class. Brad spends some time in Metro before we head off – he picks up several shirts, looks at them and puts them down again; he seems to be in a weird mood this afternoon, acting a bit cagey like there's something on his mind.

The two of us wander around the shopping mall for a while, looking for something to do. There is music playing from invisible speakers in the roof: Don Henley's 'Boys of Summer' turns into Cyndi Lauper's 'Girls Just Wanna Have Fun' which is interrupted by an announcement of some description – weird sounds, something about a sale over at City Beach, I don't really catch any of it – which turns into Wang Chung's 'Dance Hall Days', fading, finally, into an echoey and vaguely sinister series of airconditioning noises and the sound of people talking. I'm trying to get Brad interested in stuff – we go into Electronics Boutique, pick up some boxes that have video games inside, put them down again. I ask Brad what he's worried about, and he mutters something about Isabel, maybe a fight they had, but doesn't embellish.

We're standing on one of the travelators, heading towards the floor below, when Brad says, without looking at me: 'Are you fucking my brother?'

'What?' Suddenly, the shopping mall seems a lot bigger and emptier, a huge white cavern, and I feel very small in the middle of it. All I can think in the seconds that follow is that Brad knows. Kristian must have told him. *Brad knows.* He's still staring in the other direction, like he doesn't want to look at me, and the fact that he's looking away somehow makes what he's just asked me that extra bit more scary.

'Your brother?' I continue.

'Yeah.'

I start to brace myself, wondering what he's going to do, what the fuck is going to happen. Would Brad want to fight me in the middle of all these people. Are we going to have this out now? I'm still wondering what the fuck is going to happen, wondering if there's any way I might be able to get out of this, and all I can think of to say is: 'Why would I be fucking your brother?' I pretend to laugh. 'That's stupid.'

Brad knows.

When Brad turns to look at me, though, I realise that

the look he's giving me is not, in fact, all that angry, and would probably be more adequately described as confused.

'What are you talking about?' he asks.

'What did you say?'

'I said it's my fucking brother... Look, down there.'

I look down to where Brad is pointing – Kristian and a group of various other little fags are standing around outside the Universal Store. They are talking to a nearby group of girls, who are making a big deal of ignoring them without really ignoring them, acting nonchalant or something, basically waiting for something to happen. *Jesus Christ*, I'm thinking. *That was close.*

'Dude,' he says, 'Sara's only been gone two months, you can't be *that* desperate yet.' He's actually laughing now, and I continue laughing along with him, pretending that I'm not in the midst of a massive heart attack.

'Hey,' Brad calls out. 'Kristian.'

Kristian turns, sees Brad and then me. He stops where he is but doesn't say anything, just nods at the two of us. Brad goes over to him and the two of them start to talk; I can't hear what they're saying but Kristian keeps looking across at me. I'm silently willing him to stop, as the looks he's giving me seem sort of...charged. It's like he's going to give the game away or something – not that there's a game to give away, but for Brad to find out or even to suspect what happened between us would be... well...pretty bad, you'd imagine, and as I'm still recovering from Brad's question a second ago, the idea that he *might* find out, the possibility that this might occur, has begun to seem somewhat more real.

The two of them talk for a bit longer, and finally Brad turns back to me. He looks like he's about to say something, but as he starts to do so, I hear his phone ring in his pocket. He pulls it out and takes a look at the screen. 'Dude,' he tells me, 'it's Isabel. I'll be back.' Brad then wanders off in the other direction, leaving me to face Kristian.

'Hey,' I say to him.

'Hey.'

'So...read any good books lately?'

The little fag stares at me, like he's wondering if I'm for real. 'What?' he asks.

'Nothing,' I say, grinning. 'I'm kidding.'

'Okay.'

'How are you?' I ask. His friends are still distracted by the group of girls – the two groups actually seem to have merged into one, and none of them is paying that much attention to anything else.

'I'm good,' he says. 'I'm awesome.'

'That's great.'

'How are you?'

'I'm awesome too.'

'My friends are retarded,' he says. 'All they do is hang out all day. Here. In the city.'

'And you don't?'

'I hang around with them because there's nothing better to do. But it's so retarded.'

'What else would you rather be doing?'

'I don't know,' he says. 'Maybe I could walk around

all day trying to impress people with what a big, tough, *awesome* dude I am...'

'What do you mean by that?' I ask.

'I wonder,' he says, sulky.

Brad, finished now with his phone call, comes back over to where we are. 'Hey, Kristian,' he says. 'Come on, we're going.'

Kristian shrugs. 'Yeah,' he says. 'Fine. Let me just...' He motions towards where his friends are standing, drifts back over to them.

'What's happening?' I ask Brad.

'That was Isabel,' he says. 'On the phone. We had a fight the other day and she was calling me to say, well... yeah. She wants to hang out this afternoon.' He grins. 'So she wants me to come over now. I don't want to ditch you or anything...'

'Dude...it's your girlfriend, it's okay.' I grin at him, put my closed fist out so he can tap it with his.

'Yeah,' Brad says. 'But I'd better leave now because I'm meant to be taking Kristian home. I said I'd give him a lift, and Isabel's is, like, way on the other side of town...'

'I'll drive the little fucker home,' I tell Brad, thinking, even as I'm saying it, what a bold move this actually is. 'It's okay.' I'm almost shocked that I've come out with this, but then, to Brad, the idea probably doesn't seem weird at all, just something a friend would do.

'You sure?'

'Yeah, it's pretty close to here anyway.'

Brad grins at me. 'That's awesome of you, dude.'

When I tell Kristian I'm driving him home, he shrugs, acting all nonchalant, but he follows me to the WRX almost straightaway. When we're sitting in the car I lean across to kiss him once, twice, and though he seems nervous at first, he gets over it pretty quickly and after we've kissed again he asks me if we're going to do it here. He seems pretty eager, and I do actually think about it for a second, but I remind myself that:

a) this is Brad's brother,

b) that there are people we know everywhere, and

c) though I've done this before, it could really get us into a lot of trouble.

So instead, I ask Kristian, 'Do what?' and he shrugs, says, 'I don't know.' I put my hand on his arm, take it away. 'Let's go back to your place,' I say, and he nods.

The drive back to Kristian's house isn't that long but Kristian isn't really saying much, and the music on the radio kind of sucks, so I slip a CD, some Xavier Rudd, in the stereo.

'What?' I say when I notice Kristian staring at me.

'You listen to this music?' he asks.

'What's that supposed to mean?'

'Nothing,' he says, shaking his head.

'You have a problem with it?' I ask.

'No,' he says, smirking. 'It's just that it's kind of...'

'Kind of *what*?'

'You're the kind of guy who goes to music festivals in thongs and a Polo shirt, aren't you?' he asks.

'What?'

'Nothing.'

I turn the music up, nodding along to the beats, and the two of us are basically silent for the rest of the trip. When we get there, neither of his parents' cars is in the garage, and he tells me they're probably still at work, that they won't be back for a while. We head into the kitchen and he asks if I want a drink or something; I tell him no, and after making a big deal of pouring himself a glass of Coke, adding one ice cube at a time, drinking it slowly, he leads me up to his room.

Kristian kicks his shoes off, flopping down onto the bed. He looks at the floor then at me. 'We better be careful...' he says. 'In case somebody hears us.'

'I thought nobody was home,' I say.

'Put some music on,' he tells me, pointing towards the big stereo that sits on his desk. 'Just in case.'

'Fine.'

There is a stack of CDs sitting next to an iPod on the desk. I look through them and find Nelly, Eminem and... Jennifer Lopez. Fucking *J-Lo*. I *knew* he was a faggot. 'What do you want to hear?' I ask him.

'I don't know. Put on whatever you want.'

'You have a lot of hip-hop,' I say. Wealthy suburban white kids like Kristian *always* seem to have a lot of hip-hop, like they have something to prove. There's a whole attitude that goes along with it, trying to look tough and menacing and as little like a wealthy suburban white kid as possible.

'I guess,' he says. 'Do you like Eminem?'

'Eminem's a fag.'

'I asked if you liked him.'

Ouch. In spite of that dumb look he always has, I

guess Kristian can be smart when he wants to. Though this is a minor victory, insignificant in the larger scheme of things, it irritates me all the same. It irritates me that I've allowed Kristian to get the better of me.

'Let's put this on,' I say, holding up the Jennifer Lopez CD, smirking.

'I don't listen to that any more.'

'I thought you were going to say someone gave it to you. For your birthday.'

'What's your problem?'

'Nothing,' I say, slipping one of the Eminem albums into the changer, pressing play. I walk over to the bed; put my hands on his shoulders and tell him to 'suck it', which, basically, he does for the next twenty minutes. Sometime later, when the two of us are in bed – after we've kissed again but before we've started to fuck – Kristian, breathing heavily, this weird look on his face, says to me: 'I really like you, Liam.'

'What?' I ask.

'Nothing,' he says, still gasping for breath, resting his forehead on my arm. 'I'm sorry, I didn't mean to say that, it's just… I think I… I mean, I like you a lot, and I…'

'What are you getting at?' I'm actually kind of shocked to hear him saying this, even if it is in a pretty indirect way.

'I'm glad that we…' He stops, pauses. 'I mean, that you…'

'That I what?'

'That we could…'

He looks up at me again, this helpless kind of look,

like he's expecting me to say something, and in those few seconds I feel something strange, something that might almost be real affection for the little fag.

Kristian and I sit in the dark in front of the television. He let me fuck him twice before, once on his bed, once on his parents', and the expression on his face as he came for a second and then a third time was different from the vacant expression he has now. He does several hits from the bong and offers it to me but I decline and we sit in silence. Kristian flicks around the channels for a while. We watch half of an Interpol video on VH1 and then bits of a movie in which Natasha Lyonne fakes an orgasm, before we end up on Channel Ten for the late news. I seem to be watching the items that flick by through some sort of a bubble. There are reports about terrorism, a bomb that went off in an Israeli market killing ten people, including small children; the premiere of some new movie starring Angelina Jolie. While this is going on, Kristian attempts to slide closer to me on the couch but I deliberately move away without looking at him. The broadcast moves on to local news: a car accident somewhere near Chapel Hill, a new-model blue Subaru that ran into some trees, killing its occupant instantly; a Brisbane company that went public on the stock market today to better than expected results. Kristian slides up to me again and this time I stay where I am.

Ten

I'm at work when Brad calls to tell me that Lachlan has died. It's a pretty cold day and it was raining earlier this morning but people are still walking around in their summer clothes – guys in their boardshorts, girls in dresses that come off the shoulder. The weather doesn't really matter as it's always airconditioned and lit by fluorescents in here. Every scruffy skate kid walking around the mall – and there seem to be an awful lot of them – reminds me of Kristian, and I'd probably have some reaction to this but the weed Jay and I smoked in the car park before coming in dulls it somewhat.

Up until Brad's call, the morning was pretty boring. I hung out by the counter occasionally making conversation with the people that came in; Jay attached himself to a customer, some guy in ugh boots and a trucker cap, and talked to him for the better part of half an hour or so. I was thinking about how much of a fag Jay is being and wondering whether or not to give him shit about it when I heard my phone ringing. We're not meant to have them on in the store but it was just Jay and me this morning, so really, who the fuck was going to stop us?

I answered and it was Brad, sounding sort of shaky. 'Liam...Where are you now?' he asked.

'I'm at work,' I told him. 'Where do you think?'

'I have to tell you something, dude...'

'What is it?'

'It's Lachlan.'

'What about him?'

'Lachlan's dead.'

'No, he's not.'

'Dude,' Brad says, and for a few seconds I can hear only hissing on the line. 'I just spoke to his brother, okay? Lachie's brother just called me. He's...'

I have never heard Brad speaking in this tone before; there is a catch in his voice that makes it sound like he might be about to cry, which alerts me to the possibility that he might be serious, but that wouldn't make any sense.

'What happened to Lachie?' I ask.

'Last night,' says Brad. 'There was an accident. He had an accident... His car... They don't know much, but he was driving home last night and his car ran off the road and he hit a tree...'

'That's...' I really don't know what to say, and what Brad is telling me isn't really registering. There has to be more to the story, either that or Brad's joking with me, but why would Brad be joking about something like this?

'They said he was going pretty fast when it happened,' Brad continues, 'and there was a tree...and he hit the tree...y'know, head on. Someone saw it happen and they called the ambulance but...dude...'

Brad's composure seems to be faltering. I remember something from last night, that report on the news, the blue Subaru with its front end all crumpled up, floodlit and surrounded by people in uniforms. I didn't connect that car with the one that had driven me to parties, with the one that had driven the guys and me out to uni so many times; it hadn't occurred to me that anyone I knew might be involved because nobody you know ever is.

I start to feel weird and weightless as Brad tells the rest of the story, tells me that the rescue workers came but it took them a long time to pull Lachlan out of the wreckage; that, as Lachie's brother explained, he probably didn't feel it because they figured it was more than likely he'd been killed on impact. Brad tells me that the police gave Lachie's parents his mobile phone, and his brother Rory started calling the numbers in it, Lachie's friends.

'So was he drunk?' I ask.

'They don't know.'

'The police aren't saying, but his brother said they found... Rory says they found...there was a note. When they took off his jeans, y'know, at the...y'know, where they examine the body, they found a note in his back pocket.'

'What?' I ask. 'What did it say?'

'Rory didn't tell me. I don't think Lachie's parents want to... I don't think they showed it to him. To Rory.'

I don't know what I'm meant to say to any of this. After a few more seconds of silence, Brad repeats: 'Lachlan's dead.'

'But it was an accident, right?' I ask. 'I mean, they can tell. Whether it was an accident or not? They can work that stuff out.'

'Who can?' asks Brad.

'I don't know. Fucking...medical examiners or who-ever. They're meant to be able to do that. He couldn't have done it to himself.' There is a T-shirt with a picture of a large sad-eyed panda bear that is made by a designer in Melbourne and costs $145 hanging from some hooks near the far end of the store. Jay is standing near the shirt, still talking to the guy in ugh boots. I'm going to be the one to have to tell Jay about this. I don't know what I'm going to say.

I tell Brad I'll come around to his house as soon as work is over so we can talk about this some more. When he hangs up, I'm still feeling what could essentially be described as disbelief, thinking how strange it is that none of us is ever going to see Lachie again, that his presence in our lives is effectively erased. That we're not going to be meeting him for drinks after uni or giving him shit about girls or playing video games at his house ever again. This is what strikes me, more so than the fact that he might be dead, which is more of an abstract idea, something that's not yet real.

A girl with dyed-black hair and Converse sneakers on comes up to the counter and buys a studded leather belt and, still in shock, I put it in the bag for her and make the required amount of small talk, act like nothing at all has happened; still, she gives me a look of concern as she leaves. I realise that the CD stopped some time back and I haven't pushed 'play' again. Jay comes over and asks me what's wrong.

The three of us are sitting on the couch in the Caldwells' living room. MTV is on in the background but none of us is really paying any attention to it. We are all vaguely shell-shocked and trying not to look at one another. Brad's parents brought home a lot of extra Thai food from that restaurant near the uni campus, which was really pretty good of them, but none of us much feels like eating so the containers of green and red curry sit there largely untouched, along with some rice that has started to congeal.

'I heard that they did tests...' Callum says. 'You know, on his body and stuff...'

'*Dude...*' Brad cuts in.

'They did blood tests. They wanted to find out if he'd been drinking, y'know, before...'

'And?' I ask.

'Well, they found an empty bottle of Jim Beam in the back of the car and there was a lot of that in his system, as well as a lot of other stuff...'

'What kind of other stuff?'

Callum shakes his head. 'They didn't say.'

'Where did you even hear this?' I ask.

'My dad,' Callum says. 'He has this lawyer friend, does

a lot of work with the police. I guess the guy has contacts there or something.'

'Yeah, but you don't know any of that for sure,' I say. 'It could all be shit.'

'That's just what I heard,' says Callum.

'How could we not have known?' Brad asks. 'That he was going to...'

'We don't know anything for sure.'

'You'd think he would have talked to us or something,' I say.

'You know how he was acting,' Callum says. 'Like, that night. We all saw it.'

We don't say anything for a while, just stare at the television, which is a flatscreen and is so large it makes everything else seem somehow minuscule. An old Flock Of Seagulls video is followed by a new one for The Faint and then an episode of *Punk'd* in which a grinning Ashton Kutcher teams up with Britney Spears or someone who looks sort-of like Britney Spears to accomplish something that's not quite clear. Callum picks at the rice but doesn't eat any.

Brad shakes his head. 'You never really know anybody. Not even your friends.'

Callum nods slowly in agreement. I say nothing.

I don't sleep that much the night before the funeral. I call Sara, who is in Munich where it's early morning, and the two of us talk for a long time. She tries to take my mind off things by telling me stories about the place she is staying, about the girlfriend whose spare room she is sleeping in, the girl's boyfriend, who is a DJ of some sort, and about the party they're all going to in a warehouse outside of the city tomorrow night. She seems to have bounced back completely since the robbery – when I ask about it, she actually seems a little embarrassed, laughing it off, insisting that she over-reacted and is fine now. There are things I'm not saying and possibly things she's not saying and there are long periods in which neither of us says anything at all. There is a noise on the other end of the line and she tells me suddenly that she has to go, that her friend is home and they're going out. She tells me she loves me and I tell her I love her as well; we wait for a few seconds and she whispers something that might be 'I miss you' before hanging up.

The day of the funeral feels weirder than I'd been antic-ipating. It reminds me of those times towards the end of grade twelve when our exams were almost over with and we'd get to leave school halfway through the day. You'd never quite believe it was that easy, that you'd just be allowed to leave like that. It felt like we were breaking a rule of some kind, and it's weird to think back on those afternoons, especially today; those afternoons when Brad and Callum and I would all be sitting around at Lachie's house, playing some fighting game on his X-Box, teas-ing that stupid dog of his whose tongue always stuck out, sitting out by the pool, talking shit, drinking beers we'd stolen from his brother, the whole of our lives ahead of us. Today feels somehow like one of those afternoons, but also very remote from them at the same time.

The service is being held in the chapel at Grammar. I've always heard of them holding funeral services there for old boys but the concept of that always seemed wildly irrelevant.

It's around half past one; Chloë, Jay and I are out on the back deck, waiting for my parents to pick us up. Jay is sitting with his hands folded in his lap, looking slightly bemused and holding an unlit joint that he will probably put in his pocket and save for later because he is worried about my parents smelling it on him. Chloë is leaning on the railing, wearing a large pair of sunglasses that she will probably not take off for the rest of the day. The three of us are all dressed for the funeral, Chloë in a black spaghetti-strap dress that shows more skin than might necessarily be church-suitable, Jay and I in our suits. I know it's completely inappropriate, considering that the funeral of one of my closest friends is happening today, but as I checked myself out in the mirror before, I realised how good I looked in a suit and tie. I mention this to Jay and Chloë while we wait and they seem to understand. 'He picked a good time of year to do himself in,' Chloë says after a while. 'It's autumn. Black is the new black, and those suits look hot on you guys.' I'm not sure whether or not she's joking and I don't say anything.

Jay starts getting anxious about the joint and suggests that we all have a drink or something before my parents arrive. Chloë mentions that she has some Xanax if we feel like some. I ask her how that's even *possible* – firstly that she would have it, and secondly that she would share it – and she tells me that an ex-boyfriend of hers has something like three prescriptions for it – he doesn't take them, apparently, he just gets a buzz out of faking the symptoms of an anxiety disorder in order to put one over on his various psychiatrists. I tell Chloë I'm pretty sure they're not meant to kick in for two weeks or something but she insists that's Prozac, and I'm really not going to argue with her. She and Jay and I all take two each with glasses of gin and Grapefruit Tiro.

After about half an hour or so, the Xanax begins to kick in; it's not really that strong, but things start to blur around the edges and the idea that Lachlan is dead begins to seem less huge and frightening. My parents arrive late and have quite obviously been fighting about something on the way, even though they both deny it as I show them inside. Mum sees the bottle of Bombay Sapphire on the bench in the kitchen and asks if she can have one; Dad gets impatient with her and I pour her a drink with what's left of the Tiro and lots of gin.

Don't get me wrong, I get on with my parents and everything, but I really don't see them that often, and that's okay with me. My dad is a partner at Smith McTiernan & Kelly, which means he's generally either a) at the office or b) pissed off and distracted about something he was meant to have done at the office, while my mum does charity work and goes to lunch a lot. Most people, when their children move out of home, move on to a smaller house, an apartment maybe, but when my brothers and I left, my parents traded up to an even *bigger* place on the other side of the river, near Bulimba.

It's a pretty sweet house actually – they have a dock out the front, and a big empty area downstairs that's great for having parties – and even though I really don't get to go there much, it's still good having them close by today.

My mother and Jay make small talk about his uni course and an artist friend of his whose work she knows and admires; Dad starts getting huffy with everyone and herds us all towards the car. By the time we finally make it to Boys' Grammar, all of the parks inside the school seem to be taken and Dad gets grumpy about having to leave the Beamer outside on Gregory Terrace. I tell him it will be fine and that lots of other people have parked their cars here as well, but he ignores me and in fact goes back to check on the car several times throughout the course of the afternoon.

As we approach the Great Hall, there are still people milling around outside, some of them standing awkwardly with their hands behind their backs, many others crying. My whole grade seems to have turned up; all around me are guys I haven't seen since school, standing around in groups of two or three in their suits and looking comprehensively freaked out. Lachlan's mother is glassy-eyed and remote when I approach her to kiss her cheek and tell her how sorry I am, but once we get inside and the service starts, she begins to cry and is eventually crying so loudly that a woman I don't recognise gets up to escort her outside and they stay there for about ten minutes.

The Great Hall is crowded to capacity, and Jay and I end up standing in a spot near the back. I'm aware of heat and silence pressing in; it's difficult to see what's going on at the front. Lachlan's father gives a eulogy but breaks down about halfway through and has to stop. Brad has been asked to speak too but is disturbed after what happened to Lachlan's dad and when he reads the words out they sound forced and insincere. The service drags on and at intervals we are asked to sing hymns, but I spend most of the time staring at a patch of something that looks like it might be melted candlewax on the floor, unable to look up.

Later that evening, after the burial at Toowong cemetery, everyone has assembled at the Caldwells' house. I guess the setting is okay because it's neutral territory – there is no trace of Lachlan in this house, except, of course, in Brad, and me, and all the young guys here who didn't drive their cars into trees and who are going to go on living.

The really strange thing is to think of Lachlan's whole life being cut off; the girls he'll never go out with, and the graduation that's never going to happen; the wedding he won't have and the house in Red Hill he'll never buy and do up; the backyard barbecues he'll never have and the afternoons he'll never pick his kids up from school, because he never had any, because this is what he chose for himself.

There are really no procedures to follow in situations like this and it seems as though people are making it up as they go along. There is a vague sense of panic in the

Caldwells' living room, but people have started to drink, and the more they do so, the more the panic is dulled. Now that the initial shock of the day's events has subsided, emotions are beginning to overflow. At least five guys I haven't seen since school come up and tell me 'it's been too long' and 'we should see each other more often' and I tell them yeah, we definitely should, even though it hasn't really been that long and the chances of us actually following through on the promises to see one another again are essentially fairly remote.

Men are standing around in their suits with beers in hand, women in sober dresses, while Brad's friends mill around, some of them slumped on the couches, others standing bolt upright, all of them still with that disbelieving look on their faces. People aren't allowed to smoke in the Caldwells' house so a group of them have split off and are standing by the pool, and various kids are smoking with their parents and nobody comments because today the order of things is so profoundly disturbed.

At a certain point Lachlan's dad stands up, drunk, and calls for everyone's attention like he is planning to make a speech or something. Some friends convince him that it's probably not a good idea and after a while he agrees, letting them lead him back to his seat. After that, everyone looks at one another nervously and, for a while, nobody has any idea what to say.

It's later now, sometime around eight, and most of us guys have taken our jackets off. Our top buttons are undone, ties loose. Brad and I head up to the bathroom to get fucked up and maybe take some more of the edge off; Jay follows us up, with Chloë and Isabel tagging along pretty close behind. Isabel checks to see if anyone has followed us and then, when she's confident we're alone, shuts the door. She asks Brad if his parents are going to get mad if they find out that we've been smoking in here; Brad tells her that his parents almost never come into this bathroom, that it belongs to him and Kristian, but she doesn't seem that reassured.

Brad is sitting on the edge of the tub with his arm around Isabel. Behind them, you can see the lights reflecting on the river through the open window. Jay and I are standing with our backs to the sink while Chloë leans on a towel rack. None of us seems to be making eye contact and my gaze keeps returning to a large beach towel with pictures of various smiling sea creatures on it which is lying, soggy, in the middle of the floor. Brad pulls a joint already rolled from his pocket and everyone's eyes move to that.

'It could have been any of us,' says Jay after a while.

'No it couldn't.' Brad glares at him. The conversation ends there.

Later, out by the pool, Callum and I are drinking beers with Nick and Chris. Both of them are tall and blond, just like Callum, and just like me for that matter, and if you saw us all from a reasonable enough distance we would probably be indistinguishable. Nick is studying international business at UQ and Chris is doing part-time work at his father's law firm. At a party early in grade eleven, Chris got drunk and took me aside to confess that if he was ever forced to sleep with another guy, if he was forced at gunpoint, say, and got to choose from any of the guys that he knew, it would definitely be me. I wasn't sure how to respond, but the next day he freaked out about it and pleaded with me not to tell anyone. I have so far lived up to my end of the deal.

The topic of conversation out here is still Lachlan; it seems like everyone I've talked to so far tonight has a theory about what he did and why, and the more people are drinking the more of it is coming out.

'He told me he was under a lot of pressure and shit,' Callum says. 'From his parents, his dad especially. About his grades, about uni.'

'Uni?' Nick asks. 'Fuck off. Everyone's under pressure, that's no reason to...you know. It's not something that you kill yourself over, just because your parents are on your back. It's not.'

'You don't know his dad.'

'I heard he was a closet fag,' says Chris. Chris looks at me then looks away.

'What, Lachie's dad?'

'Lachie.'

Nick's eyes widen. 'You *serious*?'

'Dude,' Callum cuts in. 'We've just been to his funeral, okay? His fucking parents are inside. That's no way to talk.'

'Lachie wasn't a fag,' I say. 'Come on. He was a close friend. You'd know.'

'We didn't know he was going to go and kill himself like that.'

I glare at him. 'If that's even what happened.'

'Sorry, mate, I'm just saying... Look, no disrespect to the dead or anything, but there were stories. You know. You've heard 'em. Everyone has.'

We all shake our heads. Chris, more confident now, continues. 'All I'm saying is... Okay. You remember Felicia, how the two of them were going out? They didn't even *fuck* for like the first six months. He couldn't do it. Said he wanted to wait until the time was right.'

'Where'd you hear that?'

'Felicia's sister.'

'That bitch?'

'That's not all. You remember Schoolies? Down the coast? There was this big swimming pool at the top of our apartment building, and Troy says he saw Lachie in there one night with some dude...'

'Lachie was *not* a fag,' I say, not aware of how loud my voice is until I turn and realise that other people nearby have turned to look at me. 'He wasn't.'

'I don't know,' Nick says. 'After we won Head of the River that year, Lachie hugged me for a really long time.'

'Let's say he *was* a fag,' says Callum. 'Hypothetically. Is that really a reason to kill yourself?'

'I don't know,' Chris smirks. 'I would.'

Under normal circumstances everyone would have laughed at that, but given that we've just been to Lachlan's funeral and all, it feels pretty inappropriate. I start to wonder what would happen if I took a swing at Chris; I imagine him putting his arms up, trying to defend himself, me getting two or three good hits in at the faggot's face before he starts to fight back; Callum and Nick pulling the two of us apart, Callum telling me to 'Calm down, mate, calm down'; tempers would be frayed, friendships tested, but under the circumstances, people would understand. None of this happens though. Nobody's quite sure what to do after Chris says 'I would' and there are a few uncomfortable seconds of eye contact before we all look at our shoes.

'There are lots of reasons he could have done it,' says Callum.

'Nobody has any reason to kill themselves,' Nick says. 'No one should have to do that.' Awkward silence.

'Is everyone right for a beer?'

'I could go another one...cheers, Chris.'

Chris goes into the house. Nick and Callum and I all turn and look into the pool for a while, at the ripples that break up the lights from under the water's surface, and none of us says anything. Thinking about the conversation we've just had, I start to feel increasingly uneasy. Kristian and a group of his friends have moved outside near the pool, all of them looking slightly uncomfortable in their suits and more or less uncomprehending as to what they're doing here. Kristian seems wary, but every so often I'll catch him looking across at me. I have never felt as remote from the little faggot, from anybody, as I do at this moment.

Eleven

Since the funeral, things have been extremely tense, to say the least. Every time the boys and I get together, Lachlan's absence feels like an extra person, and we're all so freaked out about what happened that it's really hard to get back to normal. Last week, after an afternoon drinking session with Brad and Callum that lasted until four in the morning, I slept through my alarm and completely blew off a shift at work. When the manager at Metro couldn't get through to my mobile, he tried calling my parents' house instead and, as you can imagine, things pretty much went downhill from there.

My dad has always been a fan of a strong work ethic, and I was expecting him to come down hard on me, but the weird thing was that he was actually kind of sympathetic about the whole thing. He decided that it might be a good idea for me to take a break from things for a while – and his version of that was to buy me a ticket to Melbourne so I could fly down and visit Euan.

'It will be good for you to see him,' Dad said. 'Someone closer to your own age. He's a sensible one, Euan. He'll be able to help you through.'

The idea of seeing Euan doesn't appeal to me in any particular sense, but when Dad makes a decree, it's usually final, and besides, getting out of town for a while doesn't exactly seem like the worst idea right now.

It's a Thursday morning when Brad drops me off at the airport. There aren't that many people at the Virgin check-in; at the head of the queue is a group of backpackers – three girls and a guy, maybe a year or two older than I am, blond. One of the girls is carrying a wakeboard and the guy has shoulders that are badly sunburned, that look as if they're starting to peel. I wonder, vaguely distracted, whether they'd feel hot to the touch, what it would feel like to rest my forehead between his shoulderblades, and I don't realise that I've started staring until the dude looks across at me and I have to pretend that I was looking at something else. Strangely enough, though, he keeps looking and actually smiles at me, and when I smile back, he nods his head before turning away. I don't know what to make of this but at this point I'm basically too tired to care.

The girl at the check-in desk flirts with me and I flirt back, a conditioned response. Inside the departure lounge I buy a strong black coffee but drinking it has absolutely no effect. I sit down at one of the benches, attempting to read the copy of today's *Australian* that someone has left there, but every article seems to be about the Middle East or some hysterical opinion piece about Bush, and my eyes keep sliding off the page towards the windows. This is when I spot him – the dude whose name, if I remember correctly, is Andrew – sitting by the big expanse of glass overlooking the runway.

Andrew was in an introduction to ethics class of mine last year, and we sat next to each other once in a lecture. He borrowed a pen from me, told me that he'd forgotten his or…something. It was a pretty hot day, and about halfway through the lecture, we traded one of those 'how *boring* is this?' looks. When he gave my pen back, the end of it had been chewed a bit, and normally something like this would have bothered me but it didn't this time. As we were leaving, we traded some bullshit small talk about…the class? Plans for the weekend? The situation in Iraq? I have no idea, but afterwards I had this vague feeling like…like what had just happened wasn't a hundred per cent…normal, wasn't something that might just take place in the course of a normal day.

Right now he's looking out at the cloudy sky, at planes on the tarmac. He has this weird, sort of faraway look in his eyes. Distracted or…I don't know. He has dark hair, long enough that it's almost messy, and a nose that kind of sticks out. He has on a white shirt, these wooden beads around his wrists, and there's really not that much you can say except that he's good-looking and blank and, because of his blankness, seems…available.

I put the newspaper down and drift in Andrew's direction to say hi. When he sees me, he raises his eyebrows a little. He offers me his hand to shake, asks me what's happening. Andrew does, in fact, remember me from that class. He makes some joke about how he just passed it by the skin of his teeth, and I tell him yeah, it was the same for me too, which it probably was. I mention how weird it is to see him at the airport and he tells me that everybody knows everybody up here and I kind of have to agree with him. Basically, it transpires that Andrew used to live in Melbourne, and he's flying there today too.

Andrew tells me that he has a job interview down there with one of the banks and that maybe he'll catch up with some of his old friends, even though he's not really that interested in the job and not even sure if he wants to see these particular friends or not. I tell him that I'm going down to see my brother; I consider telling him about Lachlan, about getting away from all the shit that seems to have been happening up here, but decide not to.

Finally, when the flight is called, I ask him where he's staying in Melbourne.

'My parents have this apartment in town,' he says.

'You're staying with them?'

'No. They're away for a few weeks. In Cape Town. My family comes from there and my dad goes back all the time for work.'

'Right.'

'So they're letting me use the apartment.'

'We should get together when we're down there.'

'Yeah. I'm going out for drinks tonight, with some of the guys. I don't know if you're doing anything, but...'

'Sounds good. I think I'm meeting my brother but I can blow him off.'

'Happy days. I guess I'll see you down there.'

'Yeah, I guess so.'

It's raining when we land in Melbourne. The terminal is crowded and baggage claim takes forever – there are so many people that the first time my bag goes past I nearly *miss* the fucking thing and have to run around to the other side in order to grab it.

Andrew and I figure that maybe we can split a cab into the city. His building is right in town; as we stand on the street outside, he asks me where I'm meant to be staying, and I tell him I'm supposed to be going to my brother's, but I guess I don't sound too enthusiastic because Andrew tells me I should come up to his place.

'You sure?' I ask him.

'Yeah,' he says. 'And if you still want to come out with us tonight, you can crash there after.'

'Really?' I say. 'That's awesome, dude. I was dreading going to Captain Charisma's tonight.'

He grins at me. 'Know how ya feel. Come on.'

I follow Andrew through a large marble lobby, into an elevator which lets us off on one of the upper floors. The apartment is a whole lot bigger than I was expecting, a huge open space with polished floors and one wall made up entirely of windows, with a view of most of the taller buildings in the city.

As soon as Andrew dumps his bag on the floor, his phone starts to ring. He looks at the display to see who it is. 'Sorry,' he says to me as he answers, 'get yourself a drink if you want.'

There is a bottle of Absolut sitting on the kitchen bench; I pour myself a glass, put in some ice, and then collapse onto one of the couches in front of the window.

A few minutes later Andrew comes back into the room. 'So listen,' he says, 'you up for a big one tonight? I reckon we're gonna be having one.'

'Yeah,' I tell him, 'I think so.'

'That was a friend of mine,' he tells me. 'Toby. Well, he's not really a friend. More of a...like, a contact. I mentioned to him that I was coming down this weekend and he told me he has some pills... If you want...'

'That sounds good,' I tell him.

He smiles, still staring at me. 'Fantastic.' He goes to the kitchen and pours himself some of the Absolut. When he comes back, he sits down beside me and we talk. I tell him about Sara, about how she's away in Europe.

'You must be missing her,' he says.

'I guess.'

He looks at me again, this weird half-smile on his face. 'You're either missing her or you're not.'

'I am,' I tell him. 'I miss her a lot. But there are always, y'know...distractions.'

'I know what you mean,' he says.

While Andrew is pouring us some more of the Absolut, I call my brother and tell him not to expect me tonight. He doesn't seem greatly upset by this, and doesn't ask what I plan to be doing instead. He tells me that tonight probably wouldn't have worked for him anyway and that he can make bookings for tomorrow instead. I tell him to go ahead, that it sounds great, and hang up. Andrew hands me my glass and we both drink in silence. When we're done, he tells me he's having a shower. He looks at me for a second longer than might be considered appropriate, and then exits. I pour myself some more of the vodka, go over and stand by the window.

Andrew and I go to his drug dealer's apartment, which is in a fairly nice building not too far away from Andrew's. We get in the lift and the whole way up we look at our reflections rather than each other. The drug dealer is dressed in Ralph Lauren and is much more uptight than I'd imagined, and as we buy pills from him, his girlfriend, who looks like she should be doing her maths homework or something, keeps giving us these weird imploring looks. The uptight drug dealer gets a phone call and apparently has to take it outside so we smoke a joint and then drink some beers with the fourteen-year-old girlfriend, who tells us that she's moving to Sydney where she knows a guy who can get her into modelling. I consider asking her what kind of modelling, but don't.

An hour or so later we meet up with Andrew's friends at some excruciatingly trendy lounge bar in the centre of town. It's basically these three guys – metrosexuals with expensive haircuts and Tsubi shirts, aviator sunglasses and trucker hats – and I'm introduced to them but I'm already pretty drunk and their names escape me.

The guys have their girlfriends here so I'm introduced to them too; they're all good-looking, dressed in Commes Des Garçons, Issey Miyake, Easton Pearson, and the only thing that really distinguishes them is that some are blonde and some are slightly less so. The guys all shake Andrew's hand, slap him on the back, and it seems everyone has already been drinking for a while so I just grab another beer and join the party.

We all end up crammed on and around several plush red sofas in a corner of the club, and I'm next to Andrew, who keeps giving me these looks that I can't really work out, when a blonde girl in something black and very low-cut comes up to us, squeals Andrew's name and drops herself into his lap. Andrew introduces her as Natalie, an ex-girlfriend of his. Natalie, it turns out, is a model. 'I feel it's my duty to make the world a more glamorous place,' she explains before she drinks practically an entire gin and tonic in one gulp. Over the next ten minutes or so, Natalie, who is still on Andrew's lap, tells us that she's just gotten back from Hong Kong, although she doesn't mention the specifics, just that she's out tonight with some guy called Foxy who works in advertising and who is 'basically a vile yuppie but he's fucking loaded and you can't complain when he's buying the drinks, right?'

Natalie is flirting quite openly with Andrew, who isn't exactly holding back or trying to stop her. Finally she tells Andrew that she has to get back to her 'date' but that if he's in town for a while she might drop in on him and say hi. I don't know how she manages to make the phrase 'drop in' sound so dirty but she does. She kisses Andrew on the lips then me on the cheek, telling me how wonderful it was to meet me, that we'll have to catch up some time, and then she's gone.

I've lost track of how much I've had to drink by now but the night is passing by in a not unpleasant sort of a blur. I ask Andrew if he's ready to take the pills yet, and he says yes, he's definitely ready. We head to a less crowded area at the back of the club – there are a few girls here, checking the two of us out, but it's basically pretty empty. Andrew takes the plastic baggie with the pills from his pocket and hands me two, taking two himself. We wash them down with our beers and then clink the bottles together. We stare at one another for a second. I ask him if he plans to fuck Natalie this weekend, and he tells me probably not. I tell him that's good and he says yeah, touches my stomach and leaves his hand there for a second before taking it away.

He tells me, 'Look, my friends can't find out, okay?' and I tell him to chill the fuck out, that they won't, and he seems satisfied with this and he touches my stomach again, leaving his hand there longer this time.

We end up in line for some new club – I didn't catch the name, but the line is ridiculously long. Andrew, however, seems to know the dude on the door, and after the two of them trade an elaborate handshake and do some catching up, the dude lifts the barrier and it seems Andrew has managed to talk us all in. Other people in the line are giving us extremely dirty looks but fuck 'em. Once we're inside, we head to one of the upstairs levels where electroclash of some sort is playing and there is plush furniture all around and everything is bathed in blue light. I go to the bar, not because I really need another drink, but I can feel the pill starting to kick in and I need something to distract me. Andrew and his friends disappear for a while and before long I am sitting on one of the sofas and though it's difficult to hear anything over the music I'm telling a girl I've just met all about how a friend of mine has just offed himself and how messed up it all is and how badly I miss him, and the girl is literally all over me, offering sympathy, telling me how *sorry* she feels and practically crying, saying that if there's *anything* she can do... It's all a bit of a blur, but before long the two of us are on an extremely crowded dance floor and the girl is letting me kiss her and touch her breasts and I do this for a while before I get bored of it and tell her I'm going to the bar and she tells me she wants to come too, so she follows but as we're heading back through the narrow little room that connects the bar area and the dance floor, I spot Andrew, who is by himself, and motion for him to follow. When we get to the bar I manage to lose the girl and Andrew, whose pill is obviously kicking in in a very big way, puts his hand in the small of my back and I can feel how sweaty he is and the drugs have brought out something almost feral in him; his blankness has given way to something much more interesting. The two of us go back to the dance floor for a while and it seems the music is louder now, if that's even possible, and Andrew keeps pressing himself against me and then moving away, and eventually, I lean in, cup my hand over his ear and shout, 'Can we please get the fuck out of here' and he says that yes we can. His parents' apartment isn't even that far but the idea of walking there seems like a nightmare just now, so we jump the queue for cabs – making enemies for life with a pair of screaming yuppies in the process – and the driver seems determined to make an issue of it but Andrew throws a twenty-dollar note his way which basically makes him shut the fuck up. On the way up to the apartment we share the elevator with an old couple in evening clothes who look deeply, almost Biblically unimpressed. There is a mirror at the back of the elevator and I lean on that, attempting to look nonchalant; Andrew stands next to me, trying to keep a straight face, but at a certain point he loses it and starts laughing hysterically. The old couple get off on the floor before ours, and when we finally make it to the apartment Andrew can't figure out how to work the key. He keeps jiggling it around in the lock, cursing it, and I tell him to let me give it a go – forcing him out of the way so that we are pressed up against each other for a few seconds – and he calls me a dick but is smiling when he says it, and eventually I get the key to work. Andrew barely has time to flick the lights on before we collapse onto one another, kissing, but the sofa is sticking into my back so I suggest that we move into the bedroom and he says that sounds like a really good idea but he needs some water first, and come to think of it, I need some water too, so we head to the kitchen and take these long, cold gulps of it from an old Bombay Sapphire bottle he keeps in the fridge, then I grab the front of Andrew's shirt, kiss him again, and he asks me 'Do you want to?' and I smirk and ask him 'Do I want to what?' and I'm loving this, he knows it and I know it, and he shakes his head, tells me 'Fuck you', and then just like that we're kissing again, and without my really being aware of it, we've made our way to the bedroom, he pulls a bunch of condoms from his bag, and I'm helping him out of his shirt, touching his stomach, his chest, amazed at how toned they are, looking at the city lights in the window behind him and thinking about nothing at all.

What happens next catches me kind of unawares. 'Fuck, you're so hot,' Andrew is saying as he helps me undress. 'You're nasty. You nasty fucken metro fag,' he's whispering at me. I can feel his teeth on my ear, and although he's manoeuvred into a position where he's on top of me, I don't really try to struggle. I'm breathing heavily, drunk, and though I vaguely know that I should be the one in control here, some new-found strength has come over Andrew – there's something animal, even sort of scary about him as he leans down to kiss me – and I become suddenly aware of how heavy he feels on top of me.

'I really want to fuck you,' he says. 'I really want to fuck you *now*.' He stands, and, not waiting for an answer, struggles his way out of his jeans and a pair of Tommy Hilfiger boxers, sliding them both down until they are bunched up around his ankles. His dick is very hard, and though it's smaller than I'd been expecting, it sticks up, looking like the punchline to a dirty joke.

I sit, propping myself up on my elbows, and tell him: 'Wait. This isn't how it normally is for me...'

'Really?' he asks, grinning. 'How is it normally? For you?'

'I don't...' I say, drunkenly, realising how fucking whiny, how *girly* my voice has started to sound. 'I've never...'

'You've never had a guy fuck you before?' he asks, coming closer. One of his hands starts working on the buckle of my belt, the other is holding his dick as though it were a weapon of some sort. I try to move his hand out of the way but he won't let me; Andrew is a lot stronger than I'd realised. Pushing me backwards onto the bed, he manoeuvres himself so he's crouching right over me, his face so close to mine that I can smell the beer on his breath.

I'm thinking a lot of things right now. There is a big part of me would like to punch the fucker out, draw blood. As I look into his face though, into that mean and *determined*-looking grin that he still has, another part of me starts to think: *Maybe this wouldn't be so bad.*

I feel Andrew's cock pressing into my stomach, and his hand, which has worked its way inside my jeans now, is touching mine.

'You've really never let a guy *fuck* you before?' he asks. 'You silly metro fag...you've never had a taste of your own medicine?'

This is a bad dream, I'm thinking, but like in a bad dream, I don't seem to be able to move, and part of me is even wondering why I don't just give in to this. I'm drunk enough that it probably won't hurt, and besides, nobody ever has to know.

I guess Andrew must be able to feel my heart beating, because he puts his hand on my chest, leaving it there for what feels like quite a long time. 'It's gonna be fucken great,' he tells me, 'I promise.'

Something in me seems to melt – that's the only way I can think of to describe it – and when I tell him okay, it feels like it's not even me saying it. I feel something cold on his fingers as he starts to work them down below. The last thing I think as he goes to tear open the condom packet is: *This is just like being with me.*

Twelve

I wake up late the next morning, feeling sort of...disgusting. Dirty. Andrew has rolled over in his sleep and his back is facing me. I don't bother trying to wake him up. I pull on a pair of boxers and head into the kitchen, drink almost an *entire* carton of milk from the large silver refrigerator. There is a bottle of Absolut sitting on one of the countertops and, with nothing much to lose and a hangover that's not going away any time soon, I pour myself some then slump on one of the big sofas in the living room. I look out at the city, the towers of glass, the church spires, and it all seems very quiet from up here. Andrew's job interview was meant to be today, but the chances of his making it are probably fairly remote.

I hear the sound of a mobile phone ringing in the bedroom, the sound of a voice. I guess Andrew must be awake. A few minutes later he emerges, fully dressed, from the bedroom. I stare at him as he walks over to the couch and tells me: 'She's coming over.'

'What?' I ask him.

'She called me before. She's coming over here now.'

'Who's coming?'

'Natalie. My ex. You met her last night...?'

'Can't you get rid of her?' I ask. 'I mean...can't you tell her, like, no?'

'No,' he says, 'I can't. Listen, it might be better if you... I mean, if you could...'

'If I could what?'

'Just keep a low profile for a while, okay? Maybe if you just...' He looks away. 'For like an hour or something. That's all it's going to take.'

'Fuck that,' I say.

'Dude, Natalie doesn't...'

'She doesn't what? She's not going to be *cool* with it if she sees me hanging around here?'

'That's not it. She knows I've been with guys before...I mean, this one time the two of us did it with some friend of hers, some dude who was a model. Cam or something. A few times...This one night he was over at my old place –'

'Dude... Spare me, okay?'

'Sorry. But I want to talk to Natalie alone, okay? She's fucked up. It's complicated.'

'*You're* more what I'd call complicated,' I tell Andrew.

'You don't get it,' he says.

'Fuck this freak show,' I say, shaking my head. I go back to the kitchen, consider pouring myself some more of the Absolut but drink it out of the bottle instead. 'Want some?' Andrew declines, helpfully pointing out to me that I'm insane to be drinking so early in the morning. I tell him I'm going for a shower and he doesn't say anything else, just stares at me.

240

In the shower I turn the cold water on as high as it will go and let it hit me full in the face while I consider my options. I'm still feeling vaguely sore from last night; thinking of Andrew, out of his mind on the pill, fucking me on the bed, on the floor, in one of the walk-in cupboards for some weird reason, then on the bed again. Me lying back, half on and half off the mattress, the look on Andrew's face afterwards. Thinking about it for too long makes my stomach hurt so I stop.

When I emerge from the bathroom, just starting to feel like the day might be in some way salvageable, I realise that Natalie has already arrived. She's in the living room, looking taller and somehow more blonde than I remembered; right now she has mascara smeared unevenly around her eyes and an old Ramones shirt with gashes across it and one of the arms torn off, but she looks, unfortunately, pretty hot.

'Hi!' she says, shouts, dashing over to me and throwing her arms around my neck. 'You're that gorgeous friend of Andrew's! I remember you!'

'Hey,' I say, as she kisses both of my cheeks. Andrew glares at me from the other side of the room.

'It's so good to see you again!' she says. 'You have no idea. Any friend of Andrew's... I hope I'm not interrupting by the way. What were you *boys* up to before I arrived?'

'He was just heading off,' Andrew says.

'No, I wasn't.'

'I thought you wanted to get more cigarettes,' Andrew says. 'I thought you were going *out.*'

I have never mentioned *anything* about cigarettes and am about to ask Andrew what the hell he's talking about when Natalie interrupts – 'Oh my god!' she yells, making a move on me. 'Cigarettes!' She grabs my forearm, looks right into my eyes – this manic expression on her face as though we're in a movie and she's being pursued by a serial killer. 'I'm *dying* for a cigarette right now, you have no idea. Liam...that *is* your name, right? Oh my god, I'm so sorry, I'm completely hopeless with names, but it is Liam, isn't it?'

'That's the one,' I tell her.

'Liam! I knew it. Liam...' Natalie pouts, lowering her voice, purring almost, when she says my name. 'If you're going, can you buy me a pack too? Marlboro Lites? I'd be *so* grateful...' She draws in, kisses me again, lingering a little to make sure her chest presses against mine. After a few seconds of this – and something gives me the feeling this move is practised too – Natalie draws back, gasping. Her eyes suddenly widen. 'Oh god, but I need money! That's so silly of me, I'm sorry, I would have *totally* forgotten. Wait a minute. I'll find some for you.'

She dashes over to the sofa and tosses her bag – a Louis Vuitton, in case I even need to point that particular fact out – down onto one of the cushions. 'Let me look,' she says, kneeling, fishing, desperate, through the bag. She deposits random things – handbills for various clubs, a Nokia 3315, a plush Gloomy Bear doll, a condom – on the floor around her, making these exasperated little noises as she does so. 'Ohhhhhhh, goddammit! I have money in here somewhere,' she says, already gathering her stuff back together, standing. 'This is *so* dumb, I can't *believe* it.' She starts stuffing everything back in the bag. 'I *just* got back from Hong Kong and... I'm *always* putting money in here and it just disappears, and, oh, Liam, do you mind?'

'Yeah, do you mind, *Liam*?' Andrew stands, smirking at me, behind the sofa. I clench and unclench my jaw. More than anything right now I would like to pick up the bottle of Absolut and smash his smug fucking face in.

Natalie, cheerily oblivious to everything that's actually going on, cocks her head to the side, smiles. 'Do you mind ever so much? I'll pay you back, promise and swear. You have no idea how badly I need a –'

'It's fine,' I tell her. 'I've got it.' It wouldn't matter whether I'd said anything or not. Natalie is the kind of girl who guys just *do things* for. She's used to it. It's probably been this way since she was four years old and begging Daddy – 'please-oh-please-oh-please just an iceblock oh *please*, Daddy', or something along those lines. I play this game too. I'm the kind of guy who does things for girls like Natalie. Natalie knows this. There's no point even pretending.

'Oh, Liam! You're the sweetest! I thought all your friends' – she turns her attention on Andrew – 'were horrible like you are.' She jumps – actually *leaps* – onto the back of the sofa to be close to Andrew, burying her head in his chest, then pummelling it with her fists.

'You like it better when I'm horrible.'

'Oh, you're *awful*. You're a *dog*. That's what you are. You're a hound-dog! You're so mean. *You* wouldn't buy cigarettes for me, would you? Oh, how is it *possible* that he has a friend as sweet as you?'

I realise now Natalie's talking to me. Both of them are looking at me, waiting for...what? An answer? My head is feeling fuzzy from the vodka. How much did I have before? I begin to suspect I'm more drunk than I thought, and as I stand there considering my options, the two of them staring at me, I realise I have nothing to say. There's no sarcastic comeback. It dawns on me that all of this has ceased to matter. The satisfied look on Andrew's face, the cigarettes...this is a losing battle. My presence here has become unnecessary.

'He's full of...um...surprises,' I tell her.

Andrew smiles, slides his arm around Natalie. She does have a nice body. He's *loving* every second of this. '*You're* full of surprises,' he says to her.

Natalie giggles. Andrew brushes some hair off her face. 'God,' she says, 'I'm so tired. You have no *idea* what they put me through in Hong Kong. I had to wear this *ugly* wedding dress. People kept *touching* me, like, touching my face and my arms and I had no idea what any of them were saying, I just had to stand there for hours in this *ugly...*' She stops midsentence, staring fixedly out the window. 'What was I saying?'

'Marlboro Lites?' I suggest.

'What?'

'Marlboro Lites? Cigarettes?'

'Oh, perfect. That would be the best. You're so thoughtful.' She nuzzles Andrew's cheek. 'Isn't he thoughtful?'

I shake my head.

'So... I'll see you soon,' Andrew says.

'Can't wait.'

'I'll bet.'

Something in this exchange has roused Natalie. Her features are set in an expression that suggests...suspicion? That seems too complex a reaction for her right now. But she asks me: '*How* do you guys know each other again?'

'Uni,' Andrew tells her before I can say anything. He stares at me. 'We're friends from uni. Liam's checking out...Melbourne. Seeing a bit more of the *city*. It's *rude* of us to keep him, don't you think?'

'Oh, you're right. You're terrible. *I'm* terrible when I'm around you.' Natalie turns to me, suddenly animated. 'Oh,' she says, 'since you're going for a walk, if you go past the Starbucks on Collins, can you get me a skinny latte? I'd *kill* for a coffee right now, I'm so wiped out from last night, you have *no* idea.'

Andrew grins at me. Once Natalie's back is turned, I give him the finger. The essential futility of this gesture does not escape me. The game is over and I have lost. I grab my wallet and phone from where they are sitting on the countertop. I consider taking the bottle of Absolut with me but decide it might be a bad idea. Fuck it.

Out in the hallway, I'm standing, waiting for the elevator to come, which it doesn't, won't. I press the button again but nothing happens. I've been watching the little bank of lights, waiting for the elevator's approach. Three floors above me, it changes direction, starts to actually go *up* again. The elevator is doing this deliberately to teach me a lesson. There is no other possible explanation. As I wait, the anger starts to build; I'm angry with myself, angry at the futility of all this. I wonder what Natalie and Andrew are doing in there. It infuriates me that he's in there with her, but more to the point, it infuriates me that I'm even angry about it. I make a fist and punch the wall next to the elevator button once, twice. I punch it pretty hard, and it doesn't really hurt at first, but as I'm looking at my knuckles, which are scraped pretty badly, I realise they're probably going to start bleeding pretty soon.

I hear noises next to me, and when I look over I see a middle-aged woman in pearls has stopped in her tracks. When she sees me looking at her, the blood drains from her face. Quickly, she turns her attention to her handbag and makes a big deal of fishing around in it like she's lost something. When the elevator finally comes, she gets in somewhat tentatively, and spends the whole ride down staring at the panel of lights, at the floor, anywhere but in my direction.

'Look, it's a girl, okay?' I say to the woman as we're both getting out. 'I'm having problems with my girl-friend. That's why I did this.' She nods in acquiescence as if humouring a crazy person, then mumbles something at me and scurries off. Perfect.

Freshly pissed off, I head down to the Causeway, off Little Collins Street. The Causeway is a narrow little alleyway with cafés either side, and it's crowded right now with people having lunch; men in suits looking confident and full of themselves, girls with shopping bags from Prada who probably aren't eating much. Near the end, there's a record store that specialises in vinyl; I go in there and look through their stuff for a while, kidding myself that I actually might know what to do with it, but I'm still distracted by thoughts of Andrew, and the hangover from the pill is harsh to say the extreme least, so I head back out for something to eat or, better yet, something to drink.

I pick a cafe at random. There's this young guy behind the counter – my age, blond, trendy stubble – and when I ask for a Beck's he gives me this smug kind of look, like *Drinking in the middle of the afternoon, huh?* before handing it over, and I'm like, *Who are you, my father? YOU WORK IN A CAFÉ, FOR FUCK'S SAKE*, and I'm tempted to say this to him but don't. I stake out a table outside, light up a cigarette and curse myself for getting mixed up with Andrew, for letting the faggot take advantage of me last night, and for punching that wall, as my hand is now basically killing me.

Two Beck's later I'm able to calm down and start dealing with things in a more rational manner.

After about forty minutes, Andrew comes down to find me. I see him before he sees me – his hair looks wet and he's wearing a different shirt, a polo, with the collar turned up, of course. When he sees me he approaches the table slowly, smirking, and slumps into the chair opposite.

'Thought you'd be here.' He looks across the table at me, not saying anything, loving this. He has this grin, this fuck-off cheeky kind of grin that makes me almost certain that something happened between him and Natalie.

'Why did you think that?'

'I somehow knew you'd find the most expensive place on the street.'

I would have a go at him, but luckily that second beer has dulled my resentment. 'Was your girlfriend pissed about the coffee? The *skinny latte*?'

'She's not my girlfriend. And no, she didn't mention it. I think she forgot.'

'Right.'

'She has the attention span of a goldfish anyway. It's the drugs.'

'She's on drugs?' I ask, my voice low.

Now it's his turn to glare at me. A waitress comes by to take my empty bottle – I ask her for another and Andrew says he'll have one too. In the time it takes for her to bring the two fresh ones, both he and I are silent.

'Look,' Andrew says finally, his smugness disappearing, 'she came to ask me for money, all right?'

'What, is she paying off her dealer or something?'

'How did you...Were you...?'

'Jesus, I was *kidding*. Is she really?'

'No, she... It's complicated. You don't know Natalie. She can be a bitch. We broke up more than a year ago, but I'm still supposed to bail her out when she does shit like this.'

'Shit like what exactly?'

'Shit like... Okay, she told me she started doing, like, a lot of speed.'

'Big surprise.'

'She's a model. You know what they're like. Anyway, she told me she's been doing it on and off for four months or something, along with cocaine – God knows where she manages to get that, but anyway – she came by to tell me that she's low on funds...' He takes a swig from the Beck's, wipes his mouth with the back of his fist.

'Low on funds. Right.'

'...which I happen to know is bullshit. She just came back from Hong Kong and the designer paid her, like, ten thousand bucks for the *weekend*. She *always* has money. Her *parents* have money. And if she's broke, it's her own fault. She's trying it on. Thinks she can squeeze it out of me.'

'Can she?'

He shakes his head. 'She was out with that Foxy guy last night. Apparently he has a girlfriend, and he didn't want the girlfriend to find out. Natalie was probably expecting something out of it. She's *always* expecting something out of it. I don't know how she put it to him but apparently he said no. She's screwed things up. So when Foxy refused to bail her out – which I can only assume is what happened – she came to me. Which is *typical*. I was her first... I mean, I was her first serious boyfriend. Back at school. We were together for maybe... three years? A long time, anyway. And when you're with someone for that long, you expect certain... I mean, there's a certain bond that...'

'I have a girlfriend,' I tell him.

'Right. So...you understand. And I mean, when you're like...when someone's, you know... It was different back then. We used to hang out together, weekends and stuff, and she'd come and watch me rowing at school.' He looks off, down the street, not really looking at anything. 'She'd already started modelling. She was in... I don't know, some magazine, but everyone saw it, and my friends were giving me shit about it, like they'd –'

'Why are you telling me all this stuff?'

'I don't know.'

'I don't care.'

'It's complicated,' he says. 'I'm just trying to explain.'

I wonder why I should believe any of what this cunt is saying to me. Then again, when it comes right down to it, why should I even waste the energy it takes *not* to believe him? What's the point of even getting annoyed when there is no way I am ever going to see Andrew again after this weekend?

'Look,' I tell him. 'It's like I said last night. You said it yourself this morning, in fact. I'm not a fag, and neither are you. It's just about this weekend, okay?'

'Okay,' he says after a while.

'So you don't have to tell me this stuff. I don't care about you and Natalie. Let's just...y'know. Party on.'

He picks up his beer and stares into it for a long time without saying anything. 'Natalie left me some coke,' he says after a while. 'She told me it was for being such a nice boyfriend.'

'Good,' I say.

'And because I gave her four hundred bucks.'

'Pussy.'

'Do you want to come back up to my place or not?'

I pay for the beers and we go.

That night I meet my brother Euan for dinner at a new restaurant called Haute. The place is right in the middle of town and he tells me he had a bitch of a time getting reservations – whether he tells me this to impress me with his connections or to let me know I should be grateful to him I'm not sure, but with Euan it could be either. When I get there, I'm still feeling slightly wired from this afternoon but composed enough that tonight should go pretty smoothly.

When I get to Haute, my brother is already there. A gorgeous Lebanese waitress shows me to the table, where Euan is in the middle of a conversation on his mobile phone. The restaurant itself is almost painfully trendy: polished floors with a whole lot of small tables in front of a big glass window, pretty dark inside with a large white bar and light fittings that seem to resemble fireflies. The waitress asks me if I need anything and I tell her I'm fine, so she leaves me with Euan just as he is hanging up his phone and standing to greet me.

'Hello, Liam,' he says, his expression not betraying much.

'Euan. Hey.' Euan is wearing glasses, which I haven't

seen him do before, but the frames look expensive, probably Calvin Klein or something. He has on a business shirt, light pink, that looks like it probably came from Paul Smith in London and almost certainly cost more than Euan would ever be willing to admit.

'How are ya?' he asks, and reaches for my hand.

'Not bad,' I say, 'not bad.'

When we shake, I initiate one of those complicated handshakes involving thumbs and wrist movements. Euan is unable to follow through and breaks the handshake off awkwardly. Something about this makes me feel good, makes me feel like this dinner might be something I could even enjoy.

Euan looks me up and down with what might be amusement or disapproval, I really can't decide. 'You coulda dressed or something,' he says.

'I did.' I have the urge to point out that the shirt and jeans I'm wearing are both Tsubi and probably cost just as much as anything he has on, but I don't.

'Is that what the kids are wearing nowadays?'

'Nope. Just me.'

His eyes narrow a little. 'Good to see you haven't lost that sense of humour...'

'I guess you're still working on yours...' I say, my smile starting to show at the edges.

After a tense couple of seconds his expression breaks out into a big cheesy grin and he starts to laugh. 'You fucker,' he says. I grin back at him and we fall sort of awkwardly into one another for a hug. I let him pat me on the back, and when we break away, he still has that big grin on his face.

'It's good to see you,' he says. 'How long has it been?'

'Too long,' I tell him. 'We must have a lot of catching up to do.'

'Come on,' he says, motioning towards the other chair. 'I already got you a beer.'

There is a Hahn Premium waiting for me on the table, ice cold. 'I missed these most of all when I was in London,' Euan says, reaching over to clink his bottle on mine. 'So. Mum and Dad told me...you've been going through some stuff.'

I stare at him, uncertain, trying to work out where he might be going with this. 'They told me what's been happening,' he says, 'and I know it's a tough time for you. I mean, with your friend, with Lachlan...'

'What about him?' I ask.

Euan sighs. 'Mum and Dad mentioned...what happened. It's always tough to lose a friend, especially... well... Do you want to talk about it?'

'Not really,' I say.

'Let me know. If you do. If there's anything you need...'

'Will do,' I say.

Okay, so I guess there are some things we need to clarify here. When it comes down to it, I really don't hate my brother, he's just...an easy target. It's actually pretty good to see him, especially in light of the fact that it's been so long. I guess more than anything, I like the fact that he's grounded. I mean, if you were to take a look at Euan, you'd say, without a doubt, this is a person who has his shit together. Whatever else happens, I admire that about him.

'So,' I say after a few moments of silence. 'How are you?'

'Better than ever,' he says. 'It's good to be back in Australia.'

'How'd you like London?'

'Ah, London. London...was...fantastic. It's a great city. Great. Nonstop. I was glad to get out to be honest, but you have to do it someday, while you're still under twenty-five. I only wish I could have seen more. I mean, with the firm it was go go go, but I had weekends at least. We did some of the museums...clubs. Soho, that kind of shit. I wouldn't know the names of half the places. Went to a lot of great restaurants. Catharine had been there a year or so before I came over so she knew the place a bit better.'

'How'd you meet Catharine?' I ask him.

'Met her through a mate of mine. Through Seb. We worked together and he was actually going out with her first. We were doing it behind his back for a while,' he says, grinning. 'After they broke up, of course, but, y'know... Didn't want to cause hard feelings or anything.'

'So it's all good between you now?'

'Yeah, mate... He says so anyway.' He laughs. 'And he knows it's the real deal between me and Catharine. She's great. Hot as hell. You'd like her. She was gonna come tonight but she couldn't, some friend of hers is having a birthday party. But you got that photo I sent you, right?'

'Yeah,' I say. 'She's stacked.'

He shakes his head, like he's trying to defend her honour or something, but does so in such a way that I get the feeling he not only agrees with me, but is proud of the fact.

'You reckon it's serious?' I ask him.

'She's talking about getting married. We're only twenty-six but why wait? Especially now.' I want to ask him what he means by that, but I don't, letting him continue instead. He goes on talking about Catharine, about the apartment she wants to buy with him, his idea that it's better to buy a house because land will always go up in value.

I start to feel weird and tense, knowing that Euan is probably going to ask me about Sara, but with the feeling that he might be going to ask me about Kristian instead, even though there is no way he could possibly know about that.

'So when are you going to think about settling down?' Euan asks after a few seconds of silence.

'I'm nineteen, so...not any time soon.'

He laughs. 'What about you and Sara?' he asks. 'You still together?'

'Yeah,' I say. 'She's in Europe, she went backpacking for a while.'

'How long?' Euan asks, looking mildly surprised.

'Four months,' I say. 'I was planning to go with her, but I...'

'Why didn't you?'

'I don't know. I wanted to.'

He shrugs, gives me this sort of half-smile. 'These

things happen.'

'What things?'

He looks like he's about to say something, but doesn't. 'You're okay with that?' he asks instead. 'With her being all that distance away?'

'Why? What do you mean?'

'A pretty girl like Sara, alone somewhere like Europe...'

'I trust her,' I say.

He nods. 'That's good. And y'know, mate, even if it doesn't work out with this one, there are always other girls.' Normally I'd take issue with something like that, but Euan's probably right. 'We Kelly men have always had it good with the ladies.'

I grin at him; reach across the table and we tap our closed fists together. 'You're right, bro.'

'Me especially.'

'Piss off,' I say, laughing.

'Do you remember when we were kids,' he asks, 'there was that restaurant Mum and Dad always used to take us to?'

I shake my head.

'Yeah, you do. They took us there all the time, it was that place on the river along Coronation Drive. We always had the crayfish. Dad was bloody well obsessed with the crayfish there.'

'I'm not sure I remember.'

'Come on. Every second Friday we used to go there. We always fought over the window seat, and Mum always let you have it because I always said I'd beat you up.'

'You could *never* beat me up.'

'There was that waitress there...that blonde, Elizabeth. She was cute. And smart. She'd always talk to us like we were adults. She was great. Spectacular tits. I was only twelve, but Christ almighty...' Euan grins as though something extremely dirty has just occurred to him. 'You know she *wanted* me. She was my first love.'

'Yeah, right. I was the one she liked.'

'I thought you didn't remember.'

'It's coming back. And her name was Emily.'

'That's the one! But I was the one she liked. I was the older man.'

I shake my head. 'Please. I was cuter. She used to mess my hair up. And she brought me chocolates from the kitchen.'

For a second Euan actually looks upset. 'What? No, she didn't.'

'Suffer, dude. Emily was mine.'

'I refuse to believe it...'

'What was that nickname she had for me?'

My brother's phone starts to ring; he looks at the screen, tells me: 'Sorry, mate, I'd better grab this. Won't be a second.'

As he is answering, the waitress returns with fresh beers. I thank her and take a swig of mine, listening to the conversation that Euan is having. 'Seb!' he's saying. 'Mate!... No, no...mate... Dinner with my brother.' He looks at me and smiles when he says this. 'No, she couldn't come... I don't know, out with friends or something... She's coming out with us later...Yeah, no worries, mate... Bring Katie... Oh, did she?' He laughs at this. 'Did she? Ohhhh, mate. Caught out! That's no good at all...'

I take a swig of my beer, relaxing somewhat. In a couple of years' time, if I don't stuff up, I could be just like Euan, and I guess if I'm honest with myself, that doesn't seem like such a bad thing. He's the kind of guy who knows what he wants; doors open for guys like Euan. He's probably right; I might eventually break up with Sara, but even if I do, there will be other girls. Everyone does crazy shit when they're young, and I guess I'm no exception, but whatever I'm doing with Kristian, with Andrew, it's no more than that. I tell myself, as I watch Euan on the phone, look at how comfortable he seems, that after this weekend that's it. After Andrew, after I fly back to Brisbane, I'm going to start shit over again. Sara will be back soon; whatever the reason was I didn't go with her, I realise, looking at Euan, that whatever I needed to do is basically done. Here begins the rest of my life. After I get back from Melbourne.

'Doesn't matter, bring whoever...' Euan is saying. 'Well, if not now, I'm sure you will by the end of the evening... Yeah... Yeah... Haven't heard a word yet... Close of trading Friday they hadn't moved... Still a dollar forty... Don't worry, mate, this shit always works out... I stake my reputation on it...' He laughs again. 'No worries, mate... I'll give you a bell... See you there... Yeah, mate, see you there...'

Euan hangs up, apologises for taking the call, and I shake my head, tell him it doesn't matter. He picks up his fresh beer and reaches out to me, so we can clink our two bottles together again. I'm telling him about uni, about plans for the future, when our entrees arrive.

The look on Andrew's face when he pulls out of me pretty much says it all. I know that I'm going to have to ask him what's wrong, but at this point, I feel beyond that. After an hour or so of hectic fucking – with Andrew on top again, me pleading with him to go on, feeling the kinds of things that nobody has *ever* made me feel before – I'm really not up to much of anything.

After dinner with my brother last night, Andrew and I met up at some club in the city, but we only stayed for one drink before going back to his place, where he still had some of the coke Natalie gave him. That night became a repeat of the previous one – me drunkenly and half-heartedly resisting before giving into Andrew, feeling simultaneously better and worse than I'd ever felt in those hours we spent in his parents' bed in the big airconditioned apartment in the centre of that unfamiliar city.

When we woke up, midmorning, we had vodka and tonic for breakfast because there was nothing else in the house, followed by desperate, sweaty sex, the sheets twisting around my ankles as Andrew pounded me over and over, the two of us whispering stuff to each other that I could never repeat even if I could remember it. Now that it's over, my head feels light; my stomach is sticky, even though I don't remember having come, and I'm *definitely* not ready to hear about whatever is bothering Andrew.

I watch him as he pulls away, slow, looking down in the general direction of his dick. 'Fuck,' he says.

'What is it?' I ask, slow, groggy.

'Fuck, fuck, fuck,' he says again, shaking his head. 'This has never happened. I mean, this has never... Fuck.'

'What?' I ask, propping myself up on my elbows, the back of my neck tingling. 'What the hell?'

When he slides the little piece of rubber from the end of his dick, I can see quite clearly that it's broken. My whole body starts to feel heavy. I know that if I close my eyes, this whole thing, this whole fucking weekend will go away, but when I open them again, Andrew is still here, and I'm still on his parents' bed beneath him.

'What do we do?' I ask.

'This has never... I mean, fuck. I've never done it without a condom before.'

'Me either,' I say, wondering if that's true.

'This isn't a problem,' he says, running a hand through his hair, then repeating the gesture a second and a third time. 'We're fine, because I've never...'

I slump back on the bed and watch as Andrew bunches up the now entirely fucking useless piece of rubber in his fist. 'It's okay,' he keeps saying, 'it's fine', and at this point, for better or worse, I really have no other option than to trust him.

Andrew disappears into the bathroom and stays there for a long time. I hear muffled noises, howls maybe, coming from in there, but I don't attempt to get up. I try closing my eyes again – just to test my theory that this whole weekend is, in fact, nothing but a hugely elaborate hallucination on my part, but when I open them again, nothing.

I go to pour myself another drink but there's no ice left and very little of the tonic water so I pour myself straight Absolut and let the bottle roll off the bed, listening to the dull thud as it lands on the carpeted floor. I lean back against the cushioned headboard and begin to drain my glass. The blinds are drawn so the bedroom is still dark. I flick the large television set on and watch the news for a while; there's an item I think might be about suicide bombings in Israel – although I'm pretty drunk on the vodka and ignoring the noises from the bathroom is actually becoming a bit of an effort, so I can't be one hundred percent sure.

After a while, the door opens and Andrew comes back to bed. He doesn't say anything. He slides under the sheets next to me, but when he tries to put his hand on my stomach, I slide out of the way. I drain my glass and he lies there, staring at the ceiling. When I tell him I need another drink, he nods and begins fishing around for the Absolut bottle, which seems to have rolled under the bed. He goes to the bar fridge under the TV set to get ice, but I tell him we don't have any left, and he laughs.

When he comes back to bed, he hands me my drink and then says that the news is depressing and can we please not watch it because he's not in the mood to feel depressed, so I find the remote, and after flicking around the channels for a while, we watch a DVD of some movie that has breakdancers in it.

Thirteen

Nothing much is happening in the store. Jay has taken over the stereo and is blasting the new Bloc Party, an album I find oddly comforting. Half an hour or so ago, these two guys came in and one of them bought a three-hundred-dollar pair of jeans. A girl, a friend of Jay's, drifted by, and the two of them ended up talking for quite a while. I looked at her on and off while I was arranging some polo shirts on a rack; she was cute, definitely, but cute in a really obvious way, in the same way that the vast majority of the kids who hang around here are cute. It's the clothes, it's the hair, it's the attitude, it's the expression, it's the comfort that comes from knowing that you look and feel *exactly* the same as everybody else. It's the comfort of knowing that if you're able to switch yourself off and just go with the flow, you are never going to be let down. People say that everyone looks and dresses the same today, but that's not necessarily a bad thing. All it means is they know how to play the game, how to get along. Conformity is highly underrated.

Every so often, I think of Andrew – I left the apartment while he was still asleep – and the back of my neck starts to feel prickly and uncomfortable until I make myself think of something else.

A copy of a fashion magazine called *Nachtschattengewäsche* is sitting on the counter. Every time I ask Jay about it, he insists that it doesn't belong to him, so I guess someone must have left it here yesterday. I've been flipping through it distractedly most of the day; there is a picture of a bored-looking blonde girl on the front, and the grabs include THE RETURN OF CHLOË SEVIGNY and ARE YOU GETTING ANY? It's printed half in German and half in English, full of articles about skater kids in Berlin, an interview with this young actor who lists his five favourite hangouts in New York, close-up photos of things like wallpaper and nipples; a magazine so offensively hip it's difficult to read more than a little bit at the one time without starting to feel dizzy and kind of ill.

Near the back of the magazine, some new young DJ is being interviewed. There is a photo of him standing in front of some decks with his back turned, and some of the more interesting questions and answers are reproduced in bold type in various places around the page. One of the questions, near the bottom, reads: *If you could beam yourself to any place with a person and an item of your choice, where would you beam yourself to and what would you take?*

When I put this question to Jay, he stares at me like I've gone insane. 'What?'

'It's a question,' I tell him. 'From this magazine of yours.'

'It's *not* mine.' He puts down one of the shirts he's

been folding, glares at me over his aviators. 'And anyway, what the hell are you talking about?'

'What it says is...' I actually have to think about it myself, and reread the question a number of times. 'Okay, the question is, if you could have *one* person, take *one* thing you liked and go any place you wanted...who, what and where would it be?'

'Um...that's...a really hard question for this time of the afternoon.'

'No, it's not,' I tell him. 'It's easy, just think of something.'

Jay has given up any pretence of trying to do whatever it was he was doing, and is staring at me. 'So is it supposed to mean, like...any place in the world? And any person living or dead or what?'

'I guess so.'

He pauses. 'I'd have to think about it,' he says after a while. 'What would you say?'

'I don't know.'

'You're the one asking the stupid question,' he says, irritated. 'You have to be able to come up with a reasonable answer.'

I'm actually stuck. The dude in the interview says that he would like to be in Tokyo, with his laptop and the cute girl he met DJing in Barcelona last month. Seems reasonable enough.

'If you could be anywhere, wouldn't you want to be in Europe?' Jay asks. 'With Sara?'

'She's coming back soon,' I say.

'I know, but wouldn't you want to be with her anyway?'

'I don't know. I hadn't really thought about it,' I tell him, because I hadn't.

'Right.'

Later that afternoon Kristian comes in with a bunch of his skate fag friends. I have ignored about five of his phone calls since coming back from Melbourne, and while I knew seeing him again was basically inevitable, I really don't know what the fuck I'm meant to do about him. He sent me a text message about a week ago asking if I loved him; when I didn't reply, he sent another the next day apologising, telling me he had been stoned and to ignore it. I didn't reply to that one either and have heard nothing since.

The little fags basically spend about twenty minutes bouncing around the store acting like dicks; two of them pick up a trucker cap from the display and toss it to each other around the store. One of them flirts pathetically with a pair of girls who seem amused at first but eventually leave when he refuses to let up, and another tries on, like, three pairs of jeans but doesn't buy any of them. The whole time this is happening, Kristian, who is wearing a white hoodie several sizes too big for him, is hanging around the periphery of the group. Every so often he looks up at me and I do the best I can to ignore him. The skate fags eventually leave to go cause havoc somewhere else, but half an hour later, when Kristian comes back on his own, I'm really not that surprised.

I'm standing at the counter when he approaches, holding an item of clothing he's picked out at random, a shirt with a naked, writhing Japanese woman on the front.

'Um... Can I try this on?' he says.

'Okay,' I tell him. 'Follow me, um...this way.'

I lead him towards the mirrored changing rooms and he follows behind dutifully. 'Did you really want to try that on?'

'No, not really.'

'Then what's going on?'

He shrugs. 'I don't know, I just wanted to...'

'Listen,' I tell him. 'This really isn't a good place for us to be talking. I'm at work.'

'Whatever,' he says, looks down at his shoes. 'It's not like I want to... I don't know, I just wanted to talk to you about...some stuff. Could I meet up with you later? Could you meet me somewhere?'

I grit my teeth. There is no getting out of this. I am angry at the little fag for tracking me down, angry that I have let things get this far, angry about the fact that, in spite of all this, Kristian still looks pretty good.

'Fine,' I say. 'That's fine. Where do you want to meet?'

'When do you finish work?'

I look around at Jay, who is on the other side of the store. 'Wait here,' I tell him, but he follows me out anyway, stopping a few metres away from where Jay is standing.

'Jay,' I say. 'What's happening?'

'Not much. What's Brad's brother doing here?'

'He wants to...' I turn to look at Kristian, who is looking through a rack of shirts, trying and failing to look nonchalant. 'It's sort of embarrassing,' I tell Jay. 'Don't mention this to Brad, but Kristian wants to buy some illegal substances from me.'

'Is this like part of your continuing quest to corrupt the youth of the nation?' Jay asks.

'Something like that.'

'Shouldn't Kristian be old enough to get his drugs for himself?'

I shrug. 'I don't know. I think he's tried already. Anyway, I said it would be okay, so do you mind if I...' Jay shakes his head at me, like he knows what's coming. 'Can you cover for me this afternoon, dude?'

Jay says nothing.

'I'll work for you tomorrow morning, okay? I just want to get this shit sorted.'

'Why's it so urgent?' Jay asks, looking vaguely suspicious.

'He wants it pretty bad. You know how it is...' Jay is silent. 'I told him I have some weed at the house, but I have to go get it...'

Jay shakes his head. 'Whatever, shithead. You owe me for this.'

'Thanks. I appreciate it.'

'I don't know why I'm agreeing to let you go. You fucking owe me big time.'

'That's awesome of you, Jay. Really.' I reach out to tap Jay's closed fist with mine and he rolls his eyes. I walk back through the store, nodding at a pair of girls in ugh boots as I go.

Kristian looks at me, his expression a little too blank, like he's trying not to appear hopeful. Little faggot. This whole exercise is pissing me off more than I can say.

'Look,' I tell him. 'I got the afternoon off. I'll be out of here in an hour. Can you meet me then?'

'Yeah, that's fine. Where should I...?'

'Just, fucking...wait for me in the food court, okay?'

He nods his head.

'Don't be late,' I tell him. 'I'm not hanging around if you're not there.'

An hour or so later, I head towards the food court. I see Kristian before he sees me; he is sitting at a table by himself, staring at the screen of his mobile phone, a blank expression on his face. The food court is a huge, echoing space filled with people, none of whom seems to be over twenty. Groups of six and seven kids sitting at tables meant for four, couples, guys joking with one another, bored kids behind counters. I don't like this part of the mall, the smell of all that fast food makes me a little sick, and all the white – the white ceiling, the end-less white floor – makes me, for some reason, think of a morgue I saw once in a movie. I definitely do not want to talk to Kristian here.

As I am approaching his table, Kristian looks up. 'Hey,' he says, giving me a look that might be either pathetic or hopeful.

'Come on,' I tell him. 'Let's go.'

'Where?'

I shrug.

'We could go to my house,' he says. 'I mean, Brad's at

Isabel's house, my parents probably aren't home.' Jesus, I'm thinking, what would my friends and I do if *anyone's* parents were *ever* home.

'Fine,' I say.

Without a word, he follows me to my car.

When we get to the house, Kristian lets me in, tells me to wait for him in the living room, that he's going upstairs but he won't be long. I don't even know why I agreed to come here this afternoon. I take a seat on one of the big sofas and look at my reflection in the large television set, which is switched off. Henry followed Kristian and me into the house and while I wait he dashes into the room and jumps up, putting his two front paws on the couch, demanding some of my attention. I scratch behind his ear and under his stomach and he begins to pant happily, his tongue lolling out. There is really no bullshit with Henry. He is always very straightforward when it comes to letting you know exactly what he wants. I admire that about him.

After a while Kristian comes back into the room. He is no longer wearing the white hoodie; he has on a pink shirt with the words VOLCOM STONE across the front, a black leather cuff that I once stole from Metro for him around his wrist. His hair is more messed up than it was before, and when he sits on the sofa across from me, I realise he's a little thinner than I remembered but still looks, unfortunately, pretty good. For a second I wonder if I'd be able to talk him into letting me fuck him again, although for a number of reasons – the least of which being the fact that Sara is due back soon – that would probably be a bad thing.

Henry rushes over to Kristian, thrilled at the prospect of someone new to play with, and Kristian scratches under his neck for a while, saying nothing. When Henry runs away, Kristian stares at the floor for a long time before looking back up at me.

'So what is it?' I ask him. 'What was it that you wanted to talk to me about?'

'There's something I...' he begins, steadying himself. 'I mean, there's something I kind of needed to tell you.'

'What do you need to tell me?'

'I don't know if it means anything... I mean, because we're not... Like you said, we're not really...together, so it probably means nothing...'

'Dude, come on,' I say, actually sort of interested.

'I kind of...with another guy, something happened, and I thought...'

'What happened?'

'I've only been seeing him for three weeks, and I don't even think it's anything that serious, but I wanted to talk to you because...even if things between you and me aren't exactly serious, I like you, that's all. I guess I kind of think about you sometimes too and I didn't want to... with Ryan – that's his name, Ryan – I didn't want it to get too serious with him before I...y'know, before I saw you again.'

I shrug. 'And?'

'I really wanted to talk to you about everything, but

you haven't called me.'

'What?'

'We haven't talked in the last few weeks, and it's not that I care, but, y'know, in spite of Ryan and everything – and it's really not that serious with him – I think it would be good to, y'know, hang out again. I kind of miss you.' He looks at me hopefully.

'Kristian, you know we can't just *hang out* whenever you want. You know it's not like that.' Even putting it like this makes things sound more real, more tangible than I'd really considered up until now.

He looks down again. 'I'm not... I'm not saying that, it's just...'

'Why are you getting so upset?'

Kristian doesn't say anything for a while, just gives me this imploring sort of look, crying almost, like he's... what? Saddened by this? I start to go over the situation in my head and I try to figure out if there's a way I might be able to talk Kristian into at least a blow job or something again later on, but the way things are going, with him so upset and all, it doesn't look likely. I don't see what's so bad with the way things have been up until now – he gets what he wants, I get what I want, everybody wins. *Grow up, you little fucker*, I almost say to him, but don't.

'I'm just...' he says. 'This whole thing is really confusing.'

I look across at him, at his nose, the way it sticks out just a little bit, and at his bottom lip, which he is in the habit of biting when he thinks nobody is watching.

There is something innocent about Kristian, and for a moment I actually feel bad about everything I've done to him. He seems tense, but then again, people always look better when they're hurt.

'It's not confusing,' I tell him. 'It's simple. What we have... I mean, what we do, it's not serious. I have a girlfriend and you have...well, whatever...your skateboard. We're not *going out*. I'm not your boyfriend. Sure, we can get together and fuck from time to time – you're actually pretty good at that, in spite of what I might or might not have said to you in the past – but that's really as far as it goes.'

'Do you mean that?' he asks, looking like he's on the verge of crying.

I shrug. 'Yeah, I do.'

He shakes his head. 'I hate you,' he says. 'I don't get this.'

I stand. 'It's easy,' I say. 'I'm going.'

'Wait,' he says, 'can you just...'

'Hey, Kristian,' I interrupt. 'It would also be really great if you'd stop calling me. It's over.'

He gets up to follow me, and I've already made it most of the way out of the living room when he says, finally, having exhausted all his other options: 'Wait! If you go, I'll tell my brother.'

'What?' I turn.

'You heard me. I'll tell Brad,' he says, glaring at me. 'I'll tell Brad what we did. Brad's your friend, and I'll tell him.'

Kristian is standing right in front of me now and

something about him looks different. He seems desperate, panicked. I've never seen the little fag stick up for himself before, but right now, he's daring me to say something, to fight back.

'You won't tell Brad anything,' I say. I grab his wrist, which is small and bony, and try to hold onto it, but he struggles out of my grasp.

'Fuck you,' he says. 'Fuck you. I'll tell him everything… How you walk around pretending to be his mate, pretending like you're the straightest dude on earth, when you're really just a fucking fag.'

I'm really not sure how it happens and I don't even feel myself doing it, but the first punch I throw hits Kristian in the chest. The force of it takes him by surprise and seems to knock the wind out of him, and when I hit him again, harder and in the face, he drops very suddenly. After that, everything is reduced to a blur; at a certain point I'm on my knees, one either side of Kristian, and I'm hitting him in the face for a second and then a third time, and I can see that there is blood, quite a lot of it, incredibly bright on Kristian's pale skin, coming from his nose and smeared all over his chin, and he starts to cry out, making these low, animal kind of noises, and he is trying very hard to escape, to twist his way out from under me, but his arms are pinned down by my knees and I'm not letting the little fucker go. I can think of almost nothing through the anger, I just want to make Kristian hurt, to punish him, to make the little faggot suffer, and all I'm really certain of as I hit him again, this time in the cheek, is that it's not just about what he said, this is not just about Kristian, this is about everything. This is everything since Sara left and everything before. It's not just Kristian I'm doing this to. I'm doing this to myself. To everyone. I think how good it would feel to punch the little fag some more, to make him bleed, and when I take another look at his face I realise that he is crying now, sobbing and gasping for breath and telling me to 'stopitstopit pleasestopit Liamstopitplease' and eventually he is crying so much that he is no longer able to form words, just sounds, and I don't want to stop, but I do, I stop, letting my head drop for a second to get my breath back.

I have one hand on the floor and the other under Kristian's chin, which I am lifting up to make him look at me. I don't feel bad or guilty right now, just relieved. Staring down at Kristian, bloodied and still crying, his eyes shut tightly, not knowing what to expect or what I'm going to do to him next, I feel like a weight has been removed, a decision finally made. This was always going to happen.

'You won't tell Brad anything,' I say. 'Okay?' He groans, sobs. 'You won't tell anything to Brad or to anyone else.' He coughs, his eyes still closed. There is some blood in his mouth and he tries to spit it out onto the floor but can't reach because I'm still pinning him down, so the bloody spit ends up dribbling down his chin instead. 'Somebody did this to you when you were walking home, okay? You were attacked. You don't know who by.' The expression, such as it is, on his face, is difficult to describe, but after a few seconds, he gives a nod, as though some of what I'm saying is finally getting through. 'Do you understand?' I ask him. 'They did this to you because you're a faggot. That's what you're going to say.' He starts to cry even harder when I say this, but he nods all the same, careful not to hit his head on the floor. 'I'm leaving now,' I tell him, 'and you're not going to tell Brad or anyone else what we did, because we never did anything, understand?'

When I stand, Kristian remains lying where he is on the floor, not moving. I'm suddenly finding it difficult to look at him, so I turn away. I leave the Caldwells' house, walking back out through the kitchen, the courtyard, to my car. When I get in, I sit in silence for a minute or so, gripping the steering wheel, wondering what exactly has just happened. I drive back to my house and get stuck in traffic for half an hour on Coronation Drive, thinking that I should have taken Milton Road instead.

Fourteen

I'm hanging out over at Brad's house, just fucking around, like always, and though it feels weird being here again so soon after everything that happened, the other day, I've decided, was really nothing but a fever dream. I'm done now, I've managed to sweat the fever out, and now things are back to normal. I'm hanging out with Brad again like nothing ever happened.

Which, of course, it didn't.

We're playing some dumb Japanese car-racing game with the sound turned down and an old Beastie Boys album blaring from the stereo; there are two mostly empty Hahn Premiums on the coffee table in front of us, and though the whole thing should pretty much feel like old times, something I can't quite put my finger on is distracting me.

The TV screen is split into two, with Brad's half of the game on the left and mine on the right. He's staring at it with a brainless intensity and I'm doing my best to keep up with him, but even though I've played this a hundred times before, I keep fucking it up. I keep fucking it up. I'm missing the corners, crashing into the barriers;

at one point my car spins around and actually starts going fucking *backwards*, and I curse, try to steady myself again. The scenery that flashes by – these stupid clumps of pine trees, mountain passes – looks nothing like the real thing and it's actually pretty annoying. The whole game is actually pretty annoying. Brad is way ahead and is basically wiping the floor with me. On my map of the racetrack, his car is represented by a red dot, and the red dot keeps moving further and further ahead of me, to the point where it actually *disappears* from fucking view, and I'm cursing this, trying to keep my car on the road, trying to work with the controller even though it just *doesn't* want to respond.

I look across at Brad, who has a dumb grin on his face now because he knows he's winning. When I turn back to the screen, I've crashed into another of those fucking barriers – my car is spiking backwards and I try half-heartedly to correct it, swearing under my breath the whole time, but it doesn't matter much any more as Brad's car has gone through the finish line. The screen cuts to a shot of this happening, and I slump back on the couch, dropping the controller back onto the coffee table in disgust.

'Fucken *owned* you that time,' Brad says, still grinning. 'What happened to you, man?'

I shrug. This is a stupid game anyway. 'I'll get you next time, you faggot.'

'Right. You'll suck my dick the next time.'

'Dude, what's with all the gay shit?'

'Huh?'

'Stop telling me to do stuff like suck your dick,' I say to Brad. 'I *don't* want to do it, okay? Can you cut it out?'

He stares at me, mildly taken aback. 'I never asked you to... Forget it,' he says, shaking his head, laughing.

'I'm just saying. I think we're getting a little too old to always be making jokes about stuff like that.'

'You know, sometimes I have my doubts about you.' Brad swigs the last of his beer, and then shakes the bottle around, just to confirm that it's actually empty. 'You want another one of these, bro?'

'Love one.'

The two of us lope up to the kitchen without saying much, and I lean on the island while Brad cracks open two more. 'You know,' he says as he hands me my beer, 'I'm impressed.'

'With what?'

'With the fact that you waited for Sara.' When I look across at him, he has that familiar dumb grin plastered across his face. 'I think it's awesome, dude. So much crazy shit has happened this year – I mean, with Lachie, and...' He looks away for a second and then back at me. 'It's nice to know you and Sara are still so solid. I told you what you guys had was special.'

'Yeah, well, Sara's special.' I say. 'I've sorta realised...'

'Realised what?'

'That I want to be with her. That I, y'know...that I love her.'

Brad starts to laugh.

'*Dude,*' I say.

'I'm not laughing at you. I'm laughing because that's cool. That's awesome.'

'Yeah, well... I can really see myself having a future with someone like Sara.'

'Someone like Sara?' Brad asks.

'With Sara. You know what I mean.'

'Yeah, bro.' Brad smiles. 'You and Sara, me and Isabel. It's like what you said about old married men...'

As Brad is reaching across to tap his closed fist with mine, Kristian walks into the kitchen, stopping in his tracks when he sees the two of us. He stares at me for a second, apprehensive, fearful even, before saying a monotone 'hey' to the two of us. He has a split lip, and even in spite of his emo hair – a dyed-black fringe brushed down so it covers his left eye almost completely – a dark purple bruise is still evident on one side of his face.

'Everything all right, kiddo?' Brad asks him.

Kristian nods slowly, pulling out a glass from the cupboard and then taking what seems like an eternity to fill it up with ice cubes and water from the fridge. He slinks out of the kitchen without looking at me or saying a word.

'What the hell happened to him?' I ask Brad when Kristian's gone.

Brad sighs, shakes his head. 'I don't know exactly, but it's pretty fucked up. He told us that he was walking to some friend's house and he was cutting across the golf course at St Lucia when these two dudes just jumped him.'

'Fuck that, man. St Lucia? That's, like, the safest suburb in the world.'

'Yeah, that's what we thought, but I guess not. He said that the guys were trying to steal his iPod or something, but he wouldn't let them have it, he held onto it...'

'Fuck, man...'

Brad leans back on the island, tensing his fists for a second and then releasing them again. 'He put up a fight, poor little dude, but he got the shit beaten out of him. He won't tell us much more than that.'

'That's fucked up,' I say. 'Is he okay?'

'I think so. I was the one who found him that arvo – he walked home by himself, and when I got here, I found him sitting in the kitchen. He was crying and he was *covered* in blood, all over his shirt, man, his face, everywhere. I couldn't believe it – I was like, *what the fuck happened to you?* but he couldn't even tell me then.'

'That's terrible, man.'

'I got him cleaned up and drove him to the hospital, just in case, but they said he was okay. Just cuts and bruises and stuff. He's still pretty shaken up.'

'I'll bet he is, poor little dude.'

'I just wish I could find the cunts who did this to him.'

'Fucken animals.'

'Mum and Dad fucken flipped when they saw him. We called the police and got him to describe the guys, but what the fuck are the police gonna do?'

'Not much,' I say. 'Useless bastards.'

'I just know that if I ever find the cunts...' Brad sighs. 'Nothing we can do about it now, though.'

We head back down to the living room and surf through the channels, watching old Aerosmith videos and episodes of *Newlyweds*, sitting in agreeable silence.

'Almost feels like old times, hey?' I say to Brad after a while.

'Yeah, dude,' he says and smiles. 'It's friends, hey? You gotta stick together. In the end there's nothing else apart from your friends.'

'You got that right,' I say.

He reaches out to me and we share one of those familiar tricky handshakes.

'We're tight,' I say. 'Friends. Nothing else matters.'

Andrew calls me after work one afternoon, and a brief yet tense conversation ensues. He is ringing to discuss the results of some tests that I made him have – he received the all-clear – and after he relays this news to me, several minutes of awkward, gruff small talk follows.

'My girlfriend gets back from Europe soon,' I tell him. 'Any day now.'

'Awesome, dude. That's really great.'

There is silence on the line for a few seconds. 'So,' I say when it becomes clear that I'm going to have to be the one to do the talking, 'what have you been, um, doing with yourself?'

'I decided to stay in Melbourne,' he tells me. 'I was getting pretty sick of everything up north, and since I have the apartment to myself and everything... I've just been going out, getting fucked up...'

'How's...um, Natalie?'

'I don't know. She's pretty intense. She said she either wanted to get married or move to Japan. I told her I really wasn't ready for that so she moved to Japan.'

'That's too bad.'

'I've been seeing other girls, but not seriously,' he tells me. 'There's this one, Crystal. She used to be one of the Jim Beam girls. Dumbest bitch you ever met but she has tits out to here. Been out with her once or twice.'

'Sounds good.'

'She's all right. I brought her home with this other girl. Some Asian girl. It was pretty wild. Yeah. Pretty fucken wild,' he says again, though without much enthusiasm.

'I'm looking forward to seeing Sara again,' I tell him. 'I think it's going to be really great.'

'Yeah, dude,' he says, with a tone that actually strikes me as oddly sincere. 'That's awesome. You and your girlfriend. I hope that works out.'

'I'm sure it will,' I say.

'Yeah.'

Neither of us can think of anything else to say, and Andrew mutters his goodbye at almost the same time I mutter mine. There's no *we should catch up*, no *good talking to you* or *maybe I'll see you around sometime*, and the air of finality that this gives is comforting.

Fifteen

I wake up early on the morning that Sara's flight is due. Brad picks me up at eight-thirty and we drive to the airport in comfortable silence. The morning sunlight inside the terminal is very bright, and as we walk through the atrium, passing backpackers and businessmen, some people saying goodbye, others being welcomed back, the light makes everyone seem weirdly insubstantial, as though we're all transparent and the light is somehow shining through us.

Sara's parents and brother arrived at the terminal before we did, and when I spot them standing at the barrier, we approach them so we can wait together. I have a brief conversation with Mr Chase – he tells me how strange it is not to have seen me for so long, asks me how I've been keeping busy all of this time. I tell him I haven't been doing much, just studying hard; he tells me how glad he is that Sara has found a solid young man like me. The weird thing is that there is absolutely no sarcasm in his voice – as far as I can tell, he is completely sincere when he says this, which makes me sad for some reason, but I try not to dwell on it.

'We were worried about our little girl,' says Sara's mother, looking at me and then back towards the gate. 'She was so good, with everything that happened. I would have been a mess.'

'She's a tough one, Sara,' says her dad.

'Just imagine it though...being stranded like that. Think what might have happened if she couldn't reach us, if...' Sara's mother makes shuddering noises. 'It makes me sick just thinking about it.'

Mr Chase puts his hand on his wife's arm. 'Silly to worry about it now,' he says. 'It's only money.'

'You know, Liam,' Mrs Chase says, looking at me again, 'Sara told us all about how you helped her through...the night that she was stranded. She said how good it was to be able to talk to you...'

I nod, not quite sure of what to say.

'You might not realise, but just having you to talk to that night helped her through the worst of it. We're grateful to you for that.'

Mr Chase reaches out and puts his arm around my shoulder, and holds me there for a moment as something intangible passes between us. I know you're wondering if I feel guilty – for everything that I've done – to Kristian, to Brad, and especially to Sara. If you really want to know, there is probably some small part of me that feels I could have handled all of this better, but you do what you need to in order to get by. I can't say that I'm not feeling relieved now – just like I was when Brad told me that made-up story about Kristian – but the alternative is feeling guilty, and that never gets you anywhere.

Looking back on it, I feel pretty bad about some of the stuff that's happened over the last six months, but everyone does stupid shit when they're young. Sure I've behaved badly, but I'll do better next time. Just because you're stupid when you're nineteen doesn't mean you're always going to be that way. Right?

Everyone seems excited and slightly on edge, like we're not quite sure who we should be expecting, if the person coming back will be the same as the old Sara, and if not, what the new Sara is going to be like. Everyone waits around nervously; I go to one of the cafés nearby and buy a bottle of water which I don't drink, I just carry it around so I have something to hold on to.

Finally an announcement comes over the loudspeakers telling us that Sara's connecting flight from Dubai is arriving. We find a place near the gate and watch the people emerging from the long tunnel, looking at each new person who appears, trying to figure out if they're going to be Sara, if we're even going to recognise her. After a while, as the flow of people is starting to thin out, I catch sight of a familiar slim, dark-haired figure approaching.

When Sara looks up and sees us, she breaks into a run, sidestepping people in the tunnel, the smile on her face as wide as a little kid's. 'You came to meet me!' she calls out. 'Oh my god, I've missed you all so much!'

She crashes into her mother's waiting arms and they hug for a long time, then she does the same to her father and her brother before getting to me. She looks a little thinner; her hair is longer and even darker, and she is wearing a pink cardigan that I have never seen before, but to look at her, she is clearly still the same Sara. When I go to hug her, she stops for a second, stares into my face, slightly uncertain, but still smiling. 'Liam,' she says. 'I'm so glad you came.'

'Of course I came,' I tell her. 'I love you, babe.' With that, she collapses into my arms, her head resting in the crook of my shoulder.

'I really missed you,' she says.

'I missed you too.'

'There's so much stuff I have to tell you. Wow, it's so weird to see you again. You haven't changed at all. This is...wow. Liam.'

We hug for what seems like a full minute before we break it off.

'I'm so tired,' she says. 'Jesus, I'm tired. The flight took forever, I'm *so* glad to be off that plane. There was this woman...oh, I'll tell you about it later. I need to sleep for, like, six days and then I'll tell you everything. Wow, there's so much stuff to tell you, it's so good to see you again, Liam...'

After we've collected Sara's stuff from the baggage carousel – it seems she has returned with twice what she took – I lead her to her parents' car, where she collapses in the back seat. She stays unconscious until the following afternoon, but I am there when she wakes up again, and it feels good.

The first time we make love, it's driven by a hunger that I don't think either of us is quite able to explain. Sara tells me she wants to go out to lunch – she hasn't seen the city in so long that she wants to get to know it again – and when we stop by my house, ostensibly so I can change my shirt, we never make it out of the bedroom. I am standing in front of my mirror, shirtless, when Sara grabs me from behind. She rests her head on my shoulder, and the two of us stand like that for a long time, her arms tight around me, looking at our reflections.

I turn around to kiss her, and she wraps her arms around me even more tightly, kissing me back even harder – a starving, desperate kiss. 'I haven't done this for so long,' Sara says as we fall onto the bed, her breath catching in her throat, and it almost feels as though she is challenging me. I have my hand under her top, the other one is working on my belt buckle, and she groans like an animal, a noise I have never heard her make before, as I rub her breast, across her body and down to the small of her back.

I fish around for a condom on my beside table, eventually finding one between the pages of some surfing magazine, and as soon as I've slipped it on, Sara grabs me, gripping my forearms so tightly that I'm sure it must be hurting, but I really don't feel a thing. When we're done, Sara curls up around me, both of us sweating, her arm hugging my chest, and we lie like that, with the sheets twisted around us, for what feels like a very long time.

'There's something I need to tell you,' she says without warning.

I turn over and look at her, but she is staring at the ceiling rather than at me, and when it becomes clear that she's not going to go on, I ask her, 'What? What is it, babe?'

'I... Nothing happened, so you don't have to worry about that, but I almost... It almost happened, and I think I need to tell you.'

'What did?' I ask, confused now. 'What happened?'

'Do you remember that time I called you from Prague? That boy I met up with, Miles?'

'You mean the gay guy?'

'He told me he was, yes.'

'What did you...?'

'We didn't do anything,' she says, sighing, seeming to almost stiffen, 'but we spent a lot of time together, and there was one night...'

'Go on,' I tell her when she stops, wondering where this might be heading, dreading it.

'Well, there was one night when we went out for drinks, we went to a bar where there were cheap beers for students, and we weren't planning to have a big night, but we kept on buying them and... I don't know, but we were talking, he was telling me about some boy he'd been seeing back where he lived, and I was telling him all about you, and we were just talking about how weird it was, you know, to be separated from your partner like that...'

She looks up at me at this point, as though she's

hoping for some kind of acknowledgement. There's nothing I can think of to say – it's actually taking a lot of effort even to lie still right now – and she continues.

'...so before long it was two in the morning and I was *really* drunk, more drunk than I've been since I can remember, and Miles wasn't even staying at the hostel any more, he was staying with some friend, but he offered to walk me back, he was worried that I wouldn't make it by myself, and I mean... I was drunk in a strange city in the middle of the night, I was hardly going to say no. So we walked along and we were just talking and laughing, but when we got to the door of the hostel, there was... I don't know what you'd call it, Liam. I guess there was a moment...'

'A moment?' I ask.

Sara senses the anger in my voice. 'It wasn't like *that*, Liam, it was just that he looked at me...'

'He looked at you...'

'And... I'm not sure. We both just stopped talking, and for a second or two it seemed like he was about to kiss me.'

I don't say anything.

'I mean, he didn't. I didn't *let* him, but it was just the way he was looking at me, holding my hand...'

'He was holding your hand?'

'I didn't mean... It *wasn't* like that.'

'What did you *almost* do?'

'What do you mean?'

'A second ago, you told me, *I almost...* What did that mean?'

'I don't know,' she says, closing her eyes. 'I guess for a second I thought about what it might be like to kiss him.'

'Did you?'

'*No*, Liam, I'm just saying... I was drunk and I was really lonely, and Miles was such a nice boy. He walked me home...'

'So what, any guy who walks you home...?'

'It's *not* like that, Liam,' she says, raising her voice. 'Nothing happened between us. I came to my senses and I thanked him for being so nice to me, and I told him that he should probably go back to his friend's place.'

'You told him that?'

'I did, because I was thinking of you. Because being with Miles made me realise how much I missed you... how much I wanted to be with you.'

I sigh, the queasy feeling in my stomach dissipating, but only slightly. 'So what you're telling me is the truth?' I ask.

'Yes,' she says. 'I just wanted to... I wanted to make sure you knew, because... I knew you'd be suspicious. I knew that no matter what we said to each other, you'd worry that something might have, you know... happened. So I wanted to be honest with you right away.'

I lean down, kiss Sara on the forehead, and she closes her eyes.

'So that's what happened,' she says, 'and that's *all* that happened.'

'I'm glad you told me,' I say.

Her next question hangs in the air, even before it's asked. 'So, what about you?'

'What about me?'

'Is there anything you need to tell me?'

'Sara, I...'

'Because I'd understand. Six months is a long time to be away, and if you ever...with anyone, I mean... I'd be upset. But I wouldn't blame you. I'd want to know.'

'Nothing happened,' I say, without even thinking about it. 'I didn't even *look* at anyone else while you were gone.'

'You didn't?'

'No.'

'So there were no... There were really no other girls?'

'Not a one.'

'What about...?' The silence between us is thick.

'...about what?' I ask.

She shakes her head. 'Nothing. You know I trust you, Liam...'

'I trust you too, Sara.'

'You know what?' she says, looking up at me and actually smiling for the first time in a while.

'What?'

'I'm glad we could talk about this. And you know what else, I'm glad because we won't ever have to talk about these things again, will we?'

'I —'

'Because we trust each other. Right?'

I don't quite know what Sara is getting at, but I get the feeling that a lot will rest on my answer to this question. 'Completely,' I say. 'I love you,' and as I'm saying this to her, I realise that it's true. 'I'm so lucky to have found a girl like you.'

Sara rolls over, laughing, and starts kissing me again. We make love for the second time this afternoon – more slowly this time, as though we're both aware that we have as long as we like to do this. When we're done, neither of us speaks, we just look at one another and run our hands across each other's skin, almost like we're strangers just getting to know one another for the first time.

'Wow,' says Sara after a while. 'It's such a weird feeling being back.'

'I don't know,' I say. 'Things change so slowly... I guess you need to be away to see it. But then there was...'

'Lachie...' she says, letting the word hang there.

I nod slowly. 'Yeah. We should have seen it coming... tried to do something.'

'You really never know,' she says quietly. 'Even if something's right there in front of you, if you don't want to see it...' Sara takes my hand, holds it for a few seconds, then lets it go.

'You know what?' I say. 'There's something I think we should do.'

'What's that?'

'Come on,' I say. 'Let's get ready.'

'I am ready,' she says.

'Oh, really? You want to go like that? You want to drive to the airport naked?'

'Yes,' she says and laughs. 'Everyone in Europe walks around nude... It's just what's *done* over there.'

'Really?' I ask, laughing. 'So they drink wine at lunch and then walk around in the buff...'

'Yes,' she says, giggling. 'It's, like, the national pastime in Italy...'

'Right then,' I say, leaning over to tickle her. 'I'd really like to meet some more of those Italians then...'

It's late afternoon by the time we make it to the airport. We take my car, and I pull up on the grass, the two of us lying by the road, watching planes as they take off and land in the orange sky.

'Doesn't this feel like last year?' Sara asks. 'Before I left?'

'It does.'

'I remember us sitting out here, planning the trip... Oh Liam, Europe was so fantastic. I really want to go back. And I really want you to come with me.'

I nod. 'I think that would be awesome.'

'I just kept wishing you were there... There were so many things I wanted to show you.'

'You'll be able to,' I say. 'You can show me everything.'

She rests her head on my chest and we lie still, listening to the cars passing.

'My mum asked me why I waited for you...'

'What?'

'She asked... Before I left, when you decided you weren't coming. She asked why I decided to wait. She said there was a whole world of boys out there, and while

I was still young enough to have fun...'

'She said that?'

'I think what she meant was... Look, you know my mother. She just wanted me to have an adventure.'

'I thought your parents... I thought your mum liked me.'

'She does, it's not that, it's just...she doesn't understand. She kept saying to me that we'd been together so long – since school and everything – and that it was okay if I wanted to experience some more of the world. I told her none of that mattered to me because I love you.'

'I'm glad,' I say. 'I mean, I love you too.'

'Do you think we could live together?' she asks without warning.

I stop, look at Sara's face to try to determine whether she's joking, but it seems as though she might be serious. 'How do you mean?'

'Not *now*,' she says, laughing nervously, 'but in a few months maybe. Would you be ready for something like that?'

'I...'

'You don't have to answer straightaway, but being away for these past six months – travelling around on my own, it really made me aware of how grown-up I feel.'

'How do you mean?'

'I'm not a baby any more. I'm not... Since I've been back at my parents', it's started to feel *stifling*. I mean, I love them, but I think I'm really ready to start doing things on my own.'

'And by on your own, you mean living with me?'

She gives me a shifty look, like she's trying to figure out if I'm joking or not. 'You dick. You know what I *mean...*'

'I do, I know, I'm just teasing you.' I nod. 'Do you really think we could do it?'

'I think we could. Give it a few months...I could move in with you, or... I don't know. We can talk about it, but...'

'That sounds like a great idea,' I tell her, not even sure where the words are coming from. 'I think we needed that time apart. I think it made me realise how important you are to me.'

'You really mean that?'

'I do.'

I look down at her and then back up at the sunset. We hold one another more tightly, and I realise, as I feel her body warm against mine: everything is going to be okay.

Acknowledgments

Thank you to everyone who assisted and believed in me throughout the writing of this novel, especially to Madonna Duffy at UQP, who has been there since the beginning. Thanks also to my fantastic friends – there are too many of you to list but you know who you are – for always being there and for helping me maintain my sanity. I must also thank my parents, Jim and Barbara, for being wonderful, knowledgable and supportive and for always coming through in a crisis. And finally, thanks to Byron and Aretha for giving me a place to crash, and Chris Harms for allowing me to indulge publicly in my chronic music-geekery.